FORBIDDEN VOWS

AN AGE GAP, BRATVA ROMANCE

K.C. CROWNE

Copyright © 2025 by K.C. Crowne

All rights reserved.

No part of this book may be reproduced in any form or by any electronic or mechanical means, including information storage and retrieval systems, without written permission from the author, except for the use of brief quotations in a book review.

DESCRIPTION

**He's supposed to marry her sister.
But the *Pakhan* doesn't play by the rules…**
He writes them in blood.

The air is thick with champagne and lies.
I'm standing at my sister's engagement party, trapped in the gilded cage of my family's dying Irish dynasty.
Beside me, the monster I'm meant to marry.

Then—the announcement.
"Introducing Ciara's fiancé—Anton Karpov."

The world shatters.
His gaze crashes into mine like a knife to the ribs.
He remembers.
The way I moaned his name.
The way he saved my life—only to ruin it.

Shit.
This.
Can't.
Be.
Happening.
But it's real.

And so is my hatred.

Then his eyes drop.
To my hand.
To the curve of my stomach.
To the heir he doesn't know exists.

That's when the real game begins.

Readers note: This is full-length standalone, secret baby, Russian bratva, Irish mafia, age-gap romance. K.C. Crowne is an Amazon Top 6 Bestseller and International Bestselling Author.

CHAPTER 1

EILEEN

"Smile, Peach Bottom."

My sister's voice is poison wrapped in silk, the kind of sweet that kills you slow. "You'll make a passable Kuznetsov bride." Her lips curve—that razor-edged smile she's perfected since we were kids. "And me?" A diamond-crusted finger taps her champagne flute. "Well, we always knew I'd marry a Karpov."

The nickname Peach Bottom—first hissed at me when I outgrew my Catholic school skirt at fourteen—still hits like a sucker punch. Back then, it was just cruel girls laughing as my hips split the seams. Now? It's a blade to the ribs, a reminder of everything our world says I'll never be:

Graceful. Obedient. Enough.

The Irish mob has a type—delicate dolls with collarbones sharp enough to draw blood. Girls who float through rooms like ghosts, their laughter a whisper, their bodies barely leaving an imprint on the world.

Meanwhile, my body is a rebellion in flesh.

Hips that don't quit, thighs that stretch designer silk into surrender, the kind of chest that makes old women clutch their pearls. "A real woman's body," my grandmother used to say, like it was a compliment instead of a life sentence.

The Infinity Lounge thrums with danger, a symphony of smoked glass and black marble, where fortunes are made and bodies disappear. Tonight, the champagne bubbles taste like swallowed screams.

"What if I want more than to pop out heirs for some Bratva captain?" I ask.

"Then you'd better learn to love the game more than your own spine, darling. That's the only currency that buys survival here. Women like us don't get to want. We get to choose which chains suit us best. Ciara adjusts my emerald pendant—the last heirloom from our Dublin estate—with fingers that dig like talons. "The Donovans used to trade in Irish whiskey and warships," she murmurs. "Now we deal in daughters."

My sister leans in closer, her perfume—something venomous and obscenely expensive—clashing with the whiskey-soaked greed in the air. "And let's be honest, with your... distinct silhouette, you should thank your lucky stars that any Bratva captain spared you a second glance."

I don't blink. "Just say it. I'm too much woman for the Bratva."

Her gaze drags over me, slow and surgical. "We're Donovans, Eileen. In our world, crowns are reserved for the slender and silent. But maybe Sergei likes a challenge.

Maybe he'll even fund that little café dream of yours—the one Dad laughed out of the room." She shrugs, swirling her drink. "Take the win. The Kuznetsovs aren't Karpov-level rich, but they're close enough."

The condescension burns, but I'm done swallowing it. "Or maybe I'll build it myself—without a man's money or permission."

Before she can strike back, a shadow falls over us—Tommy Benedetto, all shark's teeth and snake's charm. "Ladies." His gaze lingers on me like a stain. "You two look... festive."

Ciara's laugh is polished arsenic. "Engagements, Tommy. Both of us."

His smirk twists. "Both?" The disbelief is a slap.

For a fleeting heartbeat, I envision the sharp crack of my champagne flute against his smug grin. Instead, I bare my teeth with a smile. "Surprised? Sometimes the dark horses leave you choking on their dust."

Ciara interjects, too eager. "Join us for a drink?"

"Tempting." He adjusts his cufflinks, eyes never leaving mine. "But I've got a Siberian hellcat waiting. Promised me the authentic Russian experience."

Ciara's giggle is brittle as spun sugar. "Always sampling the merchandise, aren't you?"

Tommy's grin stretches, grotesque. "Enjoy the night, ladies. Some brides get twitchy once they feel the collar click shut."

Fucking predator.

I rise, slow and deliberate, the silk of my dress whispering secrets against my thighs. "Funny, Tommy. In your world, men think they can leash us like dogs." I step closer, close enough to taste the cigars and rot on his breath. "But even a leashed bitch has teeth. And if you yank too hard?" My smile vanishes. "She just might tear out your fucking throat."

Silence.

Then—Tommy laughs, cruel and mocking. "I'm eager to see how you'll dress up as a bride — what a spectacle that will be."

His words slice through the air like a blade, an unmistakable declaration of war.

Ciara's fingers dig painfully into my arm. "Eileen, he's just teasing."

I wrench away from her grip, my momentum carrying me into the solid mass of Paddy's chest. His brow, lined with old scars, furrows deeply in concern.

"Miss Donovan—"

"Bathroom, Paddy," I cut in sharply, already striding away.

The hallway envelops me, the club's vibrant pulse now a distant murmur. A sudden flicker in the smoked glass catches my gaze—my reflection, a striking vision in emerald silk.

The dress embraces each defiant curve, accentuating a body sculpted by passionate dances through tumultuous nights, not timidity. My glossy red curls tumble provocatively around my shoulders, setting off my creamy skin and fierce green eyes that smolder with unyielding spirit.

I shove through the back door, gulping the alley's frozen air like a lifeline.

Think, Eileen. There must be a way out.

Above me, the sky is a hollow black sheet, Chicago's neon greed devouring every last star—a perfect echo of how my family aims to devour my dreams, leaving nothing but emptiness.

I press a hand to my chest, as if I could claw back the ambitions they've stolen. I belong on sunlit streets, scouting the perfect storefront, breathing in the fresh aroma of espresso beans. I should be scribbling menu ideas on napkins, collaborating with contractors, creating something truly mine.

Instead, I'm caged in a gilded cage, mindlessly selecting bone-white china patterns like a docile doll.

But dolls don't bleed.

And I haven't finished fighting.

I stand in silence, savoring a fleeting eternity. Minutes had barely slipped by when the scene before me drastically changed.

The alley erupts in metallic screams.

I whirl around to see Tommy Benedetto—this time, he's being hauled between two Bratva enforcers, his body flung about like a defeated boxer clinging to the ropes. Blood paints his designer stubble, that pretty-boy face now a swollen mess. His left eye pulses shut, the color of rotting plums.

"Wait—you've got this wrong!" Tommy's voice cracks as they throw him face-first into a rancid puddle. The pale blue

Tom Ford suit drinks up alley filth like a sponge. "I got money! Fuck, I got—"

The bigger enforcer silences him with a steel-toe kick to the ribs. I hear something crack. The other screws a silencer onto his Makarov with terrifying precision.

"Andrei said quick," he grunts, Chechen accent thick as Siberian frost.

Fuck. Bratva enforcers.

My lungs turn to ice. Three stumbling steps back—clang—my heel meets the trash can. The gunman's head jerks up. Moonlight slithers along the barrel as it swings toward me.

Run bitch!!

But my legs refuse to obey.

"Wait! You don't know who—"

"Don't care." His trigger finger pales.

Suddenly, a scent hits me—bergamot and gun oil—an instant before an iron-clad arm snakes around my waist.

I'm airborne, stilettos kicking empty air as some mountain of a man hauls me backward. My silk dress rips against brickwork.

The lead enforcer's eyes widen.

I'm tossed into a Porsche 911's butter-soft leather.

The car door slams shut behind me. In the confined space, my kidnapper's presence overwhelms—all broad shoulders and restrained power.

His tailored suit strains across biceps earned through more than just gym sessions.

When he shifts gears, tendons flex in his tanned hands, the two-headed eagle signet ring glinting with each movement.

He's Bratva royalty.

"Who the FUCK—"

A single look shuts me up.

Just like that. No words. No warning. Just those sharp eyes locking onto mine, cold and commanding, and suddenly my voice dies in my throat.

For the first time in my life—me, Eileen Donovan, who never knows when to shut up—I'm left completely, utterly speechless.

Those deep, wolfish hazel eyes, more green than gold under the dashboard lights, flash with a menacing intelligence. He appears to be in his mid to late forties, the epitome of a silver fox, with every crease around those piercing eyes adding to his lethal allure.

Moonlight caresses the silver threads in his beard, highlighting the stark contrast against his umber skin, making it captivating rather than weathered. As he turns, light dances across the defined angles of his face.

This man isn't merely distinguished; he's a predator cloaked in the guise of sophistication.

The engine snarls to life. My kidnapper throws us into reverse, tires screaming. Through the windshield, I see the enforcer lowering his gun slowly—not from mercy, but recognition.

Who the hell is this guy?

"Talk," I demand, voice shaking. "Or I'll dive at the next light."

Hazel eyes flick to mine, wolf-yellow in the dashboard glow. "You'd break that pretty neck before rolling three feet." Moscow velvet over Siberian steel. "Sit still, devochka. Tonight, I'm your guardian devil."

The speedometer kisses 90 as we vanish into Chicago's neon arteries. And I'm trapped with a man who smells like danger and $300-an-ounce cologne.

"Bullshit." My fingers dig into the Porsche's butter-soft leather. "You just kidnapped a Donovan."

His knuckles bleach white on the steering wheel, tendons standing out like steel cables beneath tanned skin. "Andrei's men would've put two bullets in your pretty skull and dumped you in Lake Michigan before you could blink."

That voice—smoke and honey with a Russian edge—vibrates through me like the Porsche's purring engine.

A traitorous shiver runs down my spine. "Who the hell are you?" I demand, louder this time.

"On a need-to-know basis." His thumb taps the wheel, a signet ring flashing—ruby-eyed eagle eating its own tail.

"Christ, did they train you at the Bratva Charm School?" I snap. "Or just the School of Cryptic Bullshit?"

The corner of his mouth twitches beneath that perfectly trimmed beard. "You walked into a warzone back there, little bird. And you're still flapping your wings like it's a fucking tea party."

I take him in properly for the first time—that aristocratic nose, the way his hazel eyes shift from moss-green to amber in the dashboard lights. Fine lines fan from his eyes, the kind earned from squinting into Siberian winds rather than laughing at parties. Silver threads glint in his dark waves, catching the light like knife edges.

And God, that scent again—leather, gunpowder, and something expensive beneath it all. My traitorous lungs drink it in.

"What I walked into," I say slowly, "was your Russian friends turning Tommy Benedetto into ground meat." My voice hardens. "A Camorra prince doesn't just get whacked without consequences."

His grip tightens. Just a fraction. Just enough. A dark chuckle. "You do understand the game."

"Enough to know you're not some Good Samaritan." I lean closer, whiskey and adrenaline burning my throat. "So who the fuck are you really?"

Those wolf's eyes flick to me, then back to the road. "Persistent little thing, aren't you?"

"Try 'woman with a working survival instinct.'"

The Porsche accelerates, pressing me into the seat. "Tough blyad," he murmurs, almost approvingly. "You're better off not knowing my name. Unless you enjoy breathing."

"Are you threatening me?"

"Stating facts." He downshifts, the engine growling like the danger lacing his words. "You're not going home tonight."

Ice floods my veins. "Excuse me?"

The silence stretches, broken only by the hum of tires on asphalt. Streetlights strobe across his face, highlighting the stubborn set of his jaw.

When he finally speaks, it's so quiet I have to strain to hear: "You're cargo now, devochka. Precious, troublesome cargo."

Several minutes later, he pulls up to a gorgeous hotel somewhere on the Gold Coast.

"What are we doing here?" My voice sounds hollow, even to me.

The building looms before us - all gleaming glass and art deco flourishes. Rooftop lights twinkle like trapped stars above us, promising a world of crystal glasses and Lake Michigan breezes.

Snap out of it, Eileen. You're not a guest.

"What are we doing here?" I repeat, sharper this time.

"You'll be safe here." His voice is calm, but his fingers flex on the steering wheel. I notice how his signet ring catches the light - that damned two-headed eagle winking at me.

"Safe?" The laugh bursts from me, raw and jagged. "That's rich coming from my kidnapper."

He turns then, slowly, like a predator sizing up prey. The movement makes his suit jacket strain across shoulders that could probably bench press me. "If I wanted you dead," he murmurs, "you'd already be feeding the fishes at Navy Pier."

"I could scream," I blurt out.

The silence that follows is heavier than the Chicago humidity. My father's voice echoes in my head - That smart mouth will get you killed someday, Eileen.

His hazel eyes darken to forest green in the dim light. "Those men back at the club? They're Andrei's attack dogs. And you just became their favorite chew toy."

He gets out of the car, then comes around to open the passenger door for me. I get out, immediately smacked in the face by the cold night air. Shivering, I follow this mysterious man into the building, noticing that he doesn't look around or seem fearful of anyone following us.

This is clearly his turf.

"Good evening," he tells the night manager, who sits behind the reception desk, half asleep. He gets a slight nod and a mumbled reply as we walk over to the elevator. "Keep your eyes on me and your mouth shut."

I can't help myself. "What, no blindfold? No handcuffs? I'm disappointed in your kidnapping technique."

The look he gives me could freeze vodka. "Keep testing me, malyshka, and you'll learn why they call me Kholodnyy."

The Cold One. The nickname slithers down my spine.

He leads me inside the elevator and the doors shut.

The elevator doors part to reveal a hallway lined with blood-red wallpaper that reminds me too much of the Infinity Lounge. His suite smells of lemon polish and something darker beneath - gun oil, maybe, or the metallic tang of old blood.

"Not bad for a criminal," I mutter, taking in the marble floors and floor-to-ceiling windows.

His laugh is dark as he locks the door behind us. A devastatingly cute dimple appears in his cheek when he smiles, barely visible beneath his stubble.

My God, there's not an unattractive inch on this man.

"Compliments will get you nowhere." He shrugs off his jacket, revealing a shoulder holster that makes my breath hitch. Try anything stupid..." He pats the gun meaningfully.

"Charming." My voice shakes despite myself. "Do you always kidnap women at gunpoint, or am I special?"

He's suddenly in my space, all heat and expensive cologne. "Special?" His breath ghosts over my lips. "You're a problem I didn't need tonight, krasavitsa."

"Can you at least tell me your first name?"

He shuts the door, then locks it, slipping the key back into his jacket pocket. "There you go with the questions, little bird."

"I have the right to know my abductor's identity."

"The kitchen is stocked. You can have the bedroom at the end of the hallway. I'm going to pour myself a scotch. Would you like one?"

"Are you deliberately trying to get me wasted?"

"No, I'm just trying to see how much is too much for you. I hear Irish girls can drink most men under the table," he shoots back with a cool grin.

Why are my legs quivering? This is not the kind of reaction my body should be having in this man's presence.

Get a grip, Eileen.

My phone buzzes in my clutch.

I hold my breath praying he doesn't notice.

His hand flashes out, confiscating it with terrifying speed.

"Give it back!" I lunge, but he's quicker, those massive arms trapping me against his chest. Every inch of him is hard muscle and barely leashed violence.

"Sit. Down." Each word is a bullet. "Unless you want Andrei's men to finish what they started."

The mention of those Bratva enforcers stills me. Against every screaming instinct, I sink onto the sofa.

I take a seat on the edge of a plush, creamy-beige sofa, my reflection staring back at me from the floor-to-ceiling windows.

He dials a number on his phone. I watch his gaze darken as it travels across the room, his mind carefully processing everything.

"Andrei, you need to call me back ASAP. Whatever that thing with Benedetto was, you need to stop it. Put it on the back burner and tell your goons to back off," he says.

Andrei. That name again.

Tommy was terrified at the mere mention of the guy back in the alley. Definitely a high-ranking member of the Russian mob. But there are so many of them waltzing around like they own Chicago these days, it's hard to keep up. Not that I truly ever cared. I should've cared. I should've paid more attention.

Within a few minutes, he calls this Andrei guy again. "For fuck's sake, you'd better call off the hit on Benedetto and the witness back at the club. Your boys will know who I'm talking about. You've really stepped into it this time. Call it off, or there will be consequences. And call me back, you idiot."

"Let's hope he gets the message sooner rather than later. For your sake."

The underlying threat does not elude me. I feel it coursing through my veins and making my blood freeze. There's a hint of danger to every word the man says, yet here I sit with my chin up and a defiant glare in my eyes.

"I don't know who you think you are, but I should warn you —I'm not the kind of woman you can kidnap and get away with it."

"Is that so? Scotch?"

The audacity of this man.

He strides toward me with a tumbler, the honey-colored scotch swirling seductively with each determined step. He offers it to me, his gaze dark and penetrating. For a fleeting moment, I consider accepting it.

Instead, I slap his hand away.

The glass flies, shattering against the parquet with a shrill crash, scotch splashing like golden rain across the floor.

A sudden chill in the air wraps around me, making me instantly regret the impulse. His calm, however, remains unbroken.

"I don't like this any more than you do," he states calmly, his voice a low rumble of controlled power. "But I have been nothing but courteous up to this point."

"You call dragging me here against my will courteous?"

His hands rise slowly, hovering near my hips without touching. "I call keeping you alive courtesy enough." That deep voice rolls over me like thunder before a storm.

I tilt my head back to glare at him, but the effect is ruined by how my breath catches. "I don't need your protection."

"Don't you?" One dark eyebrow arches. His gaze drops to my parted lips. "That pretty mouth was about to get you killed back there."

My pulse jumps at the word pretty. "And what's it getting me now?" The challenge slips out before I can stop it.

His answering smile is all predator. "Trouble, malyshka. The kind you've been begging for since you first looked at me."

"I—"

His hand finally lands on my waist, burning through the silk. "Your pupils have been dilated since the car. Your breathing changes when I get close." His thumb brushes the underside of my breast. "And right now, your heart is trying to escape through that pretty little throat."

The tension shifts palpably; the air thickens with unsaid promises. I swallow hard, my defenses wavering under the weight of his intense focus. "Observant for a kidnapper."

"I pay attention to what I want to take."

The possessiveness in his tone sends heat flooding through me. "And what exactly do you want to take?"

His lips graze my earlobe. "First? That sharp tongue of yours." A nip at my jaw sends a shiver down my spine. "Then every other part that keeps pretending it doesn't want this."

When I open my mouth to protest, he captures it in a searing kiss. There's nothing gentle about it—just hunger and possession and the faint taste of expensive whiskey. My hands fist in his shirt of their own accord.

My hips rock forward in answer before I can stop them.

His groan vibrates through me as he backs me against the wall, one muscular thigh sliding between mine.

The kiss tastes like danger and damnation.

And worst of all? I have no intention of stopping.

CHAPTER 2

EILEEN

I never thought something like this would upend me. I melt into his arms and welcome his tongue as he explores me, his hands moving up and down my body.

"You have no idea of the power you hold," he whispers against my lips.

"You're insane," I whisper back, yet hungrily welcome another kiss.

We devour one another, the hunger growing stronger with each fleeting second. I breathe him in while his fingers dig into the fabric of my dress, touching me, squeezing me, feeling my body burn against his.

"This is wrong on so many levels," I gasp as he peels my dress off.

"You can end it anytime," he says, then bites my shoulder.

My hips tilt forward, and I feel him, big and hard, nestled against my lower belly. Good God, do I need this. I want this. My body and mind have sabotaged me, joining forces for this hell of a ride.

With trembling fingers, I reach up and take off his jacket.

It lands on the floor next to my dress and stiletto heels. I'm not sure when I slipped out of the heels, but I'm losing track of time altogether. He keeps kissing me, tasting every inch of skin he can reach while I keep touching him, feeling his hard muscles against my nimble fingertips. It's an automatic process, our bodies converging, melding into each other.

"This is crazy," I manage, standing before him in nothing but my bra and panties.

A smile dances across his tender lips as he looks me over. "And you're fucking gorgeous."

"I bet you tell that lie a lot," I mutter.

He scoffs and kisses me again. This time, however, he's ravenous. Decisive and dominant. I have no choice but to submit, and I do so gladly. Screw what happened earlier. Screw what brought me here in the first place. Screw it all to hell, because this is happening.

I gasp as his hands come up, taking a firm hold of my breasts.

"No push-up," he quips, smiling devilishly as he fondles my flesh through the delicate lace. "You have no clue, do you?"

"About what?"

One hand slides around the back and unclasps my bra. It slips off, and I'm left completely exposed under his dark gaze. I tilt my head back, sucking in a deep breath as he comes down and takes my right nipple in his mouth.

"How delicious you are," he growls and moves on to my left.

Suckling. Nipping. Teasing the hell out of me until I whimper and quiver against him. My hands refuse to remain idle as I clumsily unbutton his shirt. I manage to undress him, and our clothes pile up in silent chaos on the floor.

My panties are the only thing that remains, and they're drenched.

"This is wrong," I say again, as if urging my brain to shift back into gear.

He laughs lightly as his hands roam freely over my body. Touching. Feeling. Squeezing. Pinching here and there to hear me gasp against his addictive lips.

"Like a broken record, I swear," he says.

I hear myself; I know he's right.

I shudder when his thumbs hook through the satin waistband of my panties. One swift motion is all it takes to leave me completely naked.

"Come here." He pulls me close, his hard cock throbbing against my belly.

He's huge, and my core tightens at the sheer thought of all of him inside of me. The rational part of my brain shuts down, leaving the animal within to run wild. I tremble in his embrace, kissing him back with growing hunger, while his hand slips between us. He finds me wet and burning hot for him.

He says nothing, looking deep into my eyes, while his fingers slide between my slick folds. I gasp as he teases my swelling clit with slow, circular motions. Then he penetrates me with two fingers, nearly taking my breath away.

"I told you, you're into me," he quips.

"I've lost my goddamn mind."

"He pushes me onto the sofa. I land with a soft thud as he kneels between my parted legs and firmly grips my knees to keep them that way.

"Fuuuuuck," I groan as he proceeds to furiously eat my pussy.

He kisses and suckles while licking my folds. He focuses on my clit as I raise my hips to meet his mouth. My head falls back as the tension coils, swelling and pushing me closer to the edge.

I listen to his subtle moans mingling, with the drumming of my heart echoing in my ears. He's enjoying this so much, and it makes my soul catch fire as I give myself to him. He devours my flesh, sucking my clit harder and harder until I finally snap like an elastic band.

The orgasm ripples through me and he drinks me in, savoring every drop of my climax as his tongue ravages my liquid pleasure.

"I need you inside me," I cry out. "Right now."

"Right now?" he calmly asks, my juices glistening on his lips.

"Right now."

The need is unbearable, and I watch with mindless desire as he positions himself between my legs, one hand guiding his cock toward my entrance. I catch the hunger in his dark eyes, the twinkle of precum on the bulging tip of his magnificent erection.

I almost scream when he spears me with his full length.

He fills me to the hilt; and it's as if he was designed for me specifically, a perfect match. He stretches me beyond my wildest dreams. He kisses me deeply and slowly, as he moves. I moan as I welcome that first thrust. Then the second.

By the third, I'm holding onto him, my fingers digging into his sculpted, broad shoulders. He holds me by the hip with one hand, while the other fondles and squeezes my breasts. The rhythm intensifies between us. He goes deeper and harder, and I feel like I could break in two from the pleasure. He pounds into me like a beast, and I take it all, clenching tightly around his gargantuan cock, while the pressure builds and builds.

"You're fucking perfect," he says and kisses me, suckling on my lower lip as he fucks me harder and deeper. My screams of raw pleasure are muffled by his lips as a second orgasm approaches.

Faster.

Harder.

Deeper.

"Come for me, baby; that's it," he says.

I know he can feel me coming and he's going all in. Every thrust feels like he's going to break me, but I fucking love it, I *need* it. My release comes with a cry of pleasure and a shudder. I glaze his cock as he lets himself go and fills me with his hot seed. I feel his heat filling my pussy.

He holds me tight, his lips pressed against my forehead as I cry out. I welcome the last of his thrusts while digging my nails into his rock-hard buttocks, reveling in the sensations that come over me. The afterglow sets in before I remember who I am or where I am, and what I probably should *not* have just done.

"I'm not finished with you yet," his words drip into my ear as he nibbles on the lobe.

We stay inseparable for a while. Complete strangers who cannot refrain from this madness. Soon, I feel him getting hard again. Wrapped in the wet warmth of my tender pussy, my captor is ready to take me again, to claim me.

And I'm going to let him.

~

Sunrise finds me splayed over his enormous bed, his gloriously naked body next to mine.

I keep going over what happened and how it happened, none of it making a lick of sense to me. My current predicament is obvious, though. Undeniable. I just spent the night in the company of the man who more or less abducted me from my engagement celebration. We screwed each other's brains out until we were too tired to even get out of bed, and I enjoyed every goddamn second of it.

"I don't usually do this," I mumble, my face half-submerged into the soft satin pillow. "I really don't."

"Even if you did, it wouldn't be a crime," he replies, still groggy and in the process of regaining full consciousness as well.

"Do you?"

"Do I what?"

Slowly, I roll over to look at him, only to end up wrapped in his strong arms again, my body hot and sizzling against his. And just like that, all the engines fire again, both of us damn near ready to repeat the activities of last night.

"This. Often," I whisper.

His lips stretch into a lazy grin, the fine lines around his eyes crinkling as he gazes at me. "What are you trying to find out?" he asks.

"Anything. I don't even know your name."

"We agreed to leave things that way for your safety."

I can't help but sigh. "Yeah."

There's a lot I wish to say, but I can't find the words. Not in this condition. Not with my body spent from the insane amount of sex, not with my mind frayed from the events that brought me here in the first place. The sudden violence, the kidnapping, the escape... the fact that I found myself inexplicably drawn to this dark, dangerous man.

Funnily enough, I feel safe in his arms, and I instantly felt safe last night in his presence.

Ridiculous.

His phone rings as my lips part to ask him another question.

He kisses me, ever so softly, then moves to answer the phone. He sits on the edge of the bed, and I can't see his face, only the splendid muscles on his broad back. His massive frame and chiseled shoulders. The faint scar on his lower back that is shaped like a half-moon. I reach out and run my fingers over it.

"Fucking finally," he says. "Where is he?" He pauses as the guy on the other line replies. "Good, so you got my message in time, but you couldn't be bothered to text me back. You fucking lunatic."

I'm guessing he's speaking to Andrei.

"What happened?" I whisper. He stays on the phone, the muscles stretched across his shoulder blades tensing.

"You do whatever you want with him, Andrei, but call off the hit on her, alright? Tell your boys to back off and forget she exists," he commands.

A wave of relief washes over me upon hearing that.

He shakes his head. "No, that's all you need to know right now. We'll discuss the details later, but I want you to promise me, swear to me, that she's off-limits. Good. Thank you. And don't kill that sorry son of a bitch yet. We'll figure out something else."

He sighs and sets the phone down. "That stubborn ass."

"I get to go home?" I ask, my voice hopeful.

A peculiar disappointment ties a knot in the back of my throat. Not the feeling I'd expected when finding out I could leave.

My ridiculously handsome captor gets up and turns around in all his naked glory, the look on his face telling me everything I need to know.

It ends here.

"You're free to go. I'll have a car waiting for you downstairs," he says. The tone of his voice is different. He sounds cold. Professional. Back to how he was when he first took me.

He's accomplished his mission, so there's no reason for him to be nice to me anymore. Oh, God, what a fool I was!

"So, that's it, huh?" I ask, quick to cover myself with the corner of a blanket.

He gives me a confused look. "You were so eager to leave last night. I can now grant you that wish. A 'thank you' would suffice. I'll hit the shower in the spare bedroom. Feel free to use the master bathroom."

All I can do is watch him walk away and disappear into the other room.

The ghost of his hazel-green eyes lingers while I take a deep breath and try to figure out what to do next. My phone is in the living room, along with my clothes. My heels. My purse.

My dignity.

Right there on the floor.

I feel used, but I wanted this. Hell, I wanted more. I couldn't get enough of this man whose name I still don't know.

Hence the sting—the sense of rejection.

There's no use in talking about it. What happened, happened, and there's nothing I can do about it now. I muster the strength to get up and turn on the shower. I wrap a towel around myself and retrieve my items from the living room. Ten minutes later, I'm dressed. I slip my phone back into my purse. The battery died overnight, so I don't have to worry about a throng of messages and missed calls just yet.

"There's a black town car waiting for you downstairs," my captor says as he escorts me to the elevator. He's wearing grey slacks and a black shirt. I still can't take my eyes off him, still can't help but wonder. "Thank you," he adds quietly.

"For what?" I whisper, blinking back tears I didn't even realize had formed.

"For trusting me. You're going home safely. You're going to be alright. Pretend you never saw anything in that back alley, and you'll keep being alright," he says.

"Is that a threat?"

"Not at all. It's my advice to you. You've got enough time on the drive over to your place to come up with the perfect excuse for last night's disappearance. But if you so much as hint at the truth to anyone, I'll know. The kind of people you don't want to see again will know. And I can't promise I can save you a second time."

The words hit hard and deep.

The man from last night, the man who claimed me and consumed me, is long gone. My kidnapper is back. The cold glare. The tight lip. The merciless tone. It was just an unexpected dream that reached its expected end.

I give him a slight nod and step into the elevator, catching one last glimpse of him before the doors close with a delicate chime.

I doubt we'll ever see each other again.

By the time the black car pulls up outside the Donovan mansion, I've already cried my heart out and come back to my senses.

"Thank you," I tell the driver as I get out and turn around to face what comes next.

Ugh, they're both home.

The car drives off.

"You can do this," I tell myself. "Come on."

It feels like a walk of shame, but I manage to fish my keys out of my purse and slip through the service gate, giving one of the bodyguards a slight nod as I make my way up the stone path. "Morning," I say and give him a wave.

Fuck, these heels are even worse the morning after. I damn near sprain my ankle, but I manage to reach the ground-floor hallway of the mansion without having to explain myself to the security staff. I stop by the kitchen door, catching a whiff of sausage and scrambled eggs. Voices trickle in from the breakfast room.

They're both home. Just as I suspected. There's no way I'll make it upstairs before they storm out of the breakfast room to question me, so I might as well get it over with before the outside bodyguards reach my father on the phone, informing him I just got home.

I straighten my back and take my heels off.

"Where the hell have you been?" My father's voice thunders across the room as I open the smoked glass door to let myself in.

"Good morning to you, too, Daddy," I mutter, then give my stepsister a slight nod. "Morning, Ciara. Sorry I ran off last night. Doubt you missed me, though."

Ronan Donovan coughs a few times, his face red with anger as he sits at the head of the table. Ciara raises an eyebrow at me, but says nothing, fork mindlessly wandering across her plate of French toast.

"Dammit, child, I had half our fleet out looking for you throughout the night!" my father snarls. "What do you have to say for yourself?"

"Well, I should apologize, first and foremost. My phone battery died and—"

He cuts me off. "Bullshit!" he yells, slamming his fist against the table for good measure, the plates, glasses and platters clattering from the aftershock. Ciara and I are both startled but not surprised. Ronan Donovan is renowned for his volcanic temper, especially when it comes to his daughters' safety. We're not scared of him, though. He's never given us reason to be. "Where were you?"

"You left to get some fresh air," Ciara says, annoyingly calm, "and then, nothing. Paddy couldn't find you. The poor man is sick with worry, still out combing the city looking for you. Daddy, by the way, you should call him and let him know she's safe."

"I ran into an old friend," I say, trying to keep myself cool in the face of what I know will be a blistering lecture. "We got to chatting, and next thing I know, we were at another club, downing shots and having the time of our lives."

"And you didn't think to call Ciara?" my father snaps, still boiling.

"My battery died."

"It was rude and inconsiderate. I was worried."

I roll my eyes, having a hard time with this mask I'm supposed to wear while we're all in the same room. After last night, I guess I have grown tired of putting up with certain behaviors on my stepsister's part.

"Oh, please, you were busy dancing and celebrating your engagement. I felt like I wasn't the best company for that, so I decided I was better off celebrating elsewhere. As you both can see, I'm safe and sound."

"This sort of behavior is beyond shameful," my father says. "You're a Donovan, Eileen. Act like one."

"Sorry."

"That's all you have to say for yourself?"

"What more do you want me to say?" I snap. "I'm sorry. I got carried away. There was plenty of drinking involved. I made a mistake. It won't happen again. There, happy?"

"Daddy, the tabloids will have a field day with this. It'll ruin my engagement announcement," Ciara whines, giving him the puppy dog eyes and the pout that usually get her whatever the hell she wants. "You need to do something about it," she adds. "Get ahead of the press somehow."

"Nobody snapped any photos of me," I tell her. "You're safe, Ciara. You don't have to worry about any of that."

She gives me a dirty look with her narrow, beady eyes. God, she looks so mean sometimes. "On second thought, Daddy, Eileen might be right. She's not the interesting daughter, after all. The paparazzi were all too busy hounding me last night."

"Ciara, honey, even if there were issues, I would fix them, you know that," he gently tells her. "As for you, Missy, you'd better be freshened up and looking perfect in less than thirty minutes. Your fiancé is coming over to meet you."

"Wait, what?"

It's as if the sky has just fallen on me. My shoulders feel heavy. My knees feel weak. My stomach is growling.

"Sergei. He's on his way over. We scheduled this days ago. You knew about it," my father says, leaning back in his seat with one eye set on his plate.

"Daddy, you can't. I haven't even consented to the engagement."

"Here we go again," he grumbles, shaking his head in disappointment. "We had this conversation already, Eileen. I thought you understood what's at stake here."

"I do, but—"

"Then go upstairs and wash away the shame of whatever you did last night," he shoots back. "Wear something pretty."

"You can borrow one of my perfumes," Ciara adds with a pleasant smile, which means something unpleasant is about to follow. "I'd let you borrow one of my floral dresses, but I doubt any would fit you."

"Oh, for—"

"Eileen has plenty of beautiful, custom-tailored dresses," my father interjects. "Perfect for her gorgeous Irish figure," he adds with a smile.

At least he never teased me about my curves. He loves me. All of me, albeit in his very stern and obtuse way. But he loves me. I don't like that he never rebukes Ciara about any of her weight-related jabs, but he's always had to keep the peace between us, especially after Ciara's mother abandoned them both.

"For the record, I'm still not okay with any of this," I mutter.

"After the stunt you pulled last night, Eileen Fiona Donovan, I don't give a rat's ass about what you're okay with," my father replies. "Now, go get ready. I'll have the kitchen prepare you a plate when you come back down. We'll be done by then, anyway."

I stomp up to my room to change.

"It is a pleasure to finally meet you, Eileen. Ronan has told me so much about you," Sergei Kuznetsov says as we shake hands in the tearoom.

His touch makes me recoil, and I wonder how much of this reaction is instinct and how much is simply me being against anything that my father tries to shove down my throat.

"Likewise, Mr. Kuznetsov," I reply with a pleasant smile.

"Sergei, please. We're going to be family soon enough."

Shivers— and not the good kind—travel down my spine at his words.

He's not a bad-looking man. On the contrary, I'll bet he's broken a string of hearts before ever setting foot in this house. Tall and athletic, Sergei appears to be a regular at the gym—or at least some sport that involves plenty of running. His shoulders are broad, and the custom, dark blue suit he's wearing falls elegantly over his muscular frame. His eyes are a cold blue, and a lock of blonde hair rests on his forehead.

He smiles, but it doesn't reach his eyes.

"Thank you for taking the time to come visit," I force myself to say, motioning for us to take our seats at the table by the window, where our staff has already set up a lovely tea service.

My father and Ciara join us, both of them quiet as they watch our interaction. It makes me feel like I'm some sort of exotic animal at the zoo, and they're introducing a new male to my enclosure.

"For you, Eileen, I will always make time," Sergei replies in a soft-spoken tone. I offer a nod as I pour a cup of tea for him, then for myself.

Ciara clears her throat, lips curled into a smirk as I look at her.

Calmly, I set the teapot down. "Here, help yourself," I say to her, then let my gaze wander over to my father, before letting it settle back on Sergei's handsome face. "So, I understand you're handling your family business now?"

"That's right, I recently took over the corporation," he replies, adding too much sugar for my taste to his tea.

"How did that happen?" I ask.

"Two of my brothers went back to Moscow. My younger brother passed away shortly after my father, leaving me to manage the US-based businesses on my own."

"They went back to Russia? Was the US mob corruption too much for them?"

"Eileen!" My father scolds me, but Sergei just laughs.

"I'll be honest, Eileen, it's refreshing to meet a woman like you," he says.

"She's one of a kind, isn't she?" my father adds.

Ciara rolls her eyes. "So, when's the wedding? It can't be too close to mine."

"The world doesn't revolve around you," I mutter.

Sergei shrugs. "We're just sitting down for tea. I'm sure Eileen doesn't want to be rushed into a life-altering event."

His Russian accent is slightly more pronounced than my captor's. I spent the single most incredible night of my life with that man, and I don't know his name.

"I'm glad you feel that way," I say. "People need to get to know each other better before they marry, right?"

"Oh, I have no doubts about the marriage part. Ronan gave me his word, and I gave mine. It's happening. But I want it to happen as smoothly and as beautifully as possible, so we can both enjoy our wedding day and the years to follow," Sergei replies.

My stomach is riddled with knots. Why does he make me feel so uneasy?

There's something beneath this pleasant surface of his. A dark shadow that makes the hairs on the back of my neck stand up. I don't see myself spending the rest of my life with this man. I barely see myself spending another hour in his company, but the dance must go on, per my father's order.

"When does Ciara wish to marry?" Sergei asks Dad.

"We haven't decided yet," Ciara says. "Before the end of this year, for sure. So you two can get married next summer or maybe next winter."

"Thank you so much," I reply, not skimping on the sarcasm.

She gives me a hard look, but she cannot hit back, not without drawing Daddy's ire.

"We'll have plenty of time to make our own arrangements," Sergei says, glancing my way. "You're more beautiful than what I saw in the magazines, Eileen."

"What magazines?" I ask, somewhat befuddled. "I've become quite adept at avoiding cameras, in general."

"*Elite Monthly* maybe?" Ciara suggests. "I think that's the last time my sister actually sat down for a photography session."

"It could be. My assistant did a wide internet search as soon as Ronan reached out with his marriage suggestion," Sergei replies, then looks at me again. "Beautiful, indeed."

I lower my gaze. "Thank you."

"Eileen here isn't exactly camera-friendly, but she's whip-smart and insanely ambitious," Ciara says. "If you want to make her happy, buy her food, books, and that lovely commercial space up on Huron Boulevard."

"A commercial space?"

"She's just kidding," I say and laugh nervously.

My father gets up. "Well, thank you for coming by today, Sergei. Shall we move to my office to iron out the details of this marriage then?"

"Shouldn't I be a part of that conversation?" I ask, every goddamn alarm bell ringing in my head as I look up at them.

"Oh, it's nothing to concern yourself with, Eileen. This is the business side of the arrangement," he replies.

"And I've got a fitting to get to," Ciara stands, perky and bright-eyed.

"You don't even have a wedding date," I mumble.

"What can I say? I'm excited!"

Sergei chuckles softly. "You have yet to tell me the name of your betrothed, Ciara."

"It's not something we wish to publicize just yet—" my father is about to explain, but my sister cuts him off with the enthusiasm of a little girl who just stumbled into the land of endless candy.

"I'm marrying Anton Karpov!"

For a moment, I can almost feel the air in the room shifting. The darkness that settles over Sergei's face is brief but telling. Whoever this Karpov dude is, Sergei clearly hates his guts. It's the first time I see a crack in his mask, and it's unsettling.

"Congratulations are in order then," he says, his tone flat.

Perhaps these wedding deals that Daddy made might not turn out the way he hoped.

CHAPTER 3

ANTON

Eileen has left a lasting impression on me.

I don't think she's aware of her power, of her sizzling magnetism. Then again, I didn't tell her, just as I didn't admit that I knew who she was. We agreed to anonymity, though I had her at a disadvantage the whole time.

"Where's Room 106?" I ask the receptionist as I walk in, leaving the cold morning behind in the half-empty parking lot of the shoddiest motel that my brother could find.

The guy looks at me with a dazed mist covering his bloodshot eyes. The whiff of weed is quick to follow. My boy here is as high as a kite. "Room 106?"

"Yeah, 106. I'm meeting someone there," I say.

"Uh, okay... Room 106..." He pauses, the brain process working extra slow and probably frying a couple of synapses in the process. "Right. Take the stairs over there, first floor, take a right, and it's all the way at the end of the hallway."

"Thanks."

He slouches back in his seat, hidden behind the desk and his computer monitor, while I make my way up the stairs, ignoring the musty smell that permeates every inch of this place.

My mind wanders back to Eileen.

We shouldn't have done what we did.

I shouldn't have, anyway. She doesn't know who I am, but I do know who *she* is, and, given what this year is shaping up to look like for me, it was a dangerous move. I couldn't help it. I didn't want to stop. She's so fucking delicious. But that smart mouth of hers is going to get her in some serious trouble someday. She's sharp and soft at the same time.

Fucking hell, I can still taste her on my lips.

Once I reach Room 106, I look both ways to make sure I wasn't followed before knocking on the door. I can hear a man's pained grunts echoing from inside, followed by rushed footsteps. A split second later, my brother opens the door. He looks tired and disheveled, his shirt crumpled and stained with blood, sweat, and booze, judging by the smell.

"What the hell, Andrei?" I snap and go right in, my shoulder brushing his.

"Took you long enough," he grumbles.

Thankfully, Tommy Benedetto is still alive. Beaten bloody and passed out, tied to a chair, and gagged with a hand towel, but alive. I turn around to look at my brother.

"Thank you for listening to me for once in your life," I say.

"I haven't decided what I'm going to do with him yet," Andrei replies. "Everything is very much still on the table. I just wanted to hear what you had to say about this. You insisted."

I take a deep breath, trying to keep my wits about me. More often than not, my brother has let his emotions decide his course of action. More often than not, I've had to clean up his messes to avoid an all-out war with one or another family from Chicago's underbelly, where we, too, belong. What happened last night was not one of his smarter moves, and now I must steer him back in the right direction before he gets us both killed.

"Sit down," I tell Andrei, pouring him a drink from the minibar and helping myself to a single shot of whiskey.

Andrei takes a seat in the chair by the window, his eyes never leaving me. I give him his drink and sit next to him at the small table. "Go on, tear me a new one," he says.

"I get it; I do," I begin with a casual shrug. "Tommy did a stupid thing, and I agree—offing him would be the easiest and the simplest solution." As if summoned, Tommy opens his eyes and damn near jumps out of his chair upon seeing me. "Isn't that right, Tommy?"

"Mhm-mmph!" He can't talk with the towel crammed in his bloodied mouth.

"I'm sure we're in agreement here," I say, giving him a slight nod. "Sit tight there, buddy. With a little bit of luck, you're going home today."

Andrei shakes his head. "Not until you tell me why."

"Listen, I'm all for setting an example these days. Another family disrespects you in public, you do what you have to do. And what Tommy did is not easy to forgive. But we've got a bigger issue on our hands, brother. There's been a shift in the organization."

"Yeah, yeah, I heard all about it—"

I cut him off. "No, you didn't hear all about it because I come bearing bad news. Kuznetsov is making his moves, just as I suspected."

Andrei gives me a startled look. "What moves?"

"There are several smaller players stepping onto the board, which is why I agreed to the Donovans' business offer. If you kill Tommy, you can kiss the Camorras' support goodbye. There's a power play happening, Andrei, and we need to be on top of it."

"They wouldn't dare," my brother mutters.

"They *would* dare. They keep daring. Kuznetsov will soon be announcing his engagement to Eileen Donovan."

His eyes grow wide. "Fuck."

"Precisely. And that's just the first step. You know as well as I do that some of the families within our organization have repeatedly voiced their displeasure regarding our business decisions. More than once, they have called for a vote, which, I might remind you, we narrowly won. We can't risk this getting bigger, so we can't forfeit the Camorra's support. Right now, they're still with us. But if you take Tommy out, the Kuznetsovs or anybody else looking to wage a coup will benefit from the Benedetto family's blessing."

"I don't like this," Andrei says. "In the old days, we could've resolved it easily."

"Sure, a couple of Kalashnikovs would've done the trick. It's the twenty-first century, Andrei, and we're spinning billions of dollars in and out of this city. Our alliance with the Italians is one of our strongest assets. We don't want to forfeit that."

"No, we don't." He shakes his head and runs his fingers through his dark, wavy hair. It's only a matter of time before he starts getting his first silver strands. I got mine in my early forties. He's thirty-eight, and the clock keeps ticking. "If I let Tommy go, he'll want to retaliate," Andrei says, giving him a sour look.

"He will not," I reply, then look over to Tommy. "You won't; will you, buddy? I mean, you have to realize that you're the one at fault here."

Benedetto stares at me for a moment. I'm almost expecting a rebuttal, but he just nods frantically, his eyes wide with fear. In the span of a single second, I'm transported back to last night. It was a quick decision. A hasty move. But it was the only reasonable thing to do when I saw Tommy being thrown into the back of the van and my brother's men rushing toward Eileen. Grab her and bolt. They recognized me and didn't decide to come after us. That would've led to an unnecessary mess.

"Fine. Tommy gets to live another day," Andrei concedes. "But he'll owe us big time."

"Big time," I repeat.

Andrei may be my younger brother, but we are equal partners in the business and in the family. I need his approval on certain matters, and when I interfere in his affairs, I have to make sure that I'm able to get him on board and back on my side. The others must always see a united front.

"I've called my men off the girl," my brother adds.

"Thank you."

"Who was the broad, anyway? Tommy's last catch?"

I shake my head. "No, but trust me, it would've led to a civil war had your men gotten to her. By the way, you really need to be more careful about the orders you give them. The whole no-witnesses thing doesn't apply when said witness is Eileen fucking Donovan."

"Oh, shit," my brother gasps. "The boys didn't mention that."

"They probably didn't recognize her. She's not the popular sister, the one that's always in the limelight from what I've learned. And she was petrified. I'm not sure she would've managed to identify herself in time."

I remember the way she trembled in my arms when I grabbed her in that alley, and when she came later, as I buried myself inside of her.

Damn you, Eileen, you have no idea what you've done to me.

"Then it's a good thing you intervened," Andrei sighs deeply. "Dodged quite the bullet there, eh?"

I nod in agreement. "She was kind enough to agree to keep the entire incident to herself, which will keep Kuznetsov off our backs in the future."

"And Ronan Donovan on our side still, I hope?"

"Yeah, we'll see about that," I reply.

Andrei glances back at Tommy. "I can see now why you were so adamant about this asshole. If we lose the Irish support, we'll definitely need the Italians and the Puerto Ricans to stick by our side."

With everything I've heard coming down the pipeline, I know it'll get a whole lot worse before it gets better. My brother and I have a pretty good handle on the organization, but we're not invincible or indestructible. All it takes is a few precise, calculated hits, and the scales could tip. Keeping Tommy Benedetto alive and bringing the Donovans into our fold are the first two of many steps we'll need to take.

Otherwise, the sharks will taste blood.

CHAPTER 4

EILEEN

For two months, I've been replaying that night in my head. Reliving the most intense moments of my life, from the scare with Tommy Benedetto to the lovemaking with my mystery man. Now I find myself staring at the plus sign of a pregnancy test, sweating bullets as I try to wrap my head around the whole thing.

"This is one hell of a clusterfuck," I mutter as I toss the stick in the bathroom bin and proceed to wash my hands.

I'm pregnant. And I don't even know the father's name.

Ciara has been droning on all day about finally meeting her fiancé tonight. I can hear people downstairs already, their voices mingling with the music of a small orchestra. Laughter. The clinking of glasses.

"Well, at least I know why I'm nauseated all the time," I tell my reflection in the bathroom mirror. "Kuznetsov's only part of the reason."

It's not that I don't like him. He's... nice. But he unsettles me, and I don't want to marry him. I have little to no power over my own life as a Donovan. I've known that for as long as I can remember, but still.

"Eileen, are you drowning in there?" Ciara calls out.

I roll my eyes. "I'm just retouching my makeup!" I shout back. "Go get yourself a drink or yell at the waiters or... something!"

I listen to the sound of her Jimmy Choos recede as I take another look in the mirror. My breasts were already quite large, but now they're struggling against the bra I'm wearing underneath a maroon evening dress. The fabric is a soft satin blend, and it's pinched in a manner that gives me an hourglass figure. Thank God there are no visible signs of my pregnancy yet.

How in the hell am I going to explain myself out of this one?

My father will explode.

I'll never hear the end of it from Ciara.

And Sergei... I doubt he'll want to marry me once he learns I'm carrying another man's child.

I have to get through tonight first, take it one step at a time, so I can preserve my sanity.

I smile at the mirror and practice my host-friendly smile. We're expecting about a hundred guests in the ballroom of our mansion—each a member of high society and the mob. In the Donovans' ballroom, deals are made, futures are decided, and alliances are built.

"There you are," Ciara scoffs as I meet her downstairs in the kitchen.

Around us, waiters with ruby-red velvet vests over white shirts and black pants buzz around like busy, breathless bees—carrying hors d'oeuvres and champagne platters out, bringing empty ones back in, refilling, then stopping by the chef's counter for updated instructions.

"Wow, I feel like I'm in a Michelin-starred review," I say and laugh lightly, glancing everywhere.

"Not with these canapes," Ciara says, pointing at three large plates resting on the table between us. "Look at them! I couldn't let the waiters go out with this garbage."

"I don't understand; what's wrong with them?" I ask, looking rather confused as I try to identify the problem.

They look like simple but elegant snacks—disk-shaped pastries with a dollop of cream cheese whip and different sorts of sauces drizzled on top. If anything, my mouth is watering, and I could easily consume one plate all by myself. I can't help but wonder if I'm already experiencing cravings or if I'm just hungry.

"I specifically asked for ricotta cheese mousse, and they used goat cheese!" Ciara exclaims, sounding like it's the end of the world.

"And how is that bad?"

"Because I asked for one thing, and they delivered something else. It's disrespectful."

"But tasty." I try to take the edge off, but Ciara isn't biting, pun intended.

She gives me a sour look. "You look puffy," she bitterly strikes back. "Also, you're not taking this seriously. My engagement party needs to be *perfect*, and it's anything but. Just earlier, I learned that we won't be serving my favorite Bordeaux. Daddy had them replace it with some Petrus from 1985. Yuck!"

"That's actually a superb vintage," I reply. "I would love a glass or..." My voice trails off as I'm reminded of my newly discovered condition. "Or lemonade. I think I'll stick to lemonade."

"What?" Ciara sounds confused.

"Girls, come on," my father pokes his head through the kitchen door. "The Karpovs are here. Let's make the introductions before the announcement later tonight."

"But, Daddy, the canapes—"

"Ciara, for fuck's sake!"

That's enough to silence her, at least where the food and drinks are concerned. I draw a deep breath and follow Ciara and our father through the kitchen door into the main salon. At the far end, I see the glass doors leading into the ballroom. My stomach churns at the sight of so many people already gathered in there. The main salon still feels breathable at this point, with only a handful of guests. Two men and a woman.

"Oh, my God," I gasp as I recognize the tall man with dark hair and hazel eyes, broad shoulders, and salt-and-pepper hair. The man who made me feel like the most precious of all women on a night two months ago.

"Ciara, honey, this is Anton Karpov," my father says, nodding at my mystery man. "Your future husband. Anton, meet my youngest, Ciara Donovan."

"It's a pleasure to finally make your acquaintance," Anton says.

I'm frozen in place, unable to move or say anything. All I can do is stare at this dangerously gorgeous man, fragments of our night together, causing my core to tighten and my throat to close up, my stomach to churn and my heart to flutter.

"Likewise," Ciara replies, eagerly straightening her back as she lets him take her hand in his. She giggles, careful to bat her eyelashes for maximum effect. "I've heard so many wonderful things about you, Anton."

Really, Ciara?

Like what? Like he's the leader of the Bratva? Like he's the most ruthless Russian American on this side of the country, if not the whole continent?

Dammit, why is he looking at me like that? He's so calm. No expression whatsoever. Just a slight nod of acknowledgment.

"You must be Eileen then," Anton says, his voice low.

"Yeah," I bluntly reply.

I know what this is. He got his groove on with me that night, knowing precisely who I was. He got what he wanted, and now I'm just a big, fat nobody. I feel used. I feel stupid. I feel so many uncomfortable things that I don't even know what to do with myself or how I'm going to survive the rest of this evening.

"Eileen?" my father says, intensely looking at me.

"Yeah?" I manage.

"What's up with you? You're being rude," Ciara says.

I give her a confused look, trying so hard to avoid Anton's gaze and ignoring the other two people he's with. "What do you mean?" I ask.

"My God, Daddy, I think she's already drunk," Ciara sighs deeply.

"No, I'm not."

"Then I am sure you could do better at entertaining our special guests," my father says. "After all, we're going to be family, and Anton here deserves more than a dry 'yeah.'"

"My apologies," I say, switching to a more polite version of myself—a dead-eyed version—while I try to manage the turmoil within. I give Anton a small smile. "It's an honor to meet you, Mr. Karpov. You're definitely the luckiest man in Chicago right now."

"Please, call me Anton," he says, his eyes never leaving mine. "I suppose fortune has smiled upon me lately."

Yeah, you boned one Donovan girl and you're about to marry the pretty one.

The nerve of this guy. "My stepsister will make a fine wife," I say.

There's a tremor in my voice, and I hope nobody caught it.

"I'll do my best to rise to her level as a husband," he replies.

The guy who looks like a slightly younger version of Anton clears his throat, a weak smile on his face. Does he know about Anton and me? Do brothers gossip the way sisters do? Then again, I never told Ciara about that night. Clearly, I never will.

"Right. This is my brother, Andrei Karpov. And this is his wife, Laura," Anton says.

"You look stunning," Ciara says to Laura, shaking her hand. "I love what this silver silk is doing for your figure."

"You can't even tell I just had twins, can you?" Laura chuckles softly, then glances my way. "Maroon does wonders for your complexion, Eileen. A Donovan through and through."

"Actually, my mother was Russian," I reply. She shakes my hand with a firmness that surprises me. "From the Fedorov dynasty."

"Dynasty," Andrei laughs lightly. "You could say that. They are royalty within our organization, I suppose."

Anton gives him a hard look. "Genealogically speaking, the Fedorov family are the closest relations to the Russian royal bloodline."

"They are? Well, then, that explains their entitlement," Andrei shoots back.

Clearly, these two like to poke each other, and it makes my father laugh wholeheartedly as he pats Anton on the shoulder. "Eileen is right. Her mother was a Russian beauty. A goddess in my eyes."

"My mom had big shoes to fill, but she rose to the occasion, didn't she?" Ciara cuts in.

I can hear the hurt in her voice. It's a touchy subject, our mothers. Mine died. Hers ran off. Hard pills to swallow for both of us. Maybe that's why I let Ciara sting me whenever she feels the need. She's got quite a lot to carry on her shoulders, whether she's excited about this wedding or not.

"I have to say, Ronan, this is quite the party you've put together," Anton says, steering the conversation away as he looks around, his gaze lingering on the glass doors that lead into the ballroom. "It's going to be an interesting evening, to say the least."

"And your home is absolutely beautiful," Laura adds. "I love the details on the woodwork. Don't think I didn't notice the staircase and the wall paneling."

"My splendid wife is an interior designer," Andrei says, one hand resting on the small of her back. "And she has excellent taste. I can only agree with her observations, Mr. Donovan. Truly a beautiful home."

"Please, call me Ronan," my father replies, then looks at Anton. "And you're right. It is going to be an interesting night. Sergei was unable to join us, however. He's busy scouting the West Coast for the perfect wedding location."

Anton gives him a curious look while stealing a glance at me. Ciara is practically nonexistent to him, but she's too excited to even notice. I feel awful. "Sergei? You mean Sergei Kuznetsov?"

"Yes," my father says.

"Such a shame," Andrei replies, but I can tell from the tone of his voice that he's elated by Sergei's absence.

"What involvement does Sergei have in my wedding?" Anton asks.

"Oh, not for our wedding," Ciara chimes in as she smiles at me. "His wedding to Eileen. They're not getting married until later next year, but the man wants what's best for his big, beautiful bride."

There it is. Another jab. I could call her out, but given that I'm pregnant by her future husband, I decide to let it go. It's bad enough as it is. The shame slowly eats away at me, but I keep my game face on and my chin up.

"You're marrying Sergei Kuznetsov?" Anton asks me.

"I am, yes."

"Another strategic agreement?" he asks my father.

"Precisely. My counselors advised me about it," Daddy replies. "The Kuznetsovs will support our alliance in the future, and it'll strengthen your lead in the Bratva, too."

"It will also give the Donovans a louder voice at the big boys' table," Andrei says, nodding with genuine appreciation. "Smart move, Ronan. I'll give you that. Bringing two Russian families into the fold." There's something in Andrei's tone I don't quite like, but I can't explain why.

"Shall we head into the ballroom and have a few drinks?" Ciara asks, ever the gracious hostess. "We've got a few exquisite vintages for you to try."

"Oh, do lead the way," Laura says excitedly.

I smile and let the ladies go first, while Andrei sticks to my father's side. Anton lingers, still looking at me. My skin burns all over. My heart's wrestling against my chest.

"After you," he says.

"Piss off," I snap, bolting for the ballroom.

Glancing back, I see the shadow of a smile dancing across his lips. It's going to be a long fucking night, and Anton is clearly enjoying this a little too much.

CHAPTER 5

EILEEN

The worst part is I can't drink these troubles away.

I play my part out of respect and love for my father. I smile and clink glasses, telling people I'm drinking mimosas and not plain orange juice in a champagne glass when asked. I laugh and trade jokes, pretending I'm happy to be here, supporting Ciara in her big moment. But halfway through the evening, and despite genuinely enjoying Laura's company, in particular, I feel drained.

"The Bratva men can be complicated," Laura says at one point as she casually describes her marriage to Andrei. "It was a bit of a culture shock for me, to be honest. There I was, this blonde Ivy League princess who spent most of her weekends at Daddy's country club, saying yes to a man I'd only met a few times before. I used to pity the royals and their arranged weddings."

"But you were always free to marry whoever you wanted," I point out, nursing my juice, sip after sip as I let my gaze wander across the ballroom.

"Of course," Laura says. "But I was financially dependent on my parents, and they really wanted this marriage to happen. I told myself I'd divorce the man after a year if I didn't like it. That way, my dad would get his business deals, Andrei would get his pretty American bride, and everybody would be fine if I just slipped out of the picture, you know?"

"And you've been married for how long now?"

"Ten years," she laughs. "As I was saying, there's something about these Bratva men. Andrei actually told me the night we met that he was going to make me the happiest woman alive."

I can't help but chuckle softly. "I'm guessing by a decade later that he nailed it?"

"Oh, yeah. I can't imagine my life without him. And let me tell you something else—Ciara's lucky. We weren't sure that Anton would ever get married. Any woman would be the most fortunate on earth to land that man. If Andrei is fierce and powerful, strong and determined, a protector and a provider through and through, as much as I adore my husband, I have to admit Anton is even more so."

"Is he?" I mumble, watching him as he dances with Ciara beneath the crystal chandelier.

They're the stars of the show. Their engagement has been announced, and they were met with cheers and applause, while I've been carrying a knot in my chest, trying to make it through the evening.

"Sometimes, I jokingly tell Andrei that if something should ever happen to him, I'd gladly marry his brother," Laura blurts out with a laugh. "It's just a way to tease him. I can't threaten him with Anton anymore, though. He belongs to Ciara now."

"I think Andrei knows he's got one hell of a woman on his hands," I reply with a warm smile, yet I can't look away from Anton.

The black suit that he's wearing fits him perfectly, drawing sharp, dramatic lines against his muscular frame. The red pocket square adds a touch of elegance to the man with a perfectly chiseled jawline and piercing gaze that keeps finding me wherever I try to hide in the crowd. And every time he looks at me, it's as if time stops.

"You'll have to excuse me, Laura, I need a breath of fresh air."

I leave her by the champagne bar and snake my way through the crowd. A smile here, a nod there, a shake of the hand, and I manage to slip past my father before he turns his head and sees me. Outside on the terrace, the cold night awaits with a starry sky and a silent garden.

"Deep breath," I whisper. "It's almost over."

Tears prick my eyes.

This is so unfair. The only man to ever make me feel beautiful and desired, and he's marrying the one woman who can always find a way to insult me. Their wedding will be unbearable to watch. Two months later, and I still can't get Anton out of my head, my body still responding to his mere presence. Even worse, I'm carrying his child.

"Not much of a party gal, eh?" His voice startles me.

"I didn't hear you come out," I gasp, quick to turn around and take a couple of steps back as I face him. "What are you doing out here?"

"Figured you could use some company."

"You figured wrong. I came out here because I wanted to be alone. Your fiancée is waiting for you."

Anton stares at me for what feels like forever. "Perhaps I should apologize."

"Oh?"

"It wasn't right. What I did that night."

"Answer me this: Ciara knew you were going to be her husband. We were celebrating that night. Did you know she'd be your wife?" I ask with a quivering voice.

"Yes."

The air between us thickens. Rage and hurt swirl through me, further confusing me as I carefully choose my words. "And did you know who I was when you abducted me, Anton?"

"When I saved you, you mean."

"Whatever. Did you know?"

"Yes."

"Yet you went ahead with it anyway," I say, crossing my arms. "Those were your brother's goons. His name kept popping up. You two had a beef with Tommy Benedetto. What did you do to that poor sap, anyway?"

Anton smiles, lighting a fire in my belly. "Yes, I went ahead with it anyway. And yes, those were my brother's men. We did have a beef with Tommy. Well, my brother did, but that's been resolved."

"You killed him, didn't you? I hear his family is still looking for him."

He shrugs. "If that's what you choose to think about us, who am I to contradict you?"

"You're my future brother-in-law, for fuck's sake," I snap. "It is beyond egregious. Everything you did is irredeemable!"

"Are you done?"

I huff and head for the stone steps leading into the garden. Anton follows me, the shadows growing heavier while the noise of the party fades behind us.

"I want to be alone," I tell him.

"Not before you hear what I have to say."

"You're marrying my stepsister. There is nothing left to say."

He grabs my arms and pulls me back. I whirl around, ready to slap him, but my knees turn to jelly instead, and I crash into him. He holds me close. *Too* close. His cologne is inebriating. His hot breath tickles my face. It's his penthouse living room all over again, and I have no control over my body.

"Eileen, I apologize for not telling you who I was that night. I did it to protect you and your stepsister. I needed to make sure my brother didn't make the biggest mistake of his life. Fortunately, that issue was resolved," he says. His voice makes my skin tingle all over. "I will not apologize for what happened, though. We were both willing participants. From what I remember, you were more than eager well into the morning."

"You knew you were marrying my stepsister," I say.

"I was still technically a free man. No official announcement had been made."

"It was made tonight, so what are you doing?" I reply, feeling his touch on the small of my back. It makes my core tighten and liquid heat seep into my panties.

Anton lowers his head as if he's about to kiss me.

"You're incredible, you know that?" he says, his lips brushing against the tip of my nose. "You have no idea. No clue about the power you hold."

"Please stop."

"That's not what you really want. Certainly not what your body is saying."

"It's not right," I manage, moaning softly as both his hands settle on my buttocks. He squeezes firmly, pulling me into him, and I melt against his chest, my knees soft and my senses shattered. "We can't."

"No, we can't. It's something I'll have to live with for the sake of my but remember this, Eileen. I do not regret that night we spent together, nor do I wish to ever forget it."

"I don't understand."

"Maybe someday you will," he says, then takes a step back.

I'm left feeling cold and alone as he looks at me and takes a deep breath. A door opens on the terrace and music from the ballroom fills the air.

"Anton, where are you?" Ciara calls out.

I freeze, my eyes wide with horror, but Anton gives me a smile and a reassuring wink. "Give me five minutes, then come back inside," he whispers before raising his voice so Ciara can hear him. "Right here, darling, hold on."

He dashes back to the terrace steps, while I remain sheltered under the sycamore tree with its thick, heavy crown. I count my breaths as I listen to Anton and Ciara chatting before they go back into the ballroom.

As soon as I'm alone again, I burst into tears.

CHAPTER 6

ANTON

I knew I'd see her again.

I just didn't expect to feel like I'd been struck by lightning. For two months, I'd been telling myself that it was all in the past. One night. A reasonable mistake that was absolutely worth making. Seeing her the other night, however, had proven that it was *not* in the past at all.

"Earth to Anton," Andrei says, pulling me back into the present. "What the hell is up with you these past few days?"

"I'm fine; relax," I tell him. "Eyes on the ball, brother."

We're seated at a massive conference table on the first floor of the Upton Conference Center—a favorite meeting spot for our organization. Cameras and tight security. State-of-the-art surveillance and meeting services. All Karpov-owned. When we call the Bratva families for a meeting, we make sure it's on our turf. Our terms.

We're still waiting for a couple of guests. Most everyone else is here, exchanging pleasantries and gossip.

I find myself focused on the Fedorovs, probably because of Eileen's mother. She was a Fedorov. Ivan's sister, to be specific. He's here with another sister, Petra.

He's still alive and kicking, still ruling over his family with an iron fist.

Still haunted by her death.

"Seriously, what's up with you?" Andrei asks in a low voice. "You've been distracted since the engagement party."

"It's nothing; I promise."

"It's not nothing. I saw the looks you and Eileen were giving each other. What happened that night with the Tommy bullshit?"

I give my brother a hard scowl. "This really isn't the time to talk about that."

"Fine, we can discuss it later. But right now, I need you here with me, alright? Kuznetsov isn't playing. He'll have plenty to say when he arrives."

"I'm with you," I reassure Andrei.

But I'm feeling the same uneasiness Andrei is. Kuznetsov has been making a few unsettling business moves across Chicago lately, building up competition against the Karpovs where he shouldn't. It's the beginning of a power play, and getting his hands on Eileen Donovan is just the icing on the cake. My instincts are right, at least where Sergei is concerned.

He's up to something.

"Look at the Abramovic gang, those sneers on their faces," I whisper to Andrei.

"They always act like pompous, arrogant pricks," he scoffs, following my gaze.

"It's different this time."

"Kuznetsov's influence?"

"Most likely. The Fedorovs have always been neutral, siding with the family in power, but I can't trust them anymore. Not with Sergei marrying Ivan's niece. That'll make Sergei family."

"You'll be family, too, by marriage," Andrei reminds me.

"Not good enough. Ciara's not a Donovan by blood. There are times when I think I'm marrying the wrong sister."

He gives me a startled look. "I knew it," he hisses. "You do have something going on with Eileen."

"Keep your trap shut."

Our conversation ends when Sergei Kuznetsov comes in, accompanied by one of his associates. The conference table is now fully occupied, twelve heads and their appropriate partners are present.

"Since when do you bring Americans to the table?" Oleg Aronov asks Sergei.

"Here we go," my brother mumbles. "There's always a loud-mouth Aronov at the ready."

"Ladies, gentlemen, I'm sure you all remember Paul Mattis, my business associate," Sergei replies with a flat smile as he loosens the button on his grey suit jacket. "His mother is Elena Kuznetsov, my cousin."

"Eat crow," Max Abramovic chuckles while his associate gives the Aronov boys quite the stink eye.

"Thank you all for coming," I say loudly, sitting at the head of the table. "I'm glad we're able to do this once a month without whipping out our semi-autos like the old days."

"Or the glory days," Ivan Fedorov grumbles.

"What was glorious about the Bratva being fractured, families slaughtering families for a slice of Chicago pie?" Andrei retorts. "We're all stronger together, and you know it."

Sergei smiles broadly. "That doesn't mean we have to like each other, right?"

"Anyway, I understand congratulations are in order," I say, raising my voice ever so slightly. I don't need much to command the room. The day they speak over me is the day my reign will end. "Sergei, I understand we're going to be family."

"I suppose marrying a Donovan does have its disadvantages," he sneers.

Good. I want him to hate me. I look forward to making his life miserable. A prick like Sergei Kuznetsov should never be allowed anywhere near Eileen. The mere thought of them building a family together makes my stomach turn.

"It does help with unifying the Bratva for generations to come," I say. "Someday, our last names won't matter anymore."

"Yes, we'll all be one big happy family, all of us bowing before—let me guess—your children, not mine," Sergei says.

Andrei raises a hand. "Gentlemen, come on. These engagements are a cause for celebration. Bringing the Irish into the fold was a smart move."

"*I'm* the one bringing the Irish into the fold, just like *I'm* the one enticing the Italians with more lucrative offers," Sergei shoots back. "All while you go off kidnapping their kids out of sheer spite. You're lucky the Benedetto family was willing to sit down and talk to me about the entire incident, Andrei."

"You're exaggerating," I reply. "It was a delicate situation, but we handled it."

"The only reason you didn't wake up next to a pig's head in your bed this morning is because I talked Tony Benedetto off the ledge," Sergei says. "And frankly, we're all getting a bit tired of these Karpov messes. We're the ones who have to clean up after you, it seems."

I shake my head slowly as I look at him. "Now, you're just being dramatic. Tommy was at fault. Granted, our reaction could've been more tempered, but we talked things through and sorted everything out. Whatever meeting you had with Tony was your business, not ours."

"I secured their support if the Puerto Ricans decide to move in on the waterfront businesses," Sergei says. He gets a nod of approval and confirmation from Paul Mattis, his trusted sidekick.

"The Puerto Ricans have grown brazen," Paul says. "Rumor has it, they're working with the Colombians to gang up on us. They've had emissaries visiting the Triads and the Yakuza, too, though I'm not sure how those conversations went."

Peter Popov grunts with displeasure as he pours whiskey into his coffee from a gold-plated flask he keeps in his jacket pocket. "This is it, boys. End of days. If the Chinese and the Japanese line up for the South Americans, we'll need proper leadership."

"What do you mean, proper leadership?" I calmly ask.

"Someone who doesn't have us wasting time patching shit up with the Italians or the Irish. We need both on our side," Ilinka Aslanova interjects, her cold gray eyes cutting right through me. She may be in her sixties, but the woman can make any man quiver with a lift of her eyebrow. "In fact, I think it's time we send emissaries of our own. The Mexicans might need our support, and the Polish need to be brought up to speed as well."

I look across the table, noticing a change in sympathies. Andrei and I have suspected it for a while now, but it's becoming visible. Sergei has been lobbying for support behind the scenes, and it appears it has paid off. It leaves my brother and me in a relatively delicate position. Reasserting ourselves at the top of the pack is imperative, but we can't just whip our dicks out on the table, figuratively speaking.

"What are you saying, Mrs. Aslanova?" I reply, narrowing my eyes at her.

"What I'm saying is I wouldn't send you or your brother. Andrei's got a short temper, and you... we all know how you negotiate, Anton. What we need for the months and years to come is diplomacy and a sly tongue."

"Let me guess; Sergei Kuznetsov should be our emissary," my brother laughs. "The man is naturally unlikeable. Look at Paul, practically recoiling whenever Sergei opens his mouth."

"Are you trying to be as offensive as possible?" Sergei retorts, visibly insulted.

"He's not wrong," I chuckle. "Sergei, you're a brilliant accountant, I'll give you that. Your gift with numbers is beyond impressive, and it's probably why your businesses within our organization have been thriving since you took over. But dealing with the Mexicans and the Polish, reeling the Japanese or the Chinese in, those things are not within your repertoire, buddy."

Sergei leans forward. "Ilinka doesn't want you representing us."

"Ilinka has one vote at this table. One."

"One vote can make all the difference."

I stand up, letting my anger get the better of me for a brief moment. I quickly remind myself that I cannot let Sergei win today, not even by a vote. Andrei is damn near ready to take out his weapon and empty the entire magazine into the bastard's face. In the old days, I probably would've applauded such initiative. But these are different times, and these people require a different approach.

I want Sergei to be fuming by the end of the meeting. Therefore, I need to beat him at his own game, so I take a deep breath and look closely at each of the players present.

"Alright, ladies and gentlemen. Clearly, there are some issues we need to address here. The lack of confidence in my brother's and my ability to lead the organization cannot exist. Perhaps I should remind everyone that it was the Karpovs who brought Tony Benedetto into the Cavalier a few years back to sign the Century Truce."

"That truce had sloppy terms—" Sergei interrupts, but I cut him off.

"The adult in charge is speaking. Wait your turn." I give him a dry smile, then resume my focus on the entire conference table. "From the moment I took over the chairman's seat, our organization has seen a 250 percent growth rate in every single branch of activity, a 45 percent drop in the frequency of visits from the federal authorities."

"In fact, twenty of the ninety current RICO investigations that the government's agencies have built against us were dropped in just the first half of this year," Andrei chimes in, eyes scrolling over his phone notes. "Another fifteen ended with either short-term arrests or charges dropped, tolerable settlements with the DA, and three hung juries."

"On top of that, we had five organization members elected to the city and district councils in November," I add. "That gives us additional influence over the regional authorities as far as docking and building permits are concerned. It will translate into approximately... What was the number again, brother?"

Andrei gives me a playful wink. "Twenty-seven point eight billion dollars, estimated to come in by the end of next year for three new residential and commercial projects, Lincoln Park, Douglas, and Bridgeport, to be specific."

"Our organization has seen nothing but growth and fewer run-ins with the law since the Karpovs have been sitting at the head of this table," I say. "Fewer killings, too. How many lieutenants and cousins have you buried this year?"

"Just the one," Popov admits. "Just Fyodor."

"And who killed Fyodor?" I ask.

Peter stares at his spiked coffee. "Charles Feng."

"And what happened to Charles Feng?" I reply, knowing the answer already.

Peter looks up at me. "A nice cup of polonium tea."

"What did the Triads do when the ME published his autopsy report?"

"They sent us a valuable heirloom," Andrew reminds everyone. "A gift, they called it. An apology for what Feng did to Fyodor."

"So, pardon me, Sergei," I say, looking back at Kuznetsov and enjoying watching the color drain from his face, "if I call bullshit on the doubts you're trying to cast upon Andrei and me. Unfortunately, we're not perfect. Andrei's temper did generate a small snag here and there, but it wasn't anything that we couldn't handle. The truth is, the Karpovs are an asset, whether you like it or not. So let's call a vote."

"Huh?" Andrei gives me a startled glance.

I reply with a subtle nod. I've got them right where I want them, and my brother will soon understand. There's still a risk that it might blow up in my face, but I can tell from Ilinka's face that I've got her back on our side.

"Let's call a vote," I repeat. "All those who want the Karpovs to remain at the head of this table, raise your hands."

For a long moment, they simply stare at me. A few mouths are gaping wide, but I stand my ground, calm and composed, waiting for their vote. Max Abramovic scoffs, not as bewildered as the elders present.

"I take it you don't like the roles and the responsibilities anymore," he says.

"On the contrary, I very much do. But seeing as Sergei and some of his ass lickers feel like they would do a better job, I figured I'd let the Bratva council decide. What say ye?"

Another moment passes before the first few hands go up. The usual suspects are in my corner, but Abramovic and Kuznetsov aren't alone either. The Popov and the Sokolov representatives lower their gazes. I hear Andrei's sharp exhale as Peter Popov and Ilinka Aslanova raise their hands. To Sergei's dismay, so does Oleg Aronov.

"Eight to four. Not bad," I reply with a broad smile. "Your confidence is greatly appreciated."

It's a good thing they're not aware of the massive sigh of relief that just unraveled deep inside of me. I'll let it out once they all leave the room. I have to keep it cool for now; truth be told, four dissenters will turn to more later down the line, and Andrei and I both know it.

"Shall we get back to business then?" Andrei asks.

Sergei is anything but happy. He doesn't seem too bummed out either. I can tell from the look on his face. I bet he's doing the math in his head, thinking the same as me. Four could easily become six by the next council meeting. Then six could become eight and so on. If I lose my seat, Sergei will find an opening to do more damage to my family without a single care concerning our bond with the Donovans.

I guess I'll just have to make sure I keep my seat.

CHAPTER 7

EILEEN

"This is insane," I tell my father as we wait outside the chapel for the bride to arrive. "The fact that you keep entertaining each of Ciara's whims does not bode well for you, Dad."

"Eileen, she wanted to get married quickly, and Anton agreed," Dad says.

He's paler than usual, dark circles blooming under his eyes. It's been two months since the engagement party, two months since I learned that my stepsister's husband-to-be is the father of the baby growing inside me, two months since I've been carrying this secret with an aching heart and a heavy soul.

It's supposed to be a joyous occasion, right?

Wrong.

It's been hell.

"Still, a wedding of this magnitude on such short notice," I sigh deeply. "It's not like Anton was going to change his mind."

Though secretly I wish he had.

"Ciara was adamant that we do this sooner rather than later," my father says, his gaze wandering over to the town car. "I think it was because she didn't want you to have to wait as long to marry Sergei."

Yeah, right.

"How magnanimous of her," I mutter.

"Eileen, this animosity between you and Ciara has to stop," he says, then winces. "We need to come across as a strong and tight-knit front for these Russian pricks."

"Dad, what's wrong with you?" I ask.

"Nothing."

"Dad."

"Nothing, Eileen. I'm just tired and stressed out of my mind. I'm giving away two daughters this year. I'd hoped I would have a little more time with you before you leave with Sergei. Honey, I love you more than life itself. It just hurts to let you go."

The words sound nice enough in my head.

"Here comes the bride," Dad says as Ciara steps out of a white limo.

Her bridal gown is ridiculously dramatic. She looks like a haute couture model about to make waves at the Met Gala.

It's not a dress; it's a sculpture made of white satin and too many layers of tulle and pearls.

She's beautiful. Her makeup is perfect. Her hair is dyed a cool platinum blonde and woven into an intricate bun, on top of which sits an elegant gold, diamond, and pearl tiara. The veil flows gently over her bare shoulders, diamonds dancing in her ears and around her delicate neck.

"You're absolutely gorgeous," I tell Ciara with a warm smile. A bitter taste lingers on the back of my tongue. I've been throwing up all morning.

"Thank you, Eileen," Ciara replies, measuring me from head to toe. "I wish I'd gone with the green bridesmaid dress, though. That salmon pink doesn't do your complexion any good."

"Eileen looks wonderful," my father tells her, then lovingly squeezes my shoulder. "Like a proper Irish girl, this one."

"Ready for your big day?" I ask through gritted teeth.

"I was born ready," Ciara declares as I hand her the bridal bouquet. "You go in first with the other bridesmaids. I'll be right on your heels."

"I'm so proud of you, honey," Dad tells her.

"I want to thank you for making this happen, Daddy," Ciara replies and plants a kiss on his cheek.

The more I look at him, however, the more uneasy I feel. There's definitely something wrong, something he's not telling us. Several times, I've seen him out of breath from a simple flight of stairs. A year ago, this man could run circles around others half his age. He's been eating less and less.

He's barely touched his favorite whiskey over the past month or so.

"Are you sure you're okay, Dad?" I ask again.

"Go inside, Eileen. Let's not spoil Ciara's special day," he bluntly replies.

"Come on, Eileen, lead the girls in. I've got a fabulous entrance to make," Ciara giggles.

I force myself to walk up the steps while a cold sweat works through me. I keep my head up as I grab my bouquet from the side table next to the ceremony hall's main entrance, then give the other bridesmaids a nod to follow me. I'm supposed to lead the way, yet I feel so out of place.

I take a deep breath as I push open the doors.

"Here comes the bride," I hear one of Ciara's close friends announce somewhere behind me. I roll my eyes.

In an instant, everything changes.

My breathing becomes erratic as I take it all in. The two hundred guests turn around to face us. Up ahead at the altar, I see the minister in his pristine white robe, purple and gold flowing over his shoulders. Next to him stands Anton in his tuxedo, looking so goddamn handsome it's a bloody sin. His brother and best man are beside him.

I catch Laura giving me a wink and an encouraging smile. "You can do this," she mouths at me. I return the smile, but suddenly everything starts to spin.

"Oh no, something's not right," I whisper.

Cold sweat is joined by a hot sensation swirling through my body. All of a sudden, I feel as if I swallowed a lead ball, and it's currently swelling inside my stomach. Looking over my shoulder, I see the bridesmaids following me without a care in the world, smiling and drawing admiration from the wedding guests.

I look forward again, noticing the frown on Anton's face as he watches me.

I'm still walking, right?

No, I'm falling.

The entire view shifts too quickly as someone gasps, "Oh, my gosh!"

I hit the ground and land on my side. My whole body goes limp before cold and hot hits me at the same time. I stare at the ceiling. I hear rushed footsteps, my father's voice booming across the wedding hall.

"Out of my way!" he snarls.

But it's Anton's face that pops into my field of vision first.

His hazel eyes are wide, filled with fear and concern, and that same softness I remember from the night we met.

Darkness tugs at me.

"Stay with me," he says before I can't hear him anymore.

His lips moving in silence is all I see before everything fades to black.

A sea of voices washes at the shore of my consciousness as I come to. I'm being wheeled on a gurney, red lights flashing around me.

"Oh, shit," I hear myself say as I realize what happened.

My father is close by, and so is Ciara. He looks worried. She looks inconvenienced.

"What's going on?" I ask the paramedics just as they're about to load me into the ambulance.

"You passed out," one of them says. "We're taking you to the hospital."

Behind my father and stepsister, I spot some of the guests lingering on the chapel's front steps, a few of the bridesmaids, Laura and Andrei, Paddy, my father's trusted lieutenant, and Anton, looking grim and quiet as he keeps his focus strictly on me.

"Hold on," I tell the paramedics. "I'm okay, I swear."

"My God, Eileen, it's bad enough you ruined my wedding day!" Ciara snaps, tears welling in her eyes. "Just go to the hospital and figure out what the hell is wrong with you."

"Listen to the paramedics, honey," my father adds.

I give Ciara a sad look. "I'm sorry. I didn't mean to."

"Of course you didn't," she scoffs, trying so hard not to cry.

"You can still have the wedding without me."

"Nonsense," Anton cuts in. "The wedding can wait. What matters most is that you're okay and taken care of. Everything else can wait."

"I'm so sorry," I apologize again.

My stepsister rolls her eyes and turns away, while my father keeps trying to console her.

"Do you have any allergies or preexisting medical conditions we need to be aware of?" the first paramedic asks as they load me into the back of the ambulance.

"No. I mean, yes," I say, lowering my voice. "I'm pregnant. Almost four months."

I glance back at my family, but they didn't hear me. Dad's too busy comforting Ciara, the now-sobbing jilted bride. I catch a glimpse of Anton frowning, just before the second paramedic shuts the ambulance doors and heads to the driver's seat.

"Okay, that's good to know. I'll add that to your chart," the paramedic says while he hooks me up to a monitor and starts checking my vitals.

"What's wrong with me?" I ask.

"Your vitals are okay. Your blood pressure is a little high, but that could be from your body's reaction to passing out. They'll need to do a full checkup and run blood work over at the hospital to figure it out definitively. It could've been nothing more than a fainting spell. It happens often in the first and even in the second trimester. Did you eat anything today?"

I shake my head slowly. "Too nervous."

"There you have it. Most likely, you passed out due to low blood sugar."

CHAPTER 8

ANTON

Perhaps I should be upset that the wedding was postponed. Ciara's endless tears should make me want to do something about it. Hell, maybe elope if I really wanted to marry her. But I don't. Not anymore. Not at all. And it's an unpleasant feeling to sit with and process while Ciara keeps complaining to her father about it.

"Figures," she says. "Eileen wasn't the center of attention, so she decided to ruin my wedding day."

"Ciara don't talk about your stepsister like that. Eileen has been in your corner the whole time," Ronan replies.

"Agreed," I say. "Whatever happened, clearly, she couldn't control it. Maybe low blood pressure or blood sugar."

"She didn't eat anything at breakfast," Ronan remembers with a deep frown.

Ciara exhales sharply. "She eats too much anyway."

Did she really just say that out loud? My heart's beating faster. They don't know. Ronan was too busy coddling this snarky creature to hear what Eileen told the paramedics. But I heard. I saw her luscious lips move. I've been doing the math in my head, reaching the same conclusion over and over.

"I'll tell the guests the wedding is postponed," I say, ready to end the whole thing.

"We could still have the wedding," Ciara insists.

Ronan shakes his head. "Honey, we talked about this."

"It's *my* life! *My* wedding! She can do her thing at the hospital and meet us later at the reception," she says. "I worked so hard on those menus," she whines.

"We'll set another date," I say, though there is zero intention behind my words. She's small and perky, and she looks up at me with doe eyes. Any man would fall prey to that gaze of Ciara's. Not me. I tried. But then Eileen unwittingly reminded me that I don't belong with her stepsister. "I'll let the guests know. In the meantime, I'll pay for the restaurant and tell them to head over there and enjoy the menu and the drinks, on me, for their trouble."

"Oh, Anton."

"I insist. Today is not a good day. Eileen's episode must've been a sign from above," I reply, tapping into Ronan's spiritual side. The man still goes to Sunday services. I know what buttons to push.

"He's right," the old man says, looking pale. "We should just pull the plug on everything and regroup. I need to head to the hospital to check on Eileen. You should come with me, Ciara."

"No, I'm fine." She crosses her arms, sulking.

"He's right, Ciara. You should go with him and see your stepsister," I gently suggest.

She raises an eyebrow at me. "I'll see her when she gets home."

"Ciara…" Ronan tries to plead with her, but the princess has made up her mind.

Yet another reason why this won't work. I can't end it here, though. I need to talk to Andrei. I need confirmation from the hospital, as well, one way or another. Eileen would never tell me, and the situation is far too delicate for me to take a Karpov hammer to it.

"It's alright," I tell them both. "You go to the hospital, Ronan. Let me know how Eileen is faring. And you should have a doctor look at you as well. You look rather out of sorts, my friend."

"I'm fine. It's just this whole wedding nonsense. I've got one daughter disappointed and the other in the hospital. I'm trying to figure out a way to fix everything."

"You can't; not today, anyway," I reply. "Let's take it one day at a time." I turn to Ciara. "You should go to the restaurant, at least. Have some of the pink champagne you like, and we'll talk tomorrow. How about that?"

Here come the puppy eyes again. "Aren't you coming with me?"

"I have some business issues to deal with. Might as well get it out of the way so I can fully focus on us in the weeks to come."

Ciara doesn't like being told no. But there's no wedding band on my finger yet, so she knows to contain her displeasure to mere passive-aggressiveness.

I leave Ciara with her father, then make my way back to the Karpov offices, where Andrei is already waiting. He and Laura left as soon as Eileen was taken by the ambulance—both knowing full well that there would be no wedding to attend today.

"Well, this day didn't turn out the way I'd expected," Andrei says, comfortably seated in the guest chair by the window of my office. "How's the bride-to-be faring?"

"Petulant and fussy, as usual."

I pour myself a double whiskey, then offer my brother one as well. He takes the glass with an appreciative nod. "I'll have Demi drive you and your car back to your place if you need him," Andrei says. "Might as well finish this bottle while we're here."

"It's not really professional, but for once, I agree with you," I say as I sit down at my desk.

I run my fingers along the glass top, fully aware that my brother is watching and analyzing my every move. "Why is that?" he asks.

"Why's what?"

"Why do you agree with me? You rarely drink at the office, Anton. Are you really that miffed about your wedding day?"

I shake my head slowly. "No, I'm relieved."

"Okay, you've got my attention," he chuckles. "What's going on?"

"I'm going to blow it all up."

Andrei stares at me for a long confused second. "Blow what up?"

"The marriage agreement."

"Are you fucking insane? We need the Donovans now more than ever!"

"Hear me out."

"No, Anton! You agreed to this! You can't back out of it, not with Sergei fucking Kuznetsov looking for every opportunity to screw us out of our position. The Bratva needs stability, and the South Americans are starting to tighten their ranks. It's not looking good, and the last thing we need is the Irish siding with them or staying neutral!"

I take a long sip of my whiskey, welcoming the burn as it rolls down my throat.

"Eileen's pregnant."

Andrei stills, his expression blank. I can almost hear the wheels turning in his head. "I fucking knew it," he hisses. "You slept with her that night."

"It was so much more than that."

"Holy shit, you're in love," my brother laughs nervously. "Oh, this is fucking rich."

"I overheard Eileen in the ambulance. No one else did, though. Her father doesn't know. Her sister would've had an aneurysm had she heard. Listen, this is a golden opportunity. Not just for me, but for our family."

"Hold on; give me a moment here, Anton. Let's take it one step at a time."

"Okay, let's," I reply and lean back in my chair.

"Are you sure that Eileen is pregnant?"

"Yes. I double-checked with the hospital on my way over."

Andrei's frown deepens. "What about patient confidentiality?"

"Since when did we let that get in our way?"

"Fucking hell, Anton."

"Right. Next question."

"Are you sure it's yours?" he asks, then finishes his whiskey and pours himself a triple. He's going to need it, because I haven't even gotten to my proposal yet.

I nod slowly. "Almost a hundred percent. Eileen hasn't had many trysts with other men from what her stepsister told me, which means that, aside from the night we spent together, there wasn't anybody else."

"And from the moment the engagement was announced publicly—"

"Eileen became off-limits for any man, Sergei included."

"Shit," Andrei says. "You knocked up one Donovan and you're going to marry the other one. Anton, this is one hell of a mess."

"It's not like I planned it. And besides, I don't intend to marry Ciara anymore."

He chuckles dryly. "Does Ciara know?"

"No, I didn't have the heart to tell her. Ronan wasn't looking too good either. I figured I'd give them a few days to pull themselves together."

Andrei gives me a long curious look. "How do you feel about all this?"

"I'll feel a lot better once I get you on board."

"On board with what?"

"Blowing it all up."

"There you go with that term again. What does that mean?" he asks, then takes another gulp of his whiskey, savoring the relaxing burn.

"I still need to marry a Donovan, just not the one I'm currently engaged to."

"You're out of your fucking mind."

"That's my child growing in Eileen's womb, and it's her father's support that we need."

"What about Sergei? He's already set to marry her."

"Hence why I need your support."

Andrei goes quiet for the better part of a minute. His gaze wanders across my office as he thoroughly analyzes the facts of our situation. It's quite simple, actually. Sooner or later, Ronan Donovan will find out about Eileen's condition. And so will Sergei. They'll both know it's not a Kuznetsov baby, and it will put Eileen in an extremely tight spot. I could keep my mouth shut about it, but my honor and my heart demand that I do something.

Besides, the pregnancy is the perfect excuse for me to back out of the deal with Ciara. I want Eileen. As much as I've tried to deny it, I need to be honest with myself and admit it. I've wanted her since the night I rescued her. She's taken up permanent residence in my mind.

"It's going to get messy," Andrei warns me.

"I need your help, so it doesn't get bloody, too," I say. "We can handle messy. We can also handle bloody, but we'll lose our seat at the table if it gets to that."

"We stand a better chance holding on to it with just messy," he agrees with a slow, tentative nod. "Yeah, I hear you. We'll need a multiple-angle approach, and a much better offer for Ronan."

"Something enticing enough to help him get over his injured pride," I add. "I'm well aware."

"You really want her, huh?" Andrei shoots me a half-smile, amusement twinkling in his eyes as he unbuttons his jacket.

"I do. And I'm going to get what I want."

"I believe you," he says. "Let's just make sure you don't burn bridges and take the Karpovs down with you in the process."

I'm concerned about that, too, but I don't express that to my brother.

I see her every time I close my eyes. I can still smell her perfume on my pillow back at the penthouse, even though the maid service had changed all the linens. It's the ghost of Eileen that lingers in my life, embedded in my senses. As I watched her collapse while walking down the aisle, unable to take her in my arms and protect her, unable to care for her, something snapped inside of me.

I'm not letting Eileen out of my grasp ever again.

"Sergei will be out for blood," Andrei warns me.

"I know."

I'll be ready for him when the time comes.

CHAPTER 9

ANTON

The next day, I pay Ronan a visit at his office across the street from the Marriott Marquis. The building has been in the Donovan family for generations, long before there were any other hotels on the block. It's well-guarded and heavily surveilled, but as his guest, I'm given easy access.

"How's Eileen doing?" I ask Ronan as I settle onto the guest sofa. His assistant has left us a fresh pot of coffee and an assortment of pastries on the table in front of us for the meeting.

He gives me a curious look. "I thought you'd be more interested in how Ciara's doing."

"She's not the one who was taken away in an ambulance yesterday."

"Eileen is fine."

"Good; I'm glad to hear that."

"Ciara isn't happy about any of it, though."

"I would imagine you're having a hard time reconciling the sisters right now," I reply with a bitter smile, but Ronan is anything but amused.

"You have no idea."

"I've been around both Donovan ladies long enough to figure a few things out," I say. "Ciara's a spoiled brat."

"You watch your tongue."

"It's the truth," I chuckle dryly. "She's also as sharp as a tack and more than capable of handling your businesses in the future. But I have to ask… Eileen's your biological child. Your blood. Why isn't she the principal heir?"

Ronan takes a deep breath before settling into the chair in front of me. He doesn't look any better than the last time I saw him, truth be told. There's an air of mortality looming over him.

"I wanted Eileen to take over, but she wants something else. She's got this dream about a coffee shop that just drives me nuts," he says.

"The café business, right. Premium, single origin only."

"You know about that?"

Eileen hasn't told me anything. She barely spoke to me whenever I visited Ciara. In fact, Eileen has made a specific effort to avoid me since the engagement party. I suppose it'll be harder for her to stay away from me now, however, in light of the pregnancy.

"Ciara told me about it," I lie with a smile. "I'm guessing you're not okay with that?"

"I just want my daughters to be happy and healthy, Anton. But I also need one of them to carry on my legacy. Eileen is my first and my blood, yes, and nothing would please me more than to see her take over the Donovan business. Alas, she's too kind and soft. She has different passions to pursue, though I'm not sure she'll get to do much once she's married to Kuznetsov."

"Sergei likes his women at home, barefoot, pregnant, and preferably partial to cooking," I reply. "Which is why I have a proposition for you."

"What?" His eyes grow wide as he raises an eyebrow.

Good. I need him dazzled while I roll it out.

"I'm going to break off my engagement to Ciara, and I'm going to marry Eileen instead," I tell Ronan. The words almost slip past him, but once he understands, his eyes damn near pop out of their orbits.

What follows is a deafening silence while I brace myself for his reaction. Ronan is known for his temper, and I'm not sure what to expect.

"I must be having a stroke, Anton, because I don't think I heard you right," he sounds eerily calm.

"You heard me right."

"Why on God's green earth would you even consider such a thing? Are you deliberately trying to start a war here?"

"No, on the contrary. I'm trying to avoid one," I reply, then take a deep breath. "What I'm about to say will piss you off, no doubt. I'm bringing you one hell of a problem, but I've also got the solution."

Ronan cocks his head to the side. "And what, pray tell, is the problem your so-called solution will resolve?"

"Eileen's pregnant with my child."

I can almost hear the vein snapping in his temple. He pulls in a sharp breath as the anger and outrage take over. I lean back in my seat, calm and composed.

"Before you explode, you need to hear the whole story. She had no idea who I was at the time," I say, then tell him what happened that night, leaving the spicy details out. Ronan has no choice but to listen. He's a smart man, and he's been around the block. He understands the importance of our alliance. "I care deeply for Eileen. Otherwise, I'd resolve the situation in a manner that wouldn't even involve you."

"Oh, Anton, you slick son of a bitch," Ronan scoffs, barely able to hold back. "I should kill you right here and now. No one would even bat an eye."

"My brother and the entire Bratva surely would," I reply. He's not aware of the internal issues in our organization. Sergei wouldn't try to bring him over to his side yet, not until he puts a ring on Eileen's finger and seals the deal. This is the perfect opportunity for me to do this, as uncomfortable as it may be for Ronan. "I could still resolve things in a discreet manner, but I don't want that. I want to marry your daughter. Just not the spoiled one."

"Again, mind your fucking tongue."

"Or what?" I snap. "She's brash and unkind, especially to Eileen. She may have the wits to run your business, but she doesn't know how to treat people, and that will get her killed one day."

"You underestimate her."

"Or maybe you *over*estimate her. Ciara still has a long way to go before she can take over for you, before she can command the respect of your people. You know it and I know it. Your enemies know it. Let me have Eileen's hand in marriage. I'll still be close enough to Ciara to make sure she doesn't get eaten alive. This way, Eileen's reputation remains untarnished, and Ciara can move on and find herself another man to marry, to have her perfect wedding day with."

"You're insane, Anton."

"No, I'm just determined. If I want something, I take it. Plain and simple. And what I'm taking now will only bring you benefits. Once the initial discomfort wears off, that is."

"Ciara won't accept it," Ronan shakes his head slowly.

I can't help but laugh. "Remind me of who the head of the family is here."

"You're a prick, Anton."

"Maybe so, but I'm the prick who will keep a prime seat at the table for the Donovans," I say.

"What about Sergei? You're taking his bride away."

"I'll handle the Kuznetsovs; don't worry about them. Hell, I'll do you another favor on top of all this. I'll make sure Sergei knows you had no way of stopping me. If he asks, I'll simply tell him that I know about your involvement in Belfast and that I threatened to expose you."

The color drains from Ronan's face. I was saving this for later, but I might as well close it up now and tie it with a nice, shiny bow.

"What about Belfast?" he asks.

"Belfast. Northern Ireland."

"I know where fucking Belfast is!" he snaps. "What's that got to do with—"

"Belfast, Northern Ireland, 2008," I stop him before he tries to claim his innocence. "I know that was you. Not you, personally, but one of your proxies. I came upon a paper trail, one that I bet will cause the British government to extradite you once I send it over to their offices. Who's in charge of the IRA situation over there? MI6? MI5? Or is it Scotland Yard?"

Ronan scoffs and stands up, pacing the room as he gathers his thoughts.

I've got him now.

The situation will make for some very uncomfortable family dinners in the future, but I'll wash it down with an extra shot of whiskey. No problem. As long as I get what I want.

And what I want more than anything is Eileen Donovan.

"You'll handle Kuznetsov, then," Ronan finally concedes with a nod, his back to me. "I'll deal with Ciara."

"Smart man."

"Fuck you, Anton. You just screwed us over in more ways than one."

"In the long term, you'll reap greater benefits from this adjusted alliance. You have my guarantee, Ronan. And my word is my bond."

The fact that I get to ruin Sergei Kuznetsov's day is a welcome bonus. He thought he'd weasel his way into the Donovans, just like he thought he'd weasel his way into my seat at the Bratva table.

Not while I'm still drawing breath.

If he aims for the king, he'd best not fucking miss.

"One more thing… if I were you, I'd worry less about Sergei and Ciara's reaction and worry more about Eileen's," I add with a chuckle. "She's not going to be happy about this at all."

CHAPTER 10

EILEEN

"Have you lost your mind?"

I'm sitting on the edge of my hospital bed, heat coursing through me as I try to adjust to Anton's proposal. The words coming out of his mouth might make sense to him, but all I'm hearing is that I'm screwed in a wholly different way.

Hell, I can't even be ashamed of what happened, because the repercussions have hit me so hard across the face that I can barely breathe.

"It's the only way that I can protect you," he says.

Anton stands by the door, hands casually in his pockets. Judging by the subtle smile dancing on his lips, he's enjoying this while I'm torn between swooning over him and punching him in the face. "I know it's a delicate situation, but I think this will defuse it."

"Defuse it?" I gasp, then look at my father. "What did Ciara say?"

"She won't speak to me," he replies, lowering his gaze. "Not yet anyway. She needs time to mourn, I suppose."

"So, not only did I wreck her wedding day, but—"

"Through no fault of your own, Eileen. You got sick," my father tries to soften the blow.

"We both know it was my fault," I shoot back. "This pregnancy is my fault."

Anton slowly raises a hand. "Mine, too. You aren't the only one responsible."

"Let me reiterate," I say, choosing to focus on my rather befuddled father. "Not only did I wreck my stepsister's wedding day, but I'm now supposed to marry her fiancé, because there wasn't enough strife between us to begin with."

"Ciara is no fool. She'll understand that it's for the best. For everyone involved," Dad says. "You'll be married to the father of your child, and I'll still have a Karpov for a son-in-law."

"That sounds more like a benefit to you and you alone. I didn't ask for this."

"But you're getting it anyway," Anton chimes in.

"You seem to be enjoying this a little too much. It's infuriating," I reply dryly.

He responds with a shrug. "It is a greater win for me."

"Oh right, because you're marrying the true-born Donovan now."

"Because I'm marrying a beautiful woman with a sizzling personality who happens to be carrying my child," Anton says.

"What about Sergei? How did he take the news?" I ask my father.

He shakes his head slowly. "Not well, but he had no choice in the matter. I left an offer on the table for Ciara. Once they both think about it, they'll probably come around and agree it's the best way forward."

"You would've made a fine kingmaker in a medieval court," I mutter and cross my arms. My heart is on a rampage, but I refuse to let Anton see how easy it is for him to rile me up. It's bad enough he overheard about the pregnancy. I should've kept my mouth shut, but as much as I hate to admit it, I can't bring myself to be too mad about it. Besides, I couldn't keep it a secret forever—the hospital ran blood work and I'm starting to show.

"Dad, this will blow up in your face. Mark my words. This is the second time I'm being shoved into a marriage I didn't consent to."

"Would you like me to back off and just leave you to your own devices?" he blurts out. "Would you prefer being the laughing stock of Chicago on top of being a single mother?"

"I'd never allow that," Anton intervenes.

"I really don't want or need anything from you," I say. "I can do this alone."

Dad scoffs and gives me a sour smirk. "This is a consequence of your actions, Eileen. I know what happened that night. From the moment you consented to this man, everything that's happened since is now on your shoulders. Now, you can either continue to act like a petulant child, or you can be smart like the Donovan that you are."

I lower my gaze.

I'm screwed and I know it.

"In the absence of a better choice, I guess my answer is yes," I say, caving in with a heavy sigh. "Dammit, I knew I should've eaten something that morning. Maybe if I had, none of this would've happened."

"It's too late to fuss about what could've been," Dad says. "I don't like this any more than you, Eileen, but it's the best way to mend the situation in a manner that doesn't cause too big a rift between us and the Bratva."

Anton struggles to contain his satisfaction, and I'm starting to think it has a lot to do with the strife between him and Sergei. He's passing up a cover girl bride for me. There has to be something to make it worthwhile, and pissing off Sergei Kuznetsov certainly sounds like a good deal as far as Anton is concerned.

"Smirk and gloat all you want," I tell Anton. "But don't expect a model wife."

"I expect Eileen Donovan," he replies with a casual smile.

"I'm not sure what that's supposed to mean."

"Eileen, this is the best decision we can make out of a bad situation," my father says. He gently touches my shoulder, but I yank away, unwilling to relent any more than I already have. "I'll go sign your release papers, and we'll get you home."

"Maybe put a padlock on my bedroom door once we get there," I mutter, sulking like an ill-tempered child. "Ciara might sneak in and smother me with a pillow in my sleep."

Anton joins my father outside my private hospital room while I'm left chewing things over.

I've kept my chin up throughout all of this, and I'll keep it up going forward.

If my father wants me to act like a true Donovan, that's exactly what I'll do.

CHAPTER 11

EILEEN

There are two sides of me fighting ferociously with every breath I take. And I don't see a resolution to the conflict anywhere in sight. The look on Ciara's face as I walk into the tearoom tells me it's going to get worse before it gets better.

"I owe you an apology."

"You're a fucking snake," Ciara snarls as soon as she sees me.

For a moment, I look at the teapot and cups on the table, just within her reach. My stepsister seems furious enough to hurl one or all of them at my head, so I keep a reasonable distance just in case.

"I'm sorry, I didn't mean for any of this to happen," I say.

"Eileen Fiona Donovan, you're a snake."

"Yeah, I heard you the first time. Will you just let me explain?"

She throws her hands up in the air, sheer exasperation coming off her in waves that practically ripple across the room. "What's there to explain? You lied to my face! You stole my fucking fiancé away from me!"

"It's not like that, I swear."

"What's it like, then? You saw my man, you knew you'd never get a prime piece like Anton Karpov on your own, so you decided to pull your father into the middle! Taking advantage of the fact that you're the true, blood-born Donovan!"

"Oh, my God, Ciara, no, I promise it was nothing like that! I don't even want to—"

"A fat bitch like you could never get a man like mine. So what did you do, exactly? What happened that night? Did you roofie him? How'd you get him to put a baby in you?"

My blood runs cold.

As I stare at Ciara in heavy silence, trying to wrap my head around how one person can be so mean, entitled, and hurtful, all the common sense that I've held on to for so long shatters into bits and pieces.

Judging by the look on her face, I think even she realizes that she's gone too far this time.

"I didn't know who Anton was when I slept with him. But I do know that my father told you what happened that night, just as both Anton and I described it. He saved my life. What happened at his place afterward, well, it happened. I asked him his name several times, but he wouldn't tell me. Had I known who he was, I never would've let it happen.

"Blood or not, we're still family. We grew up in the same house, under the same roof, following the same rules, and abiding by the same traditions. And, yes, we've had plenty of disagreements, and your mouth often gets the better of you—"

"Excuse me?"

"Yeah, you heard me. You can be so incredibly mean, though all I ever did was support you," I snap. "Well, this time, shit happened. But I swear to you on my mother's grave that I would've never allowed that night with Anton to end the way it did had I known who he was."

"Bullshit," Ciara spits and crosses her arms, slowly moving closer to the window. "You've always been jealous."

"I'm pregnant with his kid," I say.

She gives me a hard look. "Yeah, I got that part. I got it when your father told me I wouldn't be able to marry the man of my dreams because you screwed him first."

"The man of your dreams?" I mutter. "What is it about him that makes him the man of your dreams, Ciara?"

"He's a Karpov. He's the head of the Bratva! He's powerful and influential, rich beyond any girl's wildest dreams. He's gorgeous, and other women drool over him. Need I go on?"

"But what has he done to make you love him?"

"He chose me, not you. That's what he did."

"My God, Ciara, are you hearing yourself?" I ask and take another deep breath. "He didn't choose you. My father offered your hand, and he accepted. You're acting like I stole your goddamn high school sweetheart. I know it sucks, and I wish it had never happened. I wish I could have just kept the pregnancy secret just a little bit longer."

"Why didn't you? Why couldn't you just leave us alone?"

I shake my head slowly. "Anton overheard me with the paramedics."

"Bullshit. You did it on purpose," she hisses. "I'll tell you one thing, Eileen. We may be family, but I'll never forgive you for this. I'm not interested in your Kuznetsov leftovers either. I wanted Anton. Well, you can have him. And I pray to God that your smug satisfaction turns to ashes in your mouth."

"Trust me, there is no satisfaction here."

She rolls her eyes. "Whatever. I hope you have a shitty life together."

"You don't mean that," I reply, tears quick to sting my eyes.

She nods with furious passion. "Oh, I mean it. I'll be civil out of respect for your father. But I will never let you take anything else that is rightfully mine, Eileen. Mark my words. You will pay for this."

"Ciara–"

"I don't want to hear anymore. I need to be alone," she says, then opens the terrace doors and steps out. I can hear her cursing as she goes deeper into the garden, her voice gradually fading while my tears flow freely.

Shame burns in my chest.

There's no coming back from this, that much is clear. And no matter how many times or how clearly I explain myself,

Ciara will not see past the mistake. She's the victim, and I'm the monster. Her own anger has poisoned her, and she's displaying the fact that she was rarely told no in her life.

I find my father in his study, nursing a glass of scotch.

He looks paler than ever, his eyes bloodshot and his hand shaking as he sets the glass down on the desk.

"You shouldn't be drinking," I tell him.

"Can you blame me?" he grumbles.

"Well, no, not really. But still, you shouldn't. Have you seen your doctor lately?" I ask, as I take a seat in one of the guest chairs. "You should get yourself checked out, a full blood workup, and everything else in between."

"Eileen, what do you want?" my father sighs heavily. "I'm tired and I really don't want to talk about my dwindling health."

"I'm worried about you."

"I'm getting old!" he snaps. "I'm getting old, and it sucks! I would've liked to have seen both of my daughters happily married and well taken care of by now, but no. You and Ciara had to make everything a thousand times harder than it needed to be."

"It's the twenty-first century, Dad! You don't need to arrange marriages for your offspring anymore!" I reply, raising my voice. "My worth, Ciara's worth, they're not dependent on the men who marry us! You're not breeding champion stock here!"

"You're still Donovans, and this is still Chicago," my father says. "The old rules still apply to you. Had you been born a

Johnson somewhere in Detroit, I might've said, 'Yeah, let the girl do whatever she wants with her life.' But you're not a Johnson. You're a fucking Donovan, and so is Ciara, which means that you two get to carry my legacy forward, just like I carried it when it was my turn."

"You speak as though we're royals."

"We *are* royals in this city, and we must follow tradition. It's the only way for us to survive as a family and as a business."

I give him a tired shrug. "What about *my* life? *My* dreams? *My* business? None of that matters as long as Ronan Donovan secures his financial empire, right? As long as the other mobsters of Chicago know that you rule over your turf with an iron fist. Because that's what this is about, isn't it? It's about everybody else seeing how good and obedient your girls are."

"Eileen, someday you'll understand. I can't force you to see things from my perspective. You still lack the emotional maturity. Unlike your sister, however, you also lack a single inkling of obedience that would ensure your survival, which is why we're doing things this way. For your own good."

"For my own good."

"Yes. You're pregnant and momentarily unwed. The father is the head of the Karpov family and the current top seat in the Bratva. The mess you find yourself in is of your own making," my father coldly reiterates.

"I didn't get myself pregnant," I mutter.

"True, but I can't take that up with Anton without starting a war. And that's not what any of us need right now. So, whether you like it or not, you'll do as you're told, Eileen.

You'll marry Anton Karpov; you'll bear children and move on with your life. And you'll secure the Donovan legacy. It's either that or destitution."

"Destitution?" I ask, my eyes widening as I stare at him.

My father calmly swirls what's left of his whiskey in the glass, then downs it all at once. "That's right. I will cut you off. And I think you know me well enough to understand that it's not a threat. Your sister will be glad to have more of my fortune all to herself. But you'll be miserable. And one way or another, you'll crawl back to me and beg for mercy. So, save yourself that despair and protect the child you're carrying. The kid shouldn't be blamed or suffer because of your choices."

"Wow, laying on the Irish Catholic guilt pretty heavy there. I guess I shouldn't be surprised."

"You're damn right!" he shoots back. "Now, go rest. Eat well. And take good care of yourself. You're going to be a mother and a bride. Lord knows, I need some peace before I head out tomorrow to try and mend things with Kuznetsov."

CHAPTER 12

ANTON

"You look happy," Andrei says.

"What makes you say that?" I innocently ask.

He gives me a smooth grin as he sits across from my desk and takes a long sip of his coffee. "You sly bastard. You wanted the other Donovan girl all along, didn't you? That pregnancy was a windfall for you. The perfect excuse."

"None of this was planned. That, I can promise."

"You're still a slick bastard. You might not have planned it, but you still got exactly what you wanted."

"You give me too much credit. Eileen unwittingly played her own part."

"She certainly seems a lot nicer than her stepsister, but she's also less useful. Pretty sure old man Ronan is grooming Ciara to take over his businesses," Andrei's humor slowly fades. "And I'm equally sure that he offered Ciara's hand to Sergei fucking Kuznetsov to make up for your blunder."

"I thought we were in this together, brother."

"We are. I just didn't think Ronan would pull Kuznetsov back in."

"Ciara hasn't said yes."

"Like she has a choice?"

A heavy sigh rolls from my chest. "It would serve Kuznetsov right to get saddled with her. She's a spoiled brat."

"A smart spoiled brat. You're forgetting that part. You're also forgetting that she's not on our side anymore."

"I still think Eileen has a shot at taking over for Ronan when the time comes. I just need to convince her that she's capable."

"Is she?"

I nod with unshakeable certainty. "Absolutely. In fact, I think she could turn the whole Donovan conglomerate into a veritable empire with the right support. I just need to win her over."

"She is carrying your baby."

"If only it were that simple," I chuckle bitterly. "I put her at odds with her own family, Andrei. It's gonna cost me."

He thinks about it for a moment. "I see the way you two look at each other, though. Beyond that animosity, which, by the way, is merely a façade, there's something real, brother. She's anything but indifferent to you."

"Don't I know it. I'll break through to that warm, soft center of hers. I don't think Eileen has ever had anyone to inspire her, to support her. I've noticed Ciara's many jabs. Ronan's old-school garble. Eileen is... dammit, she could rule the fucking world if she wanted."

"You both could. And you both should."

"It's gonna get messy before we get there," I tell Andrei. "What's the word in our organization, in the meantime?"

He exhales sharply and sets his coffee on the desktop, then runs a hand through his thick, brown hair. Sometimes, all I have to do is look at him, watch him closely, to understand what he's thinking, what he's about to say. Out in public, however, Andrei is impossible to read. Dangerously unpredictable. It's one of many things I love about my brother. Behind closed doors, when it's just the two of us, he's an open book, and right now, I'm not sure I like what I'm reading.

"Kuznetsov is actively lobbying against us, which shouldn't come as a surprise. He's taking advantage of this Donovan switch to paint you as a backstabber. Untrustworthy. A snake in the grass," he says. "Paul Mattis is doing his share, too, organizing separate meetings with the other families. He's due to sit down with the Sokolovs next week. Fedorov hasn't agreed to a meeting yet, though."

"Ivan won't entertain Sergei, but Petra might."

"There will be stock options for two of our companies available at the end of the month," Andrei reminds me. "We're going public with Zanta and CypressCo. Might as well make Petra an offer. An enticing one."

I cock my head to the side. "What are we offering, exactly?"

"I suggest half price on each share and cap her at fifteen percent. We don't want Petra Fedorov to hold a majority in any of our companies, obviously."

"We might have to," I sigh deeply. "If it gets to that, let her have up to twenty percent of Cypress. Zanta is too volatile at this point."

He nods slowly. "Let's hope it doesn't get to that."

"Set up a meeting. Tell her that we're going public with CypressCo. Mention the offer and see how she reacts."

"What if she says no?"

"Just ask her," I shoot back with a smirk. "One way or another, we need the Fedorovs on our side. Whether it's the young one or the elder, we have to secure their support, because if they fall, the others won't be far behind."

"What will you do in the meantime?"

"Brace for the incoming shitstorm," I reply, only half joking. "I've got a jilted fiancée, a pissed-off baby mama, and a future father-in-law who's looking more frail with each passing day. Something tells me there will be major changes happening in the Donovan family sooner rather than later, and I need to make sure we're on top of that."

Andrei laughs, throwing his head back for good measure. "Sounds like you've got some ass-kissing to do."

"More or less."

"Which brings me back to my original point. You look happy."

"In a twisted way, I guess I am," I confess with a slight shake of the head. "She's different, Andrei. She really is. I could tell from that very first night, despite the circumstances—"

"For which I am responsible. My bad."

"Actually, I'm grateful that you were hotheaded enough to pull that stunt with Tommy Benedetto. None of this would've happened otherwise."

"Then, you're welcome," Andrei replies with a grin.

"I mean it. She's something else. Wily as hell and stubborn as a mule, but sharp as a razor. And she's kind, Andrei. Aside from Laura, do you know any other woman who you could genuinely describe as kind?"

His silence gives me his answer as he leans back into his chair and smiles softly. "I was right, Anton."

"About what?"

"You're absolutely whipped."

"Perhaps. But we're sailing some treacherous waters here, brother. I hope you can forgive me for these shifts."

Andrei gives me a long look. His eyes say more than his words ever will. "Big brother, we've stuck together through thick and thin. Lord knows, you saved my ass more times than I can count. The least I can do is ride this out with you and make sure we both come out on top. There's no way in hell I'm letting Sergei Kuznetsov bump us off the food chain."

"Then let's make sure he doesn't."

Easier said than done, of course. Sergei is an intelligent man. A savvy entrepreneur. And a fucking extraordinary psychopath. The man has outsmarted and outgunned anyone who's gotten in his way, his own family included.

I'm not scared of him, but I do worry. If the other families turn against us, holding on to the seat of power might kill us.

I'm about to marry an incredible woman and our first child is on the way.

I've got work to do.

CHAPTER 13

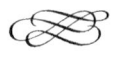

EILEEN

My wedding day is supposed to be the happiest day of my life.

Yet here I stand, at the doors of the ceremony hall, holding my bridal bouquet and my breath. I look around at the approximately fifty people present. This feels like a shotgun wedding. Hell, it really is, if I think about it.

"Oh, God," I whisper, my dress suddenly too tight.

My father hooks his arm through mine. He's yet to see a doctor, and he's looking like he's got one foot in the grave already. It's the stubborn Irish in him, through and through. "Come on, Eileen. You've got this," he whispers.

I glance down at myself. The bridal gown is beautiful. Trying it on and having it adjusted for my ever-changing figure was one of the highlights over the past few weeks. The white satin wraps around my chest and arms, leaving my shoulders and the upper part of my back bare. Everything else is an elegant tulle with thousands of pearls embroidered in delicate floral motifs. My veil flows from a gold band fastened around my updo. Curls tickle the base of my neck. I look beautiful. I should feel beautiful.

"Do I?"

"You do, my child," my father says. "For better or worse, this is your day. And you must seize it. You're a Donovan."

I look around again, spotting guests from our side of the family, some from Anton's. Ciara sits in the front row, still sulking. I bet she'll grow old and be buried with that frown on her face.

"She hates me."

Dad follows my gaze. "Ciara will get over it. Come, Eileen. Let's get you married."

I should be gliding down the aisle, weightless with joy. But I can't savor this moment. Not really. It feels as though I stole it from Ciara. Anton stole it, actually. He couldn't leave well enough alone, and now he waits for me at the end of the aisle, next to the priest and his brother.

We didn't have any bridesmaids. No pompous ceremony. Nothing too flashy. We agreed on something small and private after the debacle at the first wedding attempt.

Bitterness lingers on the tip of my tongue as I take a deep breath and let my father walk me down the aisle. The organ fades into the background as the thudding of my heart echoes in my ears.

"You look wonderful," Laura whispers from her seat.

I give her a warm smile. "Thank you."

If only I felt wonderful. For a moment, as my gaze locks on Anton, I fool myself into thinking that this might turn out beautifully, after all. The sparkle in his eyes lights a fire within my heart.

We haven't seen much of each other since I got back from the hospital. I made sure to keep busy and out of his reach, and every time we did meet, I kept it short and at a reasonable distance.

"Congratulations!" a cousin of ours whispers loudly.

I smile and nod, pretending this really is a most auspicious day. To my surprise, whenever I look at Anton, I actually believe it long enough for me to play my part, anyway. My father gives me away, quietly shaking the groom's hand before he takes his seat next to Ciara. She's got tears in her eyes, and spite curls her red lips. The off-white dress she's wearing is yet another jab. Dad gives her a gentle squeeze on the knee.

"Ready?" Anton asks me.

"As I'm ever going to be," I grumble, then put on a fake smile and face the priest.

"Dearly beloved," the priest begins as he prepares to read a few passages from the Good Book, "we are gathered here today to join…"

His voice fades as my mind and gaze wander.

I smell the candles burning. The subtle fragrance of my rose bouquet.

I hear the last of the organ music's notes dissolve into echoes across the wedding chapel.

My mother would've never allowed this to happen.

I look at Anton and take a deep breath. He looks so handsome and ready. There's so much I'd like to say to him.

"Miss Donovan?" the priest shakes me from my reverie.

I give him a startled look. "Yes?"

"This is the part where you say, 'I Do,'" Anton whispers.

Murmurs rise behind us.

For a moment, I lose myself in my groom's hazel eyes, and I actually feel like this could work out. That it could lead somewhere, despite the shoddy kickoff. Something drew us together that night. The child growing inside me is proof of that.

"I guess I do," I sigh heavily, wishing I had the luxury of genuine enthusiasm.

The priest gives me a strange look, then asks Anton the same question.

"I do," Anton says without hesitation.

The vows are spoken. It all becomes so real, so fast, that I barely have a moment to properly digest it, to fully understand how my life will change.

This is not what I wished for growing up. It's not how I imagined my wedding day would unfold.

"You may now kiss the bride," the priest concludes.

"Here's to you, Mrs. Donovan-Karpova," he says.

"How did you know I'd want to keep my name?" I whisper.

"You underestimate my ability to read you, my darling," he replies, then kisses me, sealing the deal in a way that leaves my head spinning and my core aching for more.

For a long, sweet moment, the entire world disappears. I don't hear my stepsister's bitter sighs anymore. I don't see my father's pale, ailing face. Gone are the thoughts of a miserable existence ahead, as a different image dares to flutter before my eyes. It's an image of me and Anton, at peace, loving one another while our kids run around, laughing and growing.

It sounds sweet and it's what I truly want, but I'm not sure what I'll get.

The live band performs an excellent Rat Pack revival as the lead singer croons, most of the ladies present breaking into soft smiles and slowly batting their eyelashes.

I sit beside my husband, torn between two different thoughts—can this actually work out or will it forever be a farce meant solely to advance our families' business interests?

"Daddy, I'll stop drinking when I wanna stop drinking." An already drunk Ciara yanks her glass back from our father when he tries to curb her self-destructive tendency. "My sister just got married! I'm celebrating!"

"Ciara, please," he tries again.

Ciara walks away, but not without giving me an ugly side-eye as she storms past our table. Everyone else seems to be aware of her discomfort, and judging by the looks on their faces, most of them sympathize. I'm the monster in this story.

"It's going to be fine," Laura tries to assure me.

"I need to borrow your hubby for a second," Andrei adds and whispers something in Anton's ear.

My "hubby" gives him a long look, then plants a soft kiss on my cheek and leaves the table.

"I'm serious," Laura insists, nodding at the waiter to refill her champagne glass. "Eileen, everything will work out once Ciara gets past that bruised ego. You'll see."

I can't help but laugh, though there's no humor in it. "This whole thing shouldn't have happened in the first place."

"There's a lot that shouldn't have happened in the first place," she chuckles. "But the heart wants what the heart wants. It took two to make that baby you're carrying, honey."

"Fair enough."

"And don't give me any BS about how you feel. It's obvious to the blind that you two are into each other and then some. I could tell from the moment I first saw you two interacting at Ciara's engagement party. The thought crossed my mind that your dad clearly set Anton up with the wrong Donovan sister."

I give her a startled look.

She laughs. "Oh, come on. Love is always messy and inconvenient."

"That's a big word for what's going on here."

"Eileen, listen to me. What's happening today is a good thing. You're a wonderful woman, you're smart and educated. You come from a powerful family, and you've got a heart of gold. Anton may seem like the devil to you, but the man's got a soft center, and it's burning for you. He'll lay the world at your feet."

"Then why do I feel so miserable?"

"Well, that's your choice, isn't it?"

Suddenly, the room feels too small.

"I'll be back."

Tears sting my eyes as I head out of the restaurant and into the hotel lobby.

"I want to go home," I cry to myself as I look around, searching for a place to hide.

Just then, Anton's voice wraps my heart in something warm and soft. "We'll go home, then."

"I don't wanna go home with you!" I snap, desperate to let my anger get the better of me. Maybe if I hurt him, he'll keep his distance. "You don't want this any more than I do, Anton, at least admit it."

"Remember those wedding vows we took? I didn't dream any of it, did I?"

I give him a confused look. "What?"

"I'm not gonna lie to you, Eileen, even if that's what you're asking me to do."

"I don't understand."

Anton takes me firmly by the arm and escorts me to the nearest elevator.

My heart races as we step inside, and I glance back at the restaurant doors. "What are you doing?"

"Explaining something to my wife."

I stand beside him, puzzled, as the elevator doors slide shut.

My core tightens as I take a deep breath, letting his spicy cologne fill my lungs and dissolve the tension in my muscles. Anton's mere presence is enough to literally unwind me. It's infuriating when I'm trying so hard not to like him.

As soon as we reach the top floor, Anton pulls me out of the elevator and brusquely ushers me into the bridal suite. For a moment, I'm breathless as I take everything in.

"Oh, wow," I whisper, overwhelmed by the explosion of white roses and gold-specked silk linens spread over the California king-sized bed.

It smells beautiful, the scent of roses and lily-of-the-valley filling the space, along with soft vanilla and just a hint of cinnamon. The room is huge and brightly lit, the city of Chicago glimmering beyond the floor-to-ceiling windows. The skyline burns red and yellow, while my heart burns white-hot for the man standing in front of me.

"'What exactly is the matter with you?" Anton asks, his smoldering gaze turning me to embers.

"What do you mean?"

"You don't want this any more than I do, Anton; at least admit it." He mimics my voice in an unflattering fashion that forces a giggle out of me.

"But Ciara—"

"Enough about that spoiled, entitled brat your father took in," Anton cuts me off, then pulls me into his arms. "What happened that night was all about us. What we wanted."

"But me getting knocked up was—"

"A gift from the gods. It still is," he says. His hand comes up to gently cup my cheek, and there is so much tenderness and wanting in his touch that I can feel my defenses crumbling. "Eileen, not a day has gone by that you haven't been on my mind. Stuck right here, beating loudly," he lightly pounds his fist against his chest. "You're carrying my child."

"That was a mistake, an accident."

He laughs. "It's amazing that you can say that with a straight face. I guess I'm going to have to prove a few things to get you to stop believing that you were cattle sold to the highest bidder."

"It's how I feel," I say, lowering my gaze. "I didn't plan it. You certainly didn't have it on your agenda either."

"Eileen, no matter how this came to be, a child is a miracle that we get to have in our lives," he says, warmth exuding from his voice. "It only makes me want this more, beyond any strategic benefits I may have noted earlier. Frankly, even those were just really good excuses. I want this child, and I want you."

"You do?"

"I need you to understand that no matter what happens, you and the little one are under my care, my protection."

"I just want this baby to be loved."

"You needn't worry about that, Eileen. This baby is the luckiest kid in the world. He's got you, and he's got me. I may come across as the big bad wolf to you sometimes, but I am ready and eager to be a loving father."

For a moment, I actually believe him. I want to believe him.

"I know you're trying to reassure me, but this entire situation is such a mess." He gently brings up a finger to shush me.

"Ciara will be just fine, and you are going to be great. I told you, no matter what happens, you are my family now, and I will do anything and everything to protect you. Do you hear me?"

"I—"

"Do you hear me, Eileen?"

A strange sense of comfort comes over me, compelling me to give him a soft nod.

He kisses me. Firmly. Decisively. My reason, my logic—poof—out the window.

My body takes over. The blood rushes to my head as everything I've been holding in comes out in sizzling waves. The desire, the longing, the secret wishes. It all pours out of me as I devour his lips, and he devours mine.

"You stubborn, annoyingly proud woman," Anton growls, then nibbles on my lower lip before his tongue slips through and eagerly wrestles mine.

"Anton," I whisper against his lips, tasting the whiskey and the hunger burning inside him.

His hands move up and down, feeling my curves through the layers of white satin and tulle. His fingers dig in, feverishly squeezing everything in his path. Our hips meet, and I feel him nestled against my lower body, hard as a rock, before he finds the delicate laces at the back of my dress.

He removes it with remarkable speed and swiftness.

"Look into my eyes," Anton commands me.

Shyly, I meet his gaze. "I'm looking."

"Tell me I didn't want this."

"I can't."

"Why not?"

My lips tremble as I stand before him in nothing more than my white lace bra and panties. He gingerly removes the veil and the tiara from the top of my head, followed by the pins holding my hair in place.

I haven't felt like this since the last time we were together. Like a woman.

A beautiful, highly desired woman.

A goddess.

"Because I know you do want this," I whisper.

"I want you," he says, letting his fingers trace the contours of my full breasts. "Not just for a night. Not just for a fling. I've wanted more from the moment I met you, Eileen. Even as I stood there a month ago, waiting for Ciara to walk down the aisle, I wanted you. It was always you."

He kisses me again, destroying the last bit of doubt I have left in me. I have to give Anton Karpov credit. He sure knows how to dismantle me. Completely

"This pregnancy is the best thing that ever happened to us," he says, his hand gently palming my lower belly. There's a bump forming, albeit not yet noticeable underneath a larger pair of pants or a roomy dress. "For me, it was the perfect excuse to do what I wanted to do from the moment I snatched you away that night. I'd already agreed to marry Ciara, and I'm a man of my word. But extenuating circumstances such as, well, this, allowed me to do what I did."

"Anton..."

I gasp as he loosens the satin bows keeping my panties on, tossing them to the floor. His hand slips between my legs, and he finds me wet, hot, and oh, so ready for him. "Perfection, baby. Sweet, sweet perfection," he whispers against my lips.

"Oh, my God," I manage as his fingers slide between my slick folds.

My hips sway in a slow but steady rhythm as he works my clit into a swollen frenzy. I hold on to him, reveling in the feel of his chiseled muscles and smooth skin against my fingertips. He deepens the kiss and brings his left hand up, grabbing me gently by the back of the neck.

He pulls me against his broad chest, my breasts soft and heavy, as he finger-fucks me into the sweetest madness. "I love your curves, your fullness," Anton whispers in my ear, then nibbles on the lobe, sending a myriad of shock waves down my spine. "I love every glorious inch of you, Eileen, and it's all mine."

"It's all yours," I say as I surrender to him once more.

My climax leaves me wanting more as he carries me to the bed and pins me against the silken pillows. We consume one another. Touching. Squeezing. Pinching and scratching. I wrap my legs around his waist and welcome him deep inside of me.

Our eyes are locked.

Our hearts echo furiously as he builds a rhythm for me to follow.

"I missed this," I moan as he spears me with his full length, his cock thick and pulsating feverishly inside of me. I feel every inch, every throb as I clench tightly around him.

"I've missed you, baby," Anton growls as he fucks me harder and deeper. Faster.

My fingernails dig into his shoulders as he slips a hand between us. He finds my tender clit and proceeds to tease me into a slowly unraveling madness. I cry out his name, over and over, as he pounds into me. A second orgasm builds up, the tension too much for my body to bear.

"Come for me, darling," he commands. "Give me everything."

"Oh, Anton!" I whimper as I come hard. He continues to plunge into me, giving me everything, as well. Our bodies melt into each other.

This has been a long time coming. I've been so busy being angry with him that I deliberately ignored everything else. This is what I've been dreaming of since we first parted ways.

He fills me with his seed, grunting like a beast as he bites into my shoulder. I squeeze every drop out of him, my pussy quivering, sated and glazed.

We collapse into each other, basking in the afterglow, but only for a moment.

We step into the shower. He lathers rose-scented soap all over my body. His hands are everywhere.

He goes down on me, licking and suckling my clit, three fingers in as he throws me over the edge of sanity again. My third orgasm finds me barely standing in the hot stream, rolls of steam rising all around us.

"I want you," I tell him as he takes me from behind. "All of you."

"You've got me, Eileen," he says, fingers digging ferociously into my hips.

He fits perfectly, as if he was made for me. And I dare believe that I was made for him.

"You've got me for life," Anton adds as he claims me.

Again and again all through the night.

No inhibitions.

No limits.

Just the two of us while the forgotten wedding reception fizzles away somewhere on the ground floor. We forget about everyone and everything as we make love again and again until we're spent, tangled between the satin sheets.

Maybe I was wrong; maybe this will work out, after all.

This could be my true happiness.

CHAPTER 14

EILEEN

Morning finds us hungry for more.

"Where do you get this energy from?" Anton chuckles, his laughter turning to moans of pleasure as I take him in my mouth.

My lips stretch around his cock, already hard and eager to fill me. "Just following your lead," I say, firmly gripping the base.

"You look gorgeous from this angle," he says, lovingly looking down at me.

He slides down my throat, quite the effort for me, but I love every inch. I love his soft hazel gaze as I look up at him. He's mine. All mine. I run one hand across his chiseled chest, letting my fingers play with the short, dark curls. I pinch a nipple as I deep-throat him with growing hunger.

"Hold it," Anton commands me, gripping me by the back of the head to keep me in position. I gladly obey, tears trickling from the corners of my eyes. Tears of pleasure, unbridled pleasure, as my tender pussy is hot and wet, waiting for his attention. "You were made for me, Eileen. You know that?"

"I'm getting a clue," I giggle as I lift my head. "Actually, I got plenty of clues throughout the night. Ever since you pulled me out of... oh no!"

"Just remembering our wedding reception?" he laughs.

I feel my cheeks burning as I sit up, my hair draping over my shoulders and tender breasts.

"I wonder what they'll say."

"I don't really care," Anton replies. "Not when I've got you looking like this."

"Like what?" I mumble.

Outside, the sun rises lazily over the incandescent skyline. Buildings jut from the ground into the pink-blue sky as the world gradually awakens from its slumber. The world, not us. We're not done here. Not yet.

I feel my husband's cock twitch in my hand.

"Like a goddess. All mine," he says, motioning for me to approach. "Come up here."

"You mean like this?" I innocently ask as I straddle him and slide onto his cock, letting him stretch and fill me to the brim once again.

His eyes roll with raw pleasure. "Fuck, yeah, just like that."

"I've never been on top before." The words come out before I realize it.

His eyes widen and he stares at me for what feels like forever. Neither of us move, but I can feel him throbbing inside me, growing even bigger while my pulse accelerates with each ragged breath. "What do you mean?"

"Well, it's not like I had much sexual experience before you came along."

"Eileen, are you telling me you've never ridden a cock before?"

I shake my head slowly. I feel awkward and wonderful, vulnerable and commanding all at once as I glance down at him. He looks so damn handsome from this position. It fills my soul with a newfound power that radiates through every pore.

"We need to remedy that right away, baby," he says. "Move your hips."

"Like this?" I moan as I let my hips sway back and forth.

I can feel every inch of him. My pussy wraps around his cock, taking in all of him as the friction against my clit sends electrifying jolts throughout my body. I can feel the buildup between us, the pressure thickening in my core.

"Just like that," he says, firmly holding my hips to guide me.

Slowly but surely, a rhythm develops. Back and forth I move, my eyes locked on his.

"You're mine," I tell him.

"I'm yours, Eileen." He sits up, and suddenly he's deeper. I gasp and groan, overwhelmed with raw pleasure as I wrap my arms and legs around him. "And you are mine. All of you. Oh, fuck, I need you to come. Right now."

"Yes!"

I move faster, clenched tightly around him as the edge sharpens.

My mind melts as I tilt my head back, as he hides his face in my breasts and nuzzles my flesh, while his cock reaches my innermost depths. I let go with a shudder, my climax glazing him with liquid pleasure.

Afterward, we lay in a post-orgasmic haze, my head on his chest as Anton draws slow circles on my back with his index finger.

"The real world awaits," I mumble.

"Let it." He sighs deeply. His warmth, his protectiveness are a constant source of heat for my very soul. "I'm not going anywhere, and neither are you."

"Are you saying you're not done with me yet?" I giggle.

His index and thumb grasp my chin, beckoning me to look up at him. "I'll never be done with you, Eileen."

"That sounds fantastic, but I'm serious," I let a heavy breath roll from my chest. "The real world is still out there."

"We'll face it together."

"That sounds romantic."

"It's true."

"How will this work?" I ask him.

He gives me a curious look. "What?"

"This marriage."

"I suppose just like any other marriage works, we'll figure it out one day at a time. Right now, I just want to enjoy this moment, to enjoy you."

"We've got a baby on the way."

He nods. "It'll be interesting."

"I'm scared."

He tightens his hold on me, his gaze softening. "One day at a time, Eileen."

"Ciara—"

"Forget about your stepsister, your father, and Sergei fucking Kuznetsov, for once," he snaps. "You don't owe them anything, and you never will. You're my wife now. You're a Karpov, not just a Donovan. Which means you can be who you were always meant to be."

I need a moment to wrap my head around that concept. "I don't know who I'm meant to be, Anton. I'm only just realizing it now."

"Then let's start whenever you're ready," he replies and kisses me again. I taste myself on his lips. "We don't have to rush into anything else. There's been enough of that to last us a lifetime."

"I guess..."

"I've got you, okay?" He resumes his gentle caressing motion down my back. It helps soothe my frayed nerves. "You're not alone, and you're not at your father's mercy anymore either. Give it time, Eileen. We both have quite the road ahead of us. But I've got you, and you've got me. I meant every word of those vows, and I intend to make sure that my actions match said words."

It's my turn to cup his cheek as I melt into him. "I trust you."

Even as I say the words, there's still a sliver of doubt persisting somewhere beneath the bottom layers of my consciousness. Fears that have lingered in my heart ever since I was a little girl. Fears built on the hurtful words and actions of the people who were supposed to love and protect me.

I feel as though I've just traded one cage for a slightly prettier one, somehow, and I need Anton to prove me wrong.

CHAPTER 15

EILEEN

The Karpov mansion is impressive.

It's a sprawling property with a generous Victorian-style home built on three levels, surrounded by lush gardens and sinuous stone-paved paths that make the whole thing look like something out of an *Alice in Wonderland* tribute.

I feel small as I step out of Anton's Lexus, parked at the bottom of the mansion's front steps. There's an artesian fountain right behind us, a skirt of evergreen blossoms reaching out from the bottom.

"Andrei and Laura have the east wing; we've got the west," Anton says, watching my awe leave my mouth hanging open. "The northern part of the building has everything else. Home offices, a fully equipped gym, a massive kitchen, two living rooms, a study, a library slash reading room, tearoom, dinner hall, and too many bathrooms for me to count."

"Holy smokes."

"I know it's enormous and may seem intimidating, but it's always welcoming and warm. There's plenty of natural light and friendly staff around every corner. Your every need will be taken care of. It's your home now, too," he says.

"It's beautiful."

"Come on in, Mrs. Karpova."

"Donovan-Karpova."

"That's a mouthful, baby. It's in the official documents, but you can't expect me to say the whole thing every time."

I relent, taking a deep breath and welcoming the fresh morning air. We're on the north side of Chicago, where the suburbs thin out and the atmosphere feels a lot cleaner. Hell, I could get used to this. The long drive from the city is actually worth it. "Okay, Mrs. Karpova it is," I tell my husband.

"Come on, Mrs. Karpova. We've got a bed to break in after I give you a tour of the place," he says. "Ian here will handle our luggage."

As if summoned, Ian comes down the white marble steps with a pleasant smile. "Welcome to the Karpov residence, Mrs. Karpova," he greets me. "It is an absolute pleasure to meet you."

"It's an absolute pleasure to meet you, too, Ian."

"Like Mr. Karpov said, allow me to handle your bags. Please, enjoy your new home. There will always be someone around to assist you, should you need anything."

I give him a slight nod and let Anton guide me up the steps, his arm lovingly wrapped around my waist. As soon as we enter, I feel as though I've just stepped into a fairy tale come true.

"My God, it's like a museum," I gasp.

"I'll tell you a secret," Anton says as he gives me the ground-floor tour. "What you see here was only recently brought in—for you."

"For me?" I'm breathless.

The hallways are adorned with generous satin drapes and a perfectly polished French marble floor. Busts and Baroque-style statuettes mark each of the floor-to-ceiling windows. There are Persian-inspired tapestries mounted on the accent walls in each of the common rooms, with dark wood furniture and plush seating everywhere.

"For you," Anton says.

"Oh Anton," I whisper and pull him into a kiss. "You really didn't have to."

"I kind of did," he replies. "I promised you a home where you would feel safe and happy. And what did your favorite poet say?"

"A thing of beauty is a joy forever. I can't believe you remembered that."

I told him about my love of John Keats when we were still in Paris on our honeymoon, lounging in the morning sun on the rooftop terrace of our hotel.

"I remember everything," Anton replies.

The more I see, the more I learn about the mansion—its history and the events that took place within these walls—

the more fascinated I am by the Karpovs and by the Bratva overall. I was never one for romanticizing the Chicago mob, I was, after all, raised by them. The Russian mafia, however, seem to have a certain class, a particular style in both their personal and so-called professional fields.

"We Irish are a tad simpler," I chuckle as we stop in the kitchen. The sheer size of it practically takes my breath away as I look around at the seemingly endless maze of dark red stone counters and grey wooden cabinets. "You might as well open a restaurant here; you already have everything you need."

"Yet when there's an official Karpov function with up to two hundred people attending, you'd be amazed how small this kitchen seems." He plants a kiss on my temple, then pours each of us a glass of iced tea from one of the four giant fridges.

He gives me a curious look. "What's up?"

"Nothing. Just... it sometimes feels too good to be true. This thing between us."

"Hey, we got lucky. There's no use in looking a gift horse in the mouth." He pauses and checks his phone. "Andrei wants to meet in my office. I have to go for a bit."

"That's okay."

"Let me take you to our suite upstairs first, so you can relax and get comfy. As soon as I'm done, I'll join you."

"And we can try that bed." I give him a wink.

"We can try that bed." He smiles and kisses me softly.

Three hours fly by.

Laura is kind enough to take me on a tour of the rest of the property, allowing me a unique opportunity to learn more about the Karpovs and their business dealings across the city. It's just as I suspected—dark money that partially finances social projects across Chicago, while the bulk of it is split between further shady investments with just enough legitimate fronts to keep the government at bay.

"What's your place in all of this?" I ask her as we take a seat on a bench in the back garden. It's so nice outside; I don't want to go back in just yet.

"I'm a Bratva wife, first and foremost," Laura says with a wry smile. "I represent Andrei wherever I go, so I have to look the part. Not that I mind. Besides, Andrei spares no expense for this particular endeavor. A Karpov lady has to look her best."

"And then I came along," I chuckle.

She gives me a sad look. "You've been misled your whole life, Eileen. It's not about how thin you are. You've got more style and class in your pinky finger than your stepsister does in her entire body. Trust me, you'll have no trouble fitting in whatsoever."

"I appreciate the vote of confidence."

"Besides, the Karpovs like their women shapely. More to love, they say," she laughs lightly. "Andrei, however, had to understand that my metabolism is a bit different."

"He tried to fatten you up?"

"And then some."

We're both laughing now.

"He loves me for me, not just for my body," Laura sighs deeply, her eyes sparkling with affection as she gazes out upon the garden. "And it feels good to know that no matter what I look like, my husband will always lay the world at my feet."

"So tell me, what's a day in a mob wife's life like?" I ask.

"I'm going to guess it's not much different than a mob daughter's life," Laura replies.

I shrug. "My dad was always strict, and we always had protection, but he didn't interfere too much in our daily activities."

"That's basically how it is here, with just a few exceptions. Usually, the Karpov wife doesn't leave the premises for the first few weeks. You live here, you breathe here, you get accustomed to the rhythm of everything, and then, slowly but surely, you start attending public events at your husband's side."

"Are you serious?" I gasp, suddenly feeling as though I had just been kicked in the gut.

Laura nods slowly. "I hated it. I was this close to jumping out the window one time."

"Anton can't keep me here like some kind of caged animal."

"You're a Karpov now, and it's only temporary."

I shake my head, refusing to accept such a thing. "No, this can't be. He didn't say anything about that and neither did you before now."

"It's part of the process. Had I not gotten over that stage myself, I would've warned you. But I came out with a different perspective. I embraced my role and my new life. Andrei understood that I was his, and that he was mine; there was a mutual respect between us," she says.

"Laura, I can't live like that. I have plans. I have things I want to do. My café project. I finally have the freedom and the opportunity to build something. What exactly is expected of me? To wait home for my husband every night, barefoot, with dinner ready?"

"Anton should be the one having this chat with you, not me," she decrees, a look of discontent shadowing her face. "I'd be irritated, too, if I were you."

"My God, you are serious."

"For what it's worth, everything is done this way in order to protect you."

I'm having a hard time wrapping my head around everything I've just learned. I try to reconcile the beauty of my new home with the metaphorical shackles now clasped around my ankles.

"He can't keep me prisoner in my own home," I say, a shiver running down my spine. "We just came back from our honeymoon. This doesn't make any sense."

"But it does. Not only are you the wife of the head of the Bratva, but you're pregnant. Like it or not Elieen, that makes you a target. There are people out there who would harm you and your child to unseat Anton, including your ex-fiancé."

I shake my head. "No. Sergei might not be happy about the broken engagement, but surely he'd never hurt a child?"

"He absolutely would if it's Anton's child. And he's not the only one. I know you're not naïve, having grown up in the lifestyle. You have to believe this is for your own good."

I reject the premise altogether and abruptly excuse myself. Too angry to speak or listen to reason, I resort to spending the rest of my evening in our suite, seated by the window with a cup of tea, trying to figure out how to get out of this place.

I'm asleep before Anton comes back.

∼

"My meetings took longer than I expected," Anton says the next morning at the breakfast table. "I'm sorry."

"You've got to be fucking kidding me," I snap and set my tea mug down. "You couldn't even be bothered to answer my calls or messages."

"I did."

"Only to tell me that you'd see me in the morning."

He stills by the chair he just pulled out and gives me a long, pensive look. I measure him from head to toe. He's tired. The top buttons of his shirt are loose, and his five o'clock shadow has grown thicker. Clearly, he hasn't slept all night.

"Please, forgive me," Anton says and takes his seat next to me. He covers my hand with his atop the table. "We're dealing with a few loose ends regarding our marriage, Eileen. I need to make sure you're safe."

"Well, from what Laura tells me, you intend to lock me up in the house for supposedly that very reason."

"I'm trying to avoid that. or to at least shorten the induction period," he replies. "I don't want this part any more than you do. But it has to be done. Our family is a complex matter. Our enemies are ruthless. Eileen. The last thing I want to do is anger you in any way."

"I'm not angry; I'm hurt." I sigh deeply. "You don't trust me enough to let me handle my own life?"

"No, I don't trust the monsters beyond these doors to leave you alone," he corrects. "I trust you, Eileen. You're my wife. It's going to be uncomfortable for a while, and I hope that when it's all over, you'll find it in your heart to forgive me."

"What if I want to go back to my father's?"

He shakes his head slowly. Judging by his calmness, I already know what's coming. "I think you know that's not an option now. Your father wouldn't allow it any more than I can."

"So then, I am really a prisoner here while you go out and stay gone for hours, leaving me like a silly bird in a cage."

"It's not like that," Anton says, pulling in a deep breath as I tug my hand away from his. "Eileen, I promise, if it were safe for you, I'd let you out—"

"You'd let me out? Oh, gee, thank you, master!"

"Dammit, woman, will you listen to reason for once?"

"Why didn't you tell me?"

He gives me a confused look. "Tell you what?"

"That I'd be a prisoner in my own home for the first few weeks after arriving. We had a great honeymoon; we were getting somewhere. You had plenty of opportunities all the way up to the minute I set foot in this house to tell me the truth."

"I never lied to you."

"A lie by omission is still a lie."

"It was for your own good," Anton replies.

"No, it was so you could manipulate me into thinking this could be a happy life."

He takes another deep breath. "I was hoping you'd trust me to keep you safe."

"I do trust you to keep me safe but keeping me safe and taking away my freedom doesn't have to be the same thing," I protest.

"Dammit," he hisses and takes out his phone. He unlocks the screen and shows me a photo that turns my stomach inside out, instantly freezing every drop of blood in my veins. "This came in the mail for you yesterday at this address. Ian intercepted it before the day's correspondence was brought up to our suite."

"Oh, God," I whisper.

It looks real enough.

A pair of bloodied knit baby boots. I think I'm going to be sick.

"What is this?"

"It's a direct threat, Eileen. The first of many we'll receive. All it takes is for one person to make it past your security detail at whatever shop or event you wish to attend. One moment of distraction for a knife to slip through." He gently places his palm over my belly. "This is our baby, and you're my wife. I owe you everything in my power to keep you both safe. And I'll do precisely that, even if it ends with you hating me."

"You still should have told me."

He shakes his head slowly. "You're right. You deserve full disclosure, the whole truth. This is it. Someone's making direct threats, and until I figure out who it is and neutralize them, I need you to stay put, Eileen. It won't take long to find out who is stupid enough to threaten my family. That, I can promise."

"I wanted to go out and tour a commercial space that's for sale," I mumble, lowering my gaze. "For my café."

"Right, we talked about that back in London."

"There's one available on Upton Boulevard. I can't go see it?"

Anton shakes his head again. "I'm sorry, babe. There will be others. Chicago's flipping real estate like it's a stack of pancakes. We'll find you the perfect space when it's safer. Until then, we need to be careful."

"This sucks."

I still hate my predicament, and I know I won't be able to sit still for too long, but at least I can understand why they want me to stay behind closed doors.

"At least you and Laura can keep busy together," he offers a sympathetic shrug as he pours himself a cup of coffee, "with all the social events coming up."

"What events?"

"The Karpovs' weekly tradition of Friday night poker, for starters. Then there's the big families' brunch on Sunday."

"The big families' brunch? Does that include the Kuznetsovs?" I raise a skeptical eyebrow at him.

"No. I'm personally inviting and vetting each member of the families. The Kuznetsovs are off the list for this month's brunch. Sergei needs to either prove his loyalty to my family or declare war. Hopefully, this move will force him into picking a side. At least then I'll know where he truly stands."

"Do you think it'll work?"

"I'm not sure. But I am sure that you'll pull through this with your chin up and your lovely smile lighting up every room that you walk into."

"That doesn't make me feel better about any of this."

"I know, Eileen. But don't make me ask you to trust me again. That's not how this works," Anton replies.

The tone of his voice has changed. It's heavier. Darker. It commands my attention and my obedience.

His arm snakes around my waist and pulls me against him. He crushes my lips with his, reminding me of our bond. I am his. He is mine. And I will submit to him willingly, because I chose this.

CHAPTER 16

EILEEN

Anton keeps me busy and gleefully entertained. Between the lovemaking sessions and the intimate dinners, the evenings spent in the reading room, or in the company of his brother and sister-in-law, I'm starting to feel like everything is going to be okay.

But then Anton leaves, never telling me about his business. Or where he's going. Or how long he'll be away.

I'm left behind, waiting, minding my growing baby bump and hefty appetite. Days turn into weeks. My father keeps me at bay, cutting our phone conversations short whenever I bring up the idea of going over to his place to check up on him.

"He sounds worse than ever," I tell Ian one morning as I help him set up the breakfast table. "He's sick. I know he is. But he won't tell me anything."

"Mrs. Karpova, please, allow me," Ian says with a gentle smile. "You're the lady of this house. I cannot in good conscience let you set the table."

"I want to."

"Please."

"No, dammit!" I snap, my eyes instantly filling with tears. "I'm almost six months pregnant, I haven't seen my husband in a week. Everybody's walking on eggshells around me, and I can't even leave this house! Let me at least help you set the fucking table!"

Ian stills, briefly lowering his gaze. Oh, God, is this what it's going to be like? And for how long? How long will I feel so miserable and alone? When did I allow Anton to become my sole source of peace and happiness?

"I'm sorry, Ian." I sigh deeply and take a seat at the table. "My hormones are getting the better of me."

"I completely understand, Mrs. Karpova, and I would—"

"Eileen. Please call me Eileen."

He nods. "I completely understand, Eileen, and I would gladly let you if I could. But I have clear orders, and frankly, it's for your own good."

"Yeah, I've heard that one before. One too many times."

A minute passes in the most awkward silence as Ian looks around, cutlery still in his hands. "Perhaps you'd like to assist with cutting the fruit?" he asks. "I was thinking about putting together a citrus salad for today's breakfast. Oranges, mandarins, grapes, maybe an apple or a pear for extra sweetness."

"That sounds good. I'll cut the fruit," I say, eagerly taking the ingredients out of their basket and setting them on the cutting board.

The enormous counter island is in the middle of the kitchen. It gives me a great view of every angle, including through the French doors leading out to the gardens. Ian doesn't know I'm aware of the key to the doors he keeps hidden in the cabinet above the sink.

"What else?"

"Pardon me?" he absent-mindedly asks as he continues setting the table.

"Oranges, mandarins, green grapes, a pear. It looks fabulous, but what do you think about adding some raspberries to it? They would add color and a sweet tartness."

"You're absolutely right, Mrs.–I'm sorry, Eileen. I believe we have some in the fridge."

"No, it appears we're out. I checked a while ago. I was looking for an early morning snack." I exhale sharply, feeling a pang of guilt as I lie through my teeth.

"Are you sure?"

"You don't believe me?" I ask, trying to sound offended.

"Of course, I do," Ian replies. "If you'd be so kind as to give me a minute, I'll ask one of the staff to fetch us some raspberries from the farmers' market down the road."

I give him a surprised look. "There's a farmers' market nearby?"

"Just half a mile north, actually. We source most of what's in the kitchen locally. Our fruits come from our closest neighbors. The meats, too. I'll be right back, and in less than twenty minutes, we'll have raspberries for your salad."

"Thank you, Ian. I truly appreciate it," I reply with a warm smile.

Once he's out of the kitchen, I know what I have to do. The fact that my father keeps brushing me off has become unbearable. I understand my stepsister being prickly until the day she dies, and I'm ready to accept that particular loss, but where Dad is concerned, I can't sit tight anymore. I'm worried about that man, and I need to see him face to face.

So, I slip through the kitchen doors using the hidden spare key.

Carefully, I sneak around the house and make my way into the massive garage. The keys are in the ignitions, because nobody's dumb enough to break into a Karpov property to jack a handful of luxury vehicles. That would be suicidal.

The fact that no one suspects I would ever do what I'm about to do is great, because it increases my chances of a clean escape.

The Karpov's security detail hasn't made a habit of keeping close tabs on me as long as I'm on the grounds. It's why Ian felt so comfortable leaving me alone in the kitchen—then again, he doesn't know I saw where he stashed that extra key.

By the time the bodyguards realize what's happening, it's too late. I'm already past the front gates and speeding up the main road into the city. Once I hit the beltway, they'll lose me altogether. Anton will be furious, but I have to do this.

"Ah, dammit!" I grumble as I realize I left my phone behind. I was in such a rush to seize the opportunity that I completely forgot about it. But it might be for the best. They could use my phone to track me.

I take the side streets through Chicago and pull over a couple of blocks away from my father's house. Nervous as hell, I get out of the car and look around until I'm sure that no one is following me.

I cross the street and make my way up the road, hands in my pockets, my nerves causing me to shiver a bit. I glance over my shoulder just as I'm about to turn the corner. Recognizing a few faces, I pull my hood over my head and proceed toward the back alley.

I don't spot Ian until he's standing right in front of me, a sour look on his face.

"You're going to get me in a heap of trouble here, Mrs. Karpova," he grimly declares.

"Dammit Ian," I gasp, startled by his unexpected presence.

"You shouldn't have come here."

"My family lives here. I just wanted to see my dad."

"It's not safe."

I scoff, giving him an annoyed look. "You can't stop me from seeing my family. Now get out of my way before I get pissed."

"No." He grabs me by the wrist, and my heart starts pounding.

"Wait. Ian—"

POP. POP.

Something whizzes past both of our heads at a terrifying speed.

"Shit, *run*!" Ian yells, blocking me with his surprisingly athletic frame.

"What the hell?" I croak, but there's no time to ask questions.

As we run down the street, Ian takes a gun out from a holster I had no idea he was wearing. He fires a couple of shots, and I yelp, finally spotting the people he's exchanging fire with.

Two men, tall and muscular, wearing all black. They look like Russian goons.

POP. POP.

A few more shots ring out as I run as fast as my feet can carry me, desperate to survive, desperate for my unborn child to survive.

Ian shoots back. We turn a corner to find a car waiting, engine running. Ian opens the driver's side door and shoves me into the passenger seat, before climbing in beside me. He guns the accelerator.

"Oh, shit!" I scream when the side-view mirror of the car explodes from another bullet. In a flash, we're speeding up the road, engine roaring, as we leave our assailants behind. "Oh, God, Oh, God, oh, my God…"

"A simple thank you would suffice," Ian grunts as he leans into the steering wheel.

"Thank you! Who were those people?"

"Precisely the people I expected to show up as soon as you came here," Ian says. Beads of sweat bloom across his forehead. He doesn't look well, and it quickly becomes clear why. Red blooms across his white shirt and grey vest. "Eileen, perhaps now you understand why your husband wanted you to stay put."

"Oh, my God, Ian! You've been shot! We need to get you to a hospital!" I yell.

He shakes his head, eyes sharply focused on the road. "I'm good. I just need to get you home, Eileen. Mr. Karpov is on his way as we speak."

My blood runs cold as I realize that my reckoning is coming a lot sooner than I had hoped. Glancing back, I breathe a momentary sigh of relief when it appears that no one seems to be following us.

"What about my dad?" I ask.

"They're not after him, Eileen. They're after you."

I shudder, my skin crawling as I struggle with the concept. I was raised my whole life knowing that I'd become a target for one of my father's rivals sooner or later. But that day never came, and I was always well-protected. It completely slipped my mind until now.

I am still susceptible to violence, and this serves as a grim reminder.

Once back at the mansion, I discover that Anton has doubled the security detail. I was able to speak to my father on the phone—courtesy of Anton calling him. He's fine, but worried about me. I feel like such a fool, but I'm angry.

"I think you understand now why I've been insistent on you staying put," Anton says, his gaze set on my face.

"I understood that there were risks involved in any sort of outing, but I was careful—"

"Careful? Eileen, it doesn't matter how careful you think you're being, because our enemies have eyes on every single point of interest. Your father's house included. They were already there, waiting for you.

"I didn't think they'd be at my father's house," I say meekly.

"Well, they were. And like I told you before, I will protect you and our child, no matter the cost."

"I'm the one paying, though, being kept in the dark and locked up in my own home," I mutter.

"Our enemies will stop at nothing to hurt you."

"*Your* enemies," I correct him.

Anton gives me a hard look. "*My* enemies?"

"You're the one they're trying to get to by hurting me. They're *your* enemies."

"Let me remind you that you were already pregnant with my child, and fully aware of it when you allowed Sergei Kuznetsov to visit and discuss your wedding arrangements," he shoots back. "Let's not play saints, Eileen. We each have our share of the blame here."

I lower my gaze. "You're right. I'm sorry."

"It's frustrating as hell; I get it."

"Is this what it's going to be like from now on?" I ask, my eyes filled with tears. "Constantly looking over my shoulder? Afraid to leave the house? Walking around with an army of bodyguards? Is this my life, Anton? It was never this bad in my father's business."

He takes a deep breath and sits on the sofa next to me. "It's just until I find out who's behind the threats and the attacks. Right now, I don't have any conclusive evidence against anybody in particular, especially Kuznetsov. And without proof, I can't make a case within the organization either."

"That leaves you with your hands tied and the snake still in the garden, so to speak."

"Precisely. But none of this even fucking matters if you're not safe. If our baby isn't safe. So, for the love of God, will you please do as I say? Please just follow my orders and play your part while I dig into this and find the evidence I need to get rid of Sergei, and whoever else he's got on his payroll."

There goes the small semblance of peace I thought I'd acquired. There goes my ritzy, artisanal café. My dream is to make something of myself, to bring my child into a world I could be proud of, our little corner of the universe. It's tainted now, forever shadowed by the threat of monsters lurking in the dark.

I'm stuck here.

Anton's company no longer feels like it's enough to soothe my soul. He continues to say it's only a matter of time. He keeps a certain distance from me, though he probably thinks I haven't picked up on it yet. But I have. He's here, but not really, not fully.

I can feel my happily ever after slipping away.

CHAPTER 17

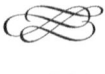

ANTON

This isn't how I wanted it to be.

A month's worth of tension has piled up between Eileen and me, causing a certain amount of distrust to fill the room whenever we're together. Physically, we're a perfect match. She's the yin to my yang and then some. She's got me hooked on her magic, and I can't get enough of her. I've yet to tell her this, but the mere sight of her and that beautiful, growing, round baby bump fills me with nothing but joy and excitement.

I can't make the most of it, though. I can't enjoy the pregnancy, nor can I truly open up to her. Hell, I doubt I even deserve a woman like Eileen.

"Dr. Hartman will see you now." A perky-looking nurse comes into the waiting room, snapping me out of my thoughts. She leads us down the hall into the ultrasound room. Once inside, she helps Eileen onto the table and then turns on the machine.

We barely spoke on the way over. In bed, we're in flawless sync. Out of bed, it feels like we're strangers stuck together by the laws of civil union.

"Good morning, Mr. and Mrs. Karpov," Dr. Hartman greets us as he walks in.

"What did the blood tests say?" I ask, skipping past the introductions, as always.

"Everything is looking good so far," he says with a gentle smile. "I'm glad to see those prenatal vitamins are keeping her minerals in check. The numbers are in both the mother's and baby's favor."

"Is there anything else we should be doing in the second trimester?"

Eileen scowls at me. "I'm right here, you know. You don't have to speak as if I'm not in the room."

The pregnancy hormones and having to stay home have my wife on a razor-sharp edge. There are good days, and then there are awful days. I do my best to keep her head above water, yet sometimes I can still feel her slipping away. What we have is fragile enough, already.

"My apologies," I reply. "Dr. Hartman, please, tell my darling wife what we can expect in the second trimester. I'm merely an observer."

The doctor laughs lightly. "It's nice to see a concerned and involved father-to-be."

Eileen ignores the doctor's comment and replies, "We would really like to be able to find out the sex today if we could."

"Alright then, let's get a sneak peek at the little one," Dr. Hartman says as he squirts gel on Eileen's belly and moves the wand around, searching for our baby.

I look at the screen, listening to the hum of the machine, but my gaze soon wanders back to Eileen. I stare at her for a moment. A beauty, even on her worst day. Her long red hair flows loosely over one shoulder. Her green eyes are focused on the screen, and her breath slows as she listens.

Soon, quick successions of *thwump, thwump, thwump* fill the room. Dr. Hartman gives a soft, "Hmm," and I notice his eyebrows raise just slightly. Eileen catches it, too.

"What is it? What's wrong?"

The doctor smiles softly and shakes his head. "Nothing is wrong at all. It's not uncommon to miss twins during the first ultrasound when they're still so small—"

"Wait, what? Did you say twins?" I ask in disbelief.

"Yes. Two babies, two strong heartbeats," Dr. Hartman says. "Here, look at this," he points to the screen, identifying two different shadows against a grainy background.

"Twins," I whisper.

It makes sense. Twins run in the family. My father was a twin, my grandmother before him. There's a set in each generation. I guess it's my turn now, and I'm elated.

"I'm going to get huge," Eileen murmurs, tears welling in her eyes. "I already feel ginormous."

"Honey, you're beautiful," I say, gently squeezing her hand. "And I'll be with you, every step of the way. I can't carry the twins for you, but I can carry you."

"You're going to be fine," Dr. Hartman says. "I think we should plan for a C-section, though, to remove some of the strain a natural birth can put on your body. In your case, Mrs. Karpova, it is probably the safer option."

"Yeah, we can do that," she absently replies.

"You can always change your mind," the nurse reminds her.

Eileen gives me a wondering look. "Are you okay with that?"

"Honey, it's your body. You're doing all of the work. I support you fully, no matter what you decide," I tell her. "I just want you to be safe, healthy, and happy, so we can raise our twins together."

"Could you be any more amazing?" She releases a shuddering breath while the nurse cleans her up and the doctor prints a copy of the ultrasound. "This is way more than what I expected."

"You're not alone," I remind her.

"Twins, Anton. We're having twins."

"Yeah, I heard."

I'm overwhelmed, too, but there's no turning back time—not that I'd want that, anyway. I wouldn't change a damn thing. I'm right where I need to be, and so is Eileen. One way or another, we're going to figure this out.

Knowing we're having twins ups the stakes even more, though. There's a side of me that has stayed hidden over the past couple of years. I didn't see a need for unnecessary bloodshed, so I stifled a most primal instinct.

I may have to let the dark side loose again in order to keep my wife and our babies safe.

CHAPTER 18

EILEEN

"I guess when God decides to throw a challenge my way, He goes all in, eh?" I laugh nervously as we arrive home.

"The very definition of fuck around and find out, right?" Anton replies, making me laugh harder.

"Oh, we sure did," I manage, as I sit on the edge of the bed.

I'm already tired, and it's not even noon. He goes over to the window and pulls the curtains wide open, letting the sunlight in. The room is bathed in a soft golden hue as I take a deep breath and try to gather my senses. Yet my thoughts continue to shoot in every direction, jumping from one extreme scenario to another.

Anton, however, is calm.

I soak in his presence, because it's the only thing that keeps me grounded when my worst-case scenarios get the better of me. "Twins. Crazy."

"Double the trouble," he replies, and kneels in front of me, his hands resting on my knees. "We'll handle it."

"Will we? Anton, we're practically strangers."

The shadow of a smile dances across his lips. "Not in the biblical sense, we're not."

"It takes so much more to raise a family," I say. "Don't get me wrong, I like what's happening here, despite the circumstances. There's no denying the chemistry, and I'm sure given enough time, we can grow together. But we don't have a lot of time to do that, do we?"

"Just because we skipped a few steps doesn't mean it won't turn out alright," he says. "I have faith in you, in us. Don't you?"

"I want to."

"What's giving you pause, then?"

I offer a slight shrug. "The fact that we skipped some pretty *important* steps. We were supposed to get to know each other first, to figure out if we are compatible, if we can actually make it work—"

"How could we have gotten to know each other if I married your stepsister, like Ronan and I had originally planned?"

I stare at him for a hot second. "Fair enough."

"Eileen, I need you to have faith in me, in us. I will do everything in my power to make sure that you and the kiddos are happy and safe," he says, the gravity of his tone having me gobbling up every word. "I will burn the whole Bratva to the ground if I have to. I won't stop until every single one of our enemies is in the ground."

"I wish violence wasn't necessary."

"Recent events argue against you, I'm afraid."

Lowering my gaze, I let a heavy sigh leave my chest. "A girl can only dream."

"It's a rough world that we grew up in," Anton says. "It's harsh and bloody. There are backstabbers at every corner. Traitors. Greedy bastards who will do anything for power, money, and influence. I don't need any of it. If someday you tell me you want to get out of the city, to leave it all behind, I will. Without hesitation."

I give him a startled look. "Are you serious?"

"Very."

It does sound enticing. Dropping everything and simply running away. But running away is exactly what we'd be doing. It wouldn't resolve the problem, and our enemies would still find a way to track us down and finish what they started. I know enough about the Russians to understand that our troubles wouldn't end with us simply leaving the city.

"I don't want to end up telling our children stories about how cowardly we were," I exhale sharply. "As much as I dislike the situation, I dislike the idea of turning tail even more. I'd cease to be a Donovan, and I certainly wouldn't make myself worthy of the Karpov name, now, would I?"

Anton's lips stretch into a delicious grin. "That's my girl."

"I still can't believe we're having twins."

"Twice as much love," he says, then laughs and kisses me deeply, cupping my face in his hands. "I will be with you every step of the way, baby. You're not alone in this."

"I'd better not be."

He gives me a hurt look. "Who would I be, if the woman I call my wife doesn't have faith in me?"

I've yet to hear what I want to hear, but I won't beg for it. Maybe I'll never hear him say it. I could convince myself that he feels it, that actions speak louder than words. That's what matters, and as far as actions go, Anton has been by my side from the moment I became his wife.

I'm married to a powerful man who makes my body sing and my heart soften whenever he's around. It's his children I'm carrying in my womb, his protection that has kept me alive and safe.

"Eileen, look at me," Anton says.

I do, losing myself in those hazel pools of his, my soul expanding like a young, growing sun.

"We've got this," he says.

I don't get the chance to reply or to express any more doubts —of which I have plenty—before he kisses me again. This time, however, it's hungrier, needier. I have no qualms about completely and shamelessly surrendering.

"We've got this," he says again as he peels my clothes off, one layer at a time.

I give in to this growing hunger, my body aching for him.

Soon enough, I'm bare and soft against his lips as he devours my pussy, one hand kneading my tender breast, while the other trails a path down my belly and nestles between my legs, just under his stubbly chin.

A moan escapes my throat as his fingers slide in. "Oh, Anton!" I cry out as his lips close around my swollen clit.

The tension builds in my core as he finger-fucks me into the next world, teasing my nerve endings until I explode and he drinks me whole.

"I'll never get tired of this," I say as he comes up and spears me with his full length.

I'm still in the throes of ecstasy, still rippling like a stone in the water as he penetrates me, his gigantic cock filling and stretching me until I melt into him altogether. He holds me tightly, arms wrapped around my body, my breasts squished against his hard chest as he goes deeper and harder.

"You're my favorite addiction," he whispers against my lips.

We kiss hungrily, starved for one another as the rhythm builds up between us. I clench myself tightly around his cock, welcoming every thrust as he pours himself into me. I listen to his ragged breath as he fucks me harder, faster.

I love the sound of skin slapping skin as he rams into me, roaring as he pumps me full of him.

Our bodies, slick with sweat and glistening in the afterglow, settle under the silken sheets while a cool breeze slips into the room through a cracked window. We're nowhere near done, though. Anton's appetite for me has grown, and I'm hopelessly desperate for more, every damn time.,

"Our lovemaking is the only thing that turns my brain all the way off," I mumble, breathing him in as I draw invisible circles with my fingertips on his bare, splendidly sculpted back.

"Well, at least I'm making myself useful," he chuckles softly.

"And then some."

He knows what I mean. He feels it, I know he does. It echoes through me into him, reverberating with every breath. There's more between us than physical chemistry, more growing than just the twins.

∽

A few weeks later, morning finds me at the breakfast table, nursing a mug of hot cocoa as I gaze out the window. Ian is back to work, fully healed from being shot. Luckily, the bullet only grazed his side. He's busy preparing the garden terrace, as we're expected to join Andrei and Laura for a family business luncheon.

"There you are," Anton says as he walks into the kitchen.

I give him a warm smile, taking a moment to admire how particularly dashing he looks in his dark blue suit. The white shirt and silver cuff links give him a regal aura, but it's his smile that makes my insides melt, every damn time.

"Good morning," I reply. He kisses me, then takes a seat at the breakfast table. "Coffee?"

"Is that what you're having?" he asks with a raised eyebrow.

"Nope."

He leans forward and takes a whiff. "Mmm. I'll have what you're having."

"Hot cocoa? Really?"

"You used the stuff from the red tin, didn't you?"

I nod. "Yes."

"Then I want some. That's premium cocoa powder from Maison D'Or. They import it from a precious little cocoa plantation in the heart of Guatemala. A single scoop is like a taste of Aztec heaven, I swear."

"You keep surprising me, Mr. Karpov," I exclaim as I fill his cup with my precious, chocolatey concoction. "And you're in luck. I always whip up a whole jug of it before I sit down for breakfast."

"I know. It's one of your little habits that always makes me smile," he says with a playful wink. I like that he's in such a good mood. "What did you mean by I keep surprising you?"

I can't help but blush. "I like to consider myself quite the coffee and chocolate connoisseur. You know about my dream project, about opening my own café someday."

"Yes, I do."

"I find it nice to know that you're also highly educated on the topic. Nobody else in this house seems to know what's in that red tin or really cares."

"Let me guess, you tried to tell Laura about how good the stuff is," he laughs lightly.

"I did."

"Laura's an Americano girl, and she'll be an Americano girl until the day she dies. Andrei, I'm afraid, is even worse. He actually calls that Starbucks stuff coffee. You're sharing a house with people who know nothing about good, quality beans, be it cacao or coffee."

I giggle softly, watching him take a long sip of his cocoa. "Either way, I'm glad you can appreciate this."

"Just as I appreciate the fact that you slipped a sprinkle of nutmeg into this, didn't you?"

I raise an eyebrow. "Like I said, you keep surprising me."

"Speaking of surprises, this is for you," Anton places a blue velvet box on the table between us.

I open it to reveal a gorgeous diamond and pearl necklace. It will look great with at least three of my cocktail dresses, which only serves to remind me that Anton pays attention. He doesn't just have good taste, he's got a working set of eyes, too. But I still feel like I'm being bought.

"Don't you like it?" he asks.

"It's beautiful."

"You don't seem that happy about it."

"I'd be happier if I could get out of this house more often," I bluntly reply. "While I fully understand the threat level, how much longer do I have to be cooped up in this place? Lunch and dinner out on the terrace don't count."

Anton gives me a long, hard look. "Where is this coming from? Because I know we're not about to have the same conversation all over again."

"I feel like you're trying to buy me, Anton, to make up for the situation. If we're going to build a marriage together, it's not going to be with diamonds and pearls."

He sits back, a muscle ticking angrily in his jaw. "I can't lavish you with presents?"

"What's the point if I can't wear them anywhere?" I level my gaze at him.

He sighs, trying and failing to hide his exasperation. "Eileen—"

"You know what, you don't have to say anything," I cut him off. "I'm tired. I'm going to go lie down for a bit. Enjoy the cocoa. I'll see you at lunch."

With that, I get up from the table and leave the kitchen, Anton staring after me, dumbfounded.

CHAPTER 19

EILEEN

As the days go by, there seems to be a sea of eggshells stretching between Anton and me. I know I can be my own worst enemy sometimes. It's something I need to work on, but Anton needs to give a little, too.

"I should've leaned into my morning sickness so I could skip all this," I mumble into my glass, causing Laura to giggle.

"You're going to go stir crazy in that room. Might as well enjoy an opportunity to socialize," she says. "Granted, not being able to drink alcohol might make the whole affair a tad gruesome, but I think you need this."

"Far be it from me to contradict you."

"Besides, you're gorgeous in this shade of green. I'm glad I got you to come out of your room tonight."

I can't help but smile.

The dress is a beautiful emerald green, creating the perfect contrast with my red hair. It brings out my eyes, too, and I'm wearing the diamond and pearl necklace that Anton got me.

The same necklace that caused me to say some rather unpleasant things. Things I feel bad about now.

"It hugs your figure in all the right places," Laura adds with an encouraging smile.

"Thank you."

Anton smiles appreciatively at me from across the room. He doesn't need to say anything. He clearly loves the way I look tonight.

"He can't take his eyes off you," Laura whispers, following my gaze. "He can never take his eyes off you, Eileen."

I chuckle. "I'm guessing you heard about the last argument we had."

"Would you even call it an argument?"

"It sure as hell wasn't a lovers' quarrel. That would require actual love in the relationship."

Laura rolls her eyes, swapping her empty champagne glass with a full one from the waiter walking by with a loaded tray. There are about a hundred people present here tonight. There's a live band playing music by the terrace windows, and the ballroom looks beautiful—the chairs are dressed in satin chair covers, sprawling springtime floral arrangements, and candles on every table.

It's meant to bring the Bratva heads closer together, but even I can sense the thick tension between them these days.

"Someday, you're going to learn enough about the Karpovs to completely redefine the concept of love you learned from whatever fairytale book you read when you were younger," Laura says, then waves and smiles at another Bratva wife.

"I'm sorry," I tell her. "I'm being a Debbie Downer, aren't I?"

"I get it," she says as she waves at somebody else.

Everybody knows and appreciates her. So many women are eager to talk to her, yet she's here with me, keeping me company instead of buzzing around and socializing like the Bratva queen she is.

"Up to a point, I'm sure you do," I reply, "but we both know I'm dealing with way more than just separation anxiety."

"Separation from your family, you mean."

"Yes."

"I know Anton and Andrei considered inviting the Donovans tonight, but it's supposed to be a Bratva thing. Inviting the Donovans would've meant inviting other non-Russian families, too, and the boys are still mending fences with the Benedetto's."

"Can't say I'm surprised after that whole debacle with Tommy Benedetto."

"I think we are all in agreement that wasn't Andrei's finest moment," Laura chuckles. "But that's my man—smart and savvy until you cross him. Thankfully, Anton was there to save the day, and you, if you remember."

"How could I forget?"

Laura sighs deeply. We both gaze across the room to where Anton and Andrei are busy talking to the Ivanovs and the Fedorovs. I've been brushing up on my Russian genealogy lately, and I'm pleased that I'm able to recognize almost half of the people present at this function. It makes me feel less lonely.

"The Karpov men didn't have it easy growing up. Their mother passed away at a time when they still needed her gentle influence. Their father was a titan, an ironclad bastard, the typical Russian warlord albeit in a pinstripe suit," Laura tells me. "Which is why both Anton and Andrei aren't the share-their-feelings type. I've been married to Andrei for quite a while now, and do you know how many times he's told me he loved me?"

I give her a curious look. "Once?"

"You underestimate him," she flashes a cool grin. "Three times."

"Wow."

"I know, right? He practically fell apart the first time he said it, shaking like a leaf in a windstorm," she says. "Watch their actions, Eileen, not their words."

I nod slowly. "I keep telling myself that. Besides, it's way too early for me to demand love from a man who barely knows me."

"Give him time," Laura replies. "He's proven himself thus far, hasn't he?"

"Yes."

"He listens when you have something to say, right?"

"Unless it's about me going out, even with a double security detail. Then he just shuts down on me. Completely."

Laura raises an eyebrow. "After the heap of trouble you got yourself and Ian into, you bet your sweet ass he's going to shut down on you. There are some things you're clearly going to have to learn the hard way."

"I don't like living in a cage. Laura. A gilded cage, granted, but it's still a cage."

"We put on a nice dress, a fancy pair of shoes, beautiful, priceless jewels. We've got disposable income at our fingertips, people tending to our every need and whim... living is about making yourself comfortable in your cage, Eileen, just as I've learned to make myself comfortable in mine."

I shake my head slowly. "Truth be told, I agree with you. Born and raised a Donovan, I feel like I traded one gilded cage for another. I guess I'm just tired of it all."

"No, what you are is anxious. Afraid. Thrown into a situation you never truly wanted. Not on these terms, anyway. I suppose you would've liked a traditional first date, a few dates with Anton before he popped the question."

"I would've liked it if our first date didn't involve him kidnapping me, that I knew his name, and if Anton had popped the question in general," I chuckle.

"Yeah, I know. They're terrible at this," she says. "Andrei practically shoved a marriage contract in my face. I told him to stick it where the sun doesn't shine and to propose to me like a real man, even though the whole thing was a setup from the start."

I'm about to ask her about those first few months of their marriage when an intense presence clouds the corner of my eye. Slowly, I turn my head and see him approaching. "Oh, shit," I mutter, damn near crushing my virgin cocktail glass with my bare hand. "Sergei."

"Relax, nobody's packing tonight," Laura whispers.

"What?"

"Guns. Knives. This is a clean event. Everybody got screened thoroughly before they even made it through the gates," she says.

"Mrs. Karpova," Sergei says upon reaching us. "It's nice to see you again; however, I wish it were under different circumstances."

"Mr. Kuznetsov," I politely reply, my skin crawling all over. I'm grateful to have Laura by my side in such an uncomfortable moment. My gaze briefly wanders across the room again, looking for Anton. I don't see him anywhere, which is probably why Sergei decided to approach me. "What do you mean?"

He smiles, but it's a flat, fake smile. "I mean under different circumstances, you and I as man and wife. Alas, that wasn't possible. No hard feelings, though?"

"Really? No hard feelings?" I snap, remembering the attack that Ian and I barely survived. "Then what were those goons doing around my father's house?"

"I can assure you I wasn't responsible for that. I've presented the Karpov brothers with all the evidence they needed to no longer consider me a threat," Sergei calmly says. "I suppose they still suspect me of dark intentions, but I've moved on. As for the goons you mentioned, I don't know anything about that. As I told your husband, I am not responsible. If the factions within our organization were offended by the whole affair, I greatly apologize, but I had nothing to do with the attack at your father's house."

"Whatever, Sergei. I was almost shot down in the middle of the street. While pregnant, might I add."

"Mrs. Karpova, I understand your frustration and I agree it was a most heinous act. As a gesture of good faith, I offered my security resources to the Karpov brothers to catch the assailants as quickly and as swiftly as possible," Sergei says.

I have a hard time believing him. Everything about him feels fake, like he's slithering around me like a snake prepping his prey, but a man of his stature is difficult to take down without any palpable evidence.

"Did they ever catch the assassins?" Laura asks, her tone much softer than mine.

He shakes his head. "I'm afraid not. But I do know they won't be foolish enough to try again. Especially now that I have been somewhat vindicated."

"What do you mean by that?" I ask.

"You haven't heard? Oh, I suppose you're still estranged from your stepsister. Ciara can be remarkably proud, but it's what I like best about her," he laughs lightly.

My stomach drops. "I don't understand."

"Your father proposed I marry Ciara in light of your unforeseen nuptials. I made her quite an attractive offer," Sergei says, his eyes carefully searching my face. "I have a good feeling about it, too. I'm confident Ciara and I will forge quite the—what do they call it? Power couple."

It's as if the entire ceiling just dropped onto my head.

For a moment, I find myself unable to breathe. My vision blurs, and the room starts spinning. A subtle nudge from Laura brings me back to earth, grounding me as I look at her in sheer horror, then back at Sergei.

"Excuse me?" I ask with a weak voice.

He seems quite satisfied with my reaction. The manipulative prick. "Ciara may very well accept my marriage proposal. If she does, plenty of fences will be mended and we will become family, after all."

"Ciara would never."

"I don't know, after the stunt you pulled with Anton Karpov, I wouldn't put it past her," his smile is sinister. "She would suit me better, anyway, and it's in her best interest, as well, if you think about it. Your father won't be around forever."

"Honestly, I wouldn't put it past her, either," Laura mumbles in my ear.

Sergei is clearly pleased with himself as he takes a moment to look around. Yet when he sees Anton coming, quickly carving a path through the thick crowd of guests, his humor fades. No wonder. The look on Anton's face speaks of bloody murder.

"Either way, it's a pleasure to see you again, Mrs. Karpova. And I do hope that you and the baby are in good health," he says.

"Babies," Laura shoots back. "They're having twins."

It's Sergei's turn to look surprised. "What can I say, other than congratulations?"

"The Karpov seed is strong," I reply. "I can't say I regret my choice."

"I'm sure you don't," he hisses before disappearing into the crowd in the opposite direction from which Anton quickly emerges.

"You missed him by a literal hairline," Laura says.

"He knew the deal when I extended the invitation," Anton growls, clearly furious. "He was to keep his distance from you. What did he say?"

"He just wanted to bring me up to speed regarding my stepsister and their potential wedding. You know, since my family couldn't be bothered to inform me."

"Oh."

The flatness of his tone makes my blood boil as I narrow my eyes at him. "You already knew, didn't you?"

"Yikes," Laura quips. "Let me take you out on the terrace for a bit, Eileen. I think you need some fresh air."

I stare at Anton for a long minute, furious. But this is a public setting. A Bratva event. I won't embarrass him or myself, not after Sergei Kuznetsov basically laughed in my face. Laura is doing the smart thing by leading me outside.

"Don't let them see us divided," I mutter as I let her accompany me out of the ballroom.

We leave Anton behind, his gaze burning into the back of my neck.

He knows a conversation is coming.

CHAPTER 20

ANTON

"Still in the doghouse?" Andrei greets me with his usual debonaire smirk as I walk into my office the next morning.

At least he brought coffee and bagels.

"It's bad this time," I mutter, taking my seat behind the desk. "Really bad."

"How bad?"

"I slept on the couch bad."

He sighs and pushes a coffee across the desk. I take it with a thankful nod and help myself to a long, hot sip. "Sorry, brother, but I did warn you."

"Yes, you did."

"You should've told her. The minute you knew Ronan offered Ciara to Sergei, you should've told Eileen. Especially since Ciara has been keeping up with her no-contact policy."

"Yes, I should've. You're absolutely right."

Andrei gives me a startled look. "Since when does the mighty Anton admit when he's wrong?"

"Hey, I'm allowed to grow, to change for the better," I reply with a faint smile. "I struggled with the decision. I wanted to tell Eileen, but seeing as she's already in such a delicate situation and I'm still trying to figure out a way to get through to her, I didn't want to upset her. Besides, that stepsister of hers can be such a pig-headed brat."

"I'll say it again. You're whipped."

I can't help but laugh. "Who'd have thought?"

"Remember when we were just getting started in the organization? What did you tell me?"

"Don't accept drinks from a bottle you didn't open."

Andrei rolls his eyes. "No."

"You don't have to pay for sex?"

"No, you ass. You said you'd never marry for love. That marriage was strictly a business arrangement. I followed in your footsteps until I married Laura and that was a kick in the balls. So, pardon me if I'm finding a ton of satisfaction in this moment."

"You go ahead and enjoy it. You've earned a minute of shameless gloating." I sigh deeply. "Eileen is so mad at me, she barely said a word this morning."

"Let me guess, you feel bad."

"I do. I've been so busy consolidating our position, looking for Sergei's weak spots, and trying to keep Eileen safe that I almost completely overlooked what she needs from me the most."

"What's that, exactly?" my brother asks. "Because I know Laura's got some pointers for you."

I shake my head, shuddering with dread. "The last thing I want is your wife tearing me a new one. Laura is a banshee in disguise, I swear. But I do know what she'd say if you were to sic her on me."

"Oh, yeah?" Andrei laughs lightly.

"And I think I know how to fix this. I'd be killing two birds with one stone, actually. Now is a good time to do it seeing as things seem to have smoothed over with the Kuznetsovs."

Andrei frowns, running a hand through his thick brown hair. "I don't think anything is ever really smooth with those fuckers."

"Nevertheless, Eileen can't keep living like this, and neither can we," I insist. "Huddled in our homes, too fearful to leave the grounds. That's like telling the whole world that we're scared of the Kuznetsovs. So, I've got an idea."

"I'm all ears."

"You're not going to like it, because I'm going to need you by my side in order for it to work."

The look he gives me is downright priceless. Part of me is stoked, because I absolutely love turning my brother inside out, especially when it comes to fixing his past mistakes. The other part of me worries that what I'm about to do might not be enough to make Eileen understand that she is everything to me. That this marriage is more than just a business transaction.

"I'm listening," Andrei grumbles.

"Eileen dreams about opening a bistro café with specialty roasts of single different origins," I say. "She's got a proper business plan put together and a strong entrepreneurial mind. Financial projections for the first five years. Investment solutions. Supplier prices. Hell, she even has a mood board and a few sketches for the interior decorator."

"Right, she mentioned something during that last lunch we had together."

"Yes, she did. I've found the perfect commercial space for her to turn that dream into reality. The perfect square footage, the perfect natural lighting, the perfect neighborhood."

"Okay, so buy it."

I give him a wry smile. "Actually, it is on the market."

"What's holding you back, then? What do you need me for..." His voice trails off while his brain catches up. I see the realization dawning in real time, his eyes widening, his jaw about to hit the floor. "Oh, hell no..."

"Tommy Benedetto owns it."

"You suck so much right now," he mumbles.

"Yeah. I'm afraid you're going to have to suck it up, little brother. You broke it, you bought it. You know the drill. There's no postponing this either. The only way Tommy will agree to sell me anything ever again is if you make a public apology. It doesn't have to be in front of a lot of people, but he'll want some Camorra witnesses present."

Andrei jumps out of his seat, close to throwing a childlike tantrum. It's not that serious, though. He's just being dramatic, hoping I might give him a pass. But I can't and I won't. I did my part in reconciling with the Benedettos after the incident was resolved. Now, it's his turn.

"You're such an ass."

"Andrei, it's time. I was sympathetic and supportive at the time. Hell, I'm sure you can remember that I'm the one who stopped a full-blown war from destroying this city," I coldly remind him. "I took quite the dent in my ego to have those conversations. It's your turn. You have to do this. It's the Karpov way."

He walks over to the window to think about it for a moment. His gaze falls over the Chicago midday skyline, the sunlight casting a warm glow upon him.

If something should happen to me, he'll be in charge until my children come of age. I need to know that I can rely on him.

"I'll do it," he says.

CHAPTER 21

EILEEN

The mountain wouldn't come to Muhammad, so I gathered the nerve to go to the mountain, instead. After some intense conversations with Ian and the security crew, I managed to convince Anton to allow them to accompany me back to my father's house.

I stand in the foyer, waiting to be received by my stepsister, while four large gentlemen from my security detail stand outside. There's a panic button device in my jacket pocket, just in case. I told them I wouldn't need it in my childhood home, but it was one of the conditions in order for this visit to happen while Anton was away on a business trip.

"Mrs. Karpova," a middle-aged woman comes downstairs to greet me. I recognize the staff uniform but I don't recognize her.

"You must be new," I say, giving her a warm smile. "I'm sorry, we haven't met."

"I'm Shelly, ma'am. I look after your father these days."

"Yes, I've heard that his health is declining, but no one is willing to give me any details," I say. "It's a miracle I was even allowed back inside my own home," I bluntly reply.

Shelly gives me a tense smile. "My apologies. Given your delicate condition, your father insisted on the secrecy."

"Where is he?"

"With his doctor, as we speak. He will join you in the tearoom soon enough. Allow me to escort you."

I look around for a long moment. Everything looks so familiar and yet so foreign at the same time. This was once the safest place in the world for me. Now, it reeks of secrets and anger, hardened feelings left stewing on a low heat until eventually boiling over.

My stepsister has a way of infecting everything and everyone with her mood.

"Where is Ciara?" I ask as I follow Shelly across the hall and into the tearoom. I know this place by heart, but I abide by the house rules. Technically speaking, while I did retain my last name, I'm not considered a resident anymore.

"She'll be here shortly," Shelly replies.

I take a seat by the window, soaking in the sun with a soft smile, both hands cradling my growing bump.

Finally, just as my mind wanders away from the stress of reuniting with my family and back to Anton and my new family, the door opens.

"Ciara," I murmur as I get up.

Ciara comes in, looking slim and pretty, as always. The ballerina dress she's wearing is a lovely shade of pink, which brings out her eyes and plumped glossed lips.

"Honestly, I thought you'd be much bigger," she says with a flat tone, barely looking at me as she joins me at the table.

I take my seat again and give her a long look. "And here I thought you'd set the weight-related jabs aside for once."

"It's actually a compliment," she says with a forced smile. God, she's hurting so much underneath this snarky façade of hers. "You look great, Eileen. Marriage and pregnancy both suit you."

"Thank you. And thank you for taking the time to see me."

"It's time to bury the hatchet, I suppose. I've done my grieving, my angry shouting, my therapy hours. We're good."

"Are we?"

Ciara takes a deep breath and lowers her gaze. "I know you and I never really saw eye to eye on a lot of things. I should've respected your choices a lot more over the years. You know how stubborn and intense I can be."

"Oh, yeah," I chuckle softly.

"I get that you didn't mean to take my fiancé away," Ciara says. "It was a hard pill to swallow, but everything turned out okay in the end, didn't it?"

"Sort of. I heard about your possible engagement."

Ciara stills for a moment, a cold grin slitting her pretty face. "Sergei Kuznetsov is quite the catch, it turns out. The engagement ring he gave me was twice as snazzy as the one I got from Anton."

"So it's happening for sure then? Ciara, are you certain you want to do this?" I ask her with genuine concern. "That man tried to kill me."

"Rumors. Unfounded rumors. Sergei didn't do anything."

"Is that what he told you?"

"It's what I know," she replies, her tone sharper than before.

"How's Dad?" I decide to change the subject, hoping to avoid an all-out confrontation.

"He could be better," Ciara says quietly.

It's the way she avoids looking right at me that gets my suspicion up. "What does that mean? He wouldn't tell me anything, either. He's my father and I worry about him. I deserve to know what's going on with his health."

"What do you want me to say? His health is declining. Old age, the stress of mob life. Your whole stunt with Anton didn't sit well with him, either. I'd hoped my engagement might spruce him up a little, but it doesn't seem to be helping."

"Where is he? He's supposed to be here with us."

"Didn't Shelly explain all this already?"

I shake my head in anger. "Ciara, I've had enough. Hate me for the rest of your life regarding Anton, I won't blame you. But do not ever cut me out of the Donovan family ever again. I gave you space, I gave you time. I'm done. From now on, we'll be communicating like adults, especially when it comes to family matters."

"Why don't you bang your fist on the table, too, for good measure?" she chuckles dryly.

"You think this is funny?"

Her humor fades into a stone-cold expression. "What's funny is you walking in here like you still own the place, so to speak. You don't. You're a Karpov, now."

"Still a Donovan."

"You're a Karpov! And given the disrespect that the Karpovs have shown to Sergei, be thankful that I even allowed you back into this house!"

"Wow, you're not even married yet, but you seem to be taking your role seriously as a Kuznetsov wife."

"You weren't married yet when you got knocked up by a Karpov," Ciara shoots back.

Every goddamn word stings. I'm trying so hard not to lash out, but it's getting damn near impossible to keep my temper in check. The pregnancy hormones aren't helping, either.

"It is how it is, Eileen. We were raised as sisters, but we've never been on the same page, not really. And yeah, I do take my role seriously. I'm going to be a loyal, supportive wife. Besides, Sergei got lucky. Daddy wants me to take over."

"I never wanted the Donovan business."

"Yeah, you made that clear a long time ago. Don't be surprised if you get completely left out of the picture once

I'm married. Sergei didn't take kindly to Anton's betrayal, and rumor has it the Karpovs won't be leading the Bratva for much longer, either. With the Donovans' support behind him, Sergei could very well take over."

Blinded by her own pride and ambition, she doesn't even realize when she overshares in an attempt to gloat. She's giving me useful information, which I will absolutely relay to Anton and Andrei. Surely, the brothers know that Kuznetsov is angling for a power play, but we weren't so sure about where my father's support would be.

"Dad's still kicking," I decide to rain on Ciara's parade. "So there isn't much you can do without his say-so. I'm his blood, and he would never toss me to the wolves just to appease your psycho, two-faced future husband."

"I suggest you mind your words!" Ciara explodes. "I won't tolerate any disrespect from the likes of you!"

"The likes of—" I raise my voice, but my father booms across the room, cutting me off and making mine sound tiny.

"ENOUGH!"

Ciara and I both freeze. Slowly, we turn around to find my father in the doorway. He's barely standing, one hand on the

frame to steady himself. My heart sinks, and I can feel the breath leaving my body as I whisper, "Dad."

Tears spring to my eyes. He looks awful. He's declined so much in the last two months, that it's as if death itself stands right behind him, its hand touching his shoulder. He's lost a ton of weight, and he's pale as a corpse. His breath is ragged, and his eyes are hollow.

"Dad," I say it louder this time. "What is wrong with you?"

"What is wrong with me? What is wrong with you, Eileen? Is this how you intend to reconcile with your stepsister? Through a shouting match?"

"We got carried away—" Ciara tries to play it off, but he interrupts her with a sickly grunt.

"Don't even. I warned you. Keep your tongue mellow. Eileen isn't the type to blow up without provocation, Ciara. We both know you started it," he says. "For heaven's sake, girls, how the hell can I leave this world with you two still bickering like this?"

"Are you planning to leave this world anytime soon?" I quietly ask.

"Are you blind, child?" he scoffs. "I'm obviously not in the best shape of my life. The last thing I want is to leave you two behind with nothing but strife and harsh words. You need to make amends with one another and you need to make them now."

"Where's your doctor? I'd like to speak to him," I say.

"Pfft, good luck," Ciara sighs. "He keeps citing doctor-patient privilege, and Daddy won't tell me anything, either."

"Is that true?"

"I'm ill. What more do you need to know?"

I gasp, struggling with the entire concept. "Ill with what? Is there a treatment? Anton has plenty of connections in the medical system," I say.

"Do you think I like being poked and prodded?"

"Nobody likes that part," I shoot back. "But it's necessary." I pause to cradle my growing bump. "Don't you want to meet your grandchildren, Dad?"

He stills, prompting a harsh laugh from Ciara. "Wow. Go straight for the heart," she whispers. "Maybe that'll get the old bull running again."

"Whatever it takes," I whisper back.

"What are you having? Boy or girl?" Dad asks, his voice noticeably lower.

"We weren't able to get a good look at the last ultrasound but we did find out that we're having twins," I reply with a warm smile.

He gives a silent gasp before his hand goes up to his chest. It was meant to be a wonderful surprise, yet his reaction strikes me with a pang of worry.

"Twins."

"Dad, are you okay?" Ciara asks with a trembling voice.

"Yeah, I'm..."

Within less than a second, I watch as my father collapses onto the floor. I hear Ciara's scream as I bolt toward him. I kneel down and turn him over. He appears even paler, barely conscious. His chest makes terrible, raspy sounds as he breathes, while his hands quiver uncontrollably.

"Where's his doctor?" I demand.

"Dad!" Ciara calls out to him.

"Where's his doctor?" I ask again.

She gives me a terrified look. "I... I don't know."

"Find him, I'll call 911."

For the first time, Ciara doesn't fight me on something I ask of her. My heart is pounding, my fingers trembling as I keep one hand on my father's chest and use the other to reach for my phone.

"Hang in there, Dad," I tell him.

∼

Two hours later, Ciara and I are in the ER waiting room. I can hear the doctors and nurses talking. Orders bouncing back and forth. Machines beeping.

Ciara takes a seat closest to the door, looking lost.

"He's going to be alright," I try to comfort her, but she waves me off.

"You weren't there. You didn't see him fading away, day after day. You didn't hear me begging him to run a few more tests, seek a second opinion."

"You all shut me out," I reply. "How is this my fault?"

"It isn't," she shakes her head slowly. "Dad didn't want anyone to tell you."

"That proud, stubborn old fool."

Dad's personal physician enters the waiting room. I catch a glimpse of my dad behind him, an oxygen mask on his face, hooked up to multiple machines monitoring his vitals. The image causes further chaos and panic in my mind.

"Dr. Rattner, what is wrong with him?" Ciara jumps to her feet, her eyes wide with fear.

"It's the worst episode yet, I'm afraid," he says.

"What is the issue, exactly?" I ask.

"He hasn't been the most cooperative patient," Dr. Rattner says. "Recent blood tests and the EKG show weakness in his heart. There could be some neurological damage, as well. We're going to run a few more tests, including a CT scan. He's also scheduled for an MRI later today."

"Is he going to be okay?" Ciara inquires.

Dr. Rattner gives her a sympathetic smile. "I wish I could say yes, but I'm not sure, not right now, anyway. We're finding several issues, but without a known cause, prescribing a particular treatment might do more harm than good. He's stable for now, but we're going to keep him under observation over the next couple of days, at least. The CT scan and MRI should tell us more. Hopefully."

"And if it doesn't?" I ask, my brow furrowed. I can hear Ronan snarling at the nurse when she tries to draw his blood.

"I'm counting on you two ladies to convince him to stick around and let me do my job," Dr. Rattner replies. "The last time we brought him in for a similar, albeit less severe issue, Mr. Donovan discharged himself before nightfall."

I give Ciara a troubled look. "For real?"

"It's like he's asking the Grim Reaper to pick him up, I swear," she nods with exasperation.

"I'll talk to him. *We'll* talk to him," I tell Dr. Rattner. "Do you have any idea of a diagnosis so far?"

"We're not sure," he says.

"Last time we were here, Sergei was with us. We were having lunch out in the garden," Ciara mumbles. "You said it could be severe arrhythmia, right, Doc?"

I look at Ciara again. "He had lunch with Sergei?"

"No, *we* had lunch with Sergei, my fiancé. He's been coming around the house every other day for the past couple of months. Sergei is the one who put us in touch with Dr. Rattner."

"Mr. Kuznetsov and his family have been on my patient roster for the better part of the last two decades," Dr. Rattner says. "The arrhythmia was just a guess. We're still not sure."

"How are you not sure?" I wonder aloud. "A specialist of your caliber, with your resources and knowledge. I'm stumped, Doc."

"I am, too," he admits. "But I need Mr. Donovan to cooperate, as well. There is only so much I can do here without his support and cooperation."

Ciara exhales sharply. "Yeah, we really need to drive that point home for Dad. Eileen and I will talk to him. When can we see him?"

"As I said, they're still running a few tests, but I assume he'll be moved into a private room in the next couple of hours.

You're both welcome to wait here or downstairs in the cafeteria. I'll send a nurse to get you once he's in a room."

I nod before Dr. Rattner turns and heads back into the ER.

Everything I've seen and heard up to this point is deeply unsettling. I don't like Sergei being so close to my family. Granted, I can't exactly stop the process, given that he's going to marry my stepsister. My father's pig-headed nature isn't helping matters, either. He's old-school, maybe a little *too* old-school for this day and age.

I just wish he had a bit more fight left in him,, because he was right about one thing. I shudder to think what will happen to Ciara and me when he's gone. For better or worse, even married to a Kuznetsov and a Karpov, respectively, my stepsister and I still benefit from the presence of Ronan Donovan—alive and able to issue orders across the board.

The Bratva needs the Irish support.

And we still need our dad.

CHAPTER 22

EILEEN

"How's Ronan doing?" Anton asks, joining me for breakfast on the patio.

It's nice and warm, a blue sky stretching above us while the birds sing their songs from the sycamore trees in the garden. I wish I could enjoy it more, but recent events have added a sour hint to a life already more complicated than it should be.

"We still don't know what's wrong with him, but at least he consented to a few more tests," I say, absent-mindedly pushing a strawberry across my plate.

My appetite has been dwindling from all the stress. I know I need to eat better for the babies, but between my father's mystery illness and the attempts on my life, I'm finding self-care to be more of a chore than something I can enjoy.

"They don't even have a clue?"

I shake my head. "Suspected arrhythmia. Possible heart failure. Apparently, there's something wrong with his lungs, too. They're trying a temporary treatment to see how he reacts to it, I guess. They think it might help them narrow it down."

"Sounds like they're treating the symptoms, not the root cause."

"Dr. Rattner said the same thing."

Anton gives me a curious look. "What do you think about him?"

"About Dr. Rattner? He seems like he definitely knows what he's doing. The man does have prestige in the field. If you're worried about the fact that he's working for the Kuznetsovs, I considered the possibility of foul play, too, but I got a second opinion. I consulted with Dr. Jeffords at the Mayo Clinic. He confirmed Rattner's professionalism and his preliminary findings."

"And how are you holding up?"

"I'm just thankful that Ciara and I are sort of speaking again. Dad keeps saying how concerned he is about the two of us getting along after he's gone. I told him to stop talking like that. Round and round in circles we go."

He gives me a soft smile. "I hope you've come closer to forgiving me for not telling you about Ciara and Sergei."

"Oh, don't get me wrong, I'm still mad about that, but I do understand why you kept it from me. Ignorance wasn't bliss, however, in this case. Had I not intervened, I don't know if Ciara alone would've been able to convince Dad to consent to further tests."

"I didn't mean to keep things from you, Eileen, my intentions were good."

"We can't build our marriage on secrets," I tell him. "The business you're in, the people you deal with, the danger, I get it. I was raised in that environment, and I probably understand better than most. Which is why I need you to be more open with me. I can't trust you, otherwise."

He nods slowly. "You're absolutely right. I was trying to shield you from harm, even though you've proven, over and over again, that you are a strong woman. Probably the strongest woman I've ever met."

"Thank you."

"With that in mind, come with me. There's something I need to show you," Anton says.

I can't help but groan and roll my eyes at him. "Please, enough with the expensive gifts. I told you already that's not what I want from you. I don't need jewels, I don't need money, I don't need any of that stuff."

"Just come outside with me," he chuckles.

"What is it this time, a new car?"

"Eileen Donovan-Karpova, will you please get up and come outside with me? Put your shoes on, while you're at it."

Too tired to argue, I do as he asks.

"I don't like this," I mutter as we head out the door.

Ian is already outside, waiting for us behind the wheel of Anton's Bentley. "Ready?" he asks with a sunny disposition.

"Whatever this is, I don't want it, Anton."

∼

I take it back.

As soon as I see the building, I know exactly what it's about. My heart begins to beat faster, the anticipation quick to take over as I look to Anton for guidance.

"What are we doing here?" I ask him, though I'm already certain of the answer.

Ian waits in the car, while my husband and I go up the stairs, entering through the glass double doors. It's vacant, plain white walls and an original-looking wooden floor, but I can already picture the renovations. Salmon pink ceramic floor tiles with gold veins, an off-white wallpaper with gold-threaded coffee bean motifs, dark wood furniture, and plush, cream-colored seating. My mind is going is mentally decorating the place as I try to contain my enthusiasm.

"I think you already know what we're doing here, Eileen," Anton replies.

"I think I need you to say it. Why must I always ask you to say certain things?"

He stops and looks at me, a look of bewilderment on his face. "Must I always say them, even when you know what they are?"

"Yes!" I exclaim, laughing.

"I know you already know."

"I think I do, but I still want you to say it. I *need* you to say it. Tell me, Anton, tell me everything, please."

"There they are!" Tommy Benedetto says cheerfully as he joins us, his shoes clicking heavily across the floor. "The happy Karpov lovebirds!"

"Oh," I mumble, surprised. "You're—"

"Alive? Yeah. I assume Anton told you the whole story."

"I did not," my husband says. He gives me a curious side-eye, waiting for my reaction.

I keep my expression neutral, not wanting to ruin the moment. Besides, I'm itching with curiosity. "What brings you here, Tommy? Though I'm obviously glad to see you're well."

"This is my place. I own it," he replies. "Well, not for much longer," he adds, giving Anton a wink.

"Interesting. I actually tried to lease it a while back," I tell him.

"Yeah, I told my property manager that I wasn't interested in leasing this unit," Tommy says. "I was actually considering a flash sale when Anton approached me."

He goes on to tell me about how Anton didn't come alone, but with Andrei by his side, ready to issue a formal apology. I listen with wide eyes, struggling not to burst out laughing as I envision the look on Andrei's face throughout that conversation.

"His ego must be shattered," I say with a sly grin.

Tommy chuckles dryly. "It was the right thing to do. I even asked a couple of my cousins to join me as official witnesses, because I wasn't sure anybody would believe me."

CHAPTER 23

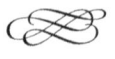

ANTON

"I'm still in awe of you," Eileen says, her head resting on my bare chest.

"In awe?"

Running my fingers through her long, red hair, I gaze down at this beautiful woman, silently thanking fate for twisting things to bring us together. It's all been worth it. I can handle anything, including discord within the Bratva, if it means having Eileen in my arms.

"I was never fully sure you were listening," she says, "but you were. You were just searching for the right way to prove it."

"And did I? Prove it, that is?"

"Oh, you most certainly did, and then some." Eileen laughs lightly. "I still can't believe it. I've been dreaming about having my own café for a long time. My dad kept postponing it, giving me all sorts of nonsensical reasons, and then you came into the picture. The trouble with Sergei, the attempts on my life, the discord between Ciara and me... for a while there, I thought I'd be stuck in this house for the rest of my life. Don't get me wrong; it's a beautiful house, but—"

"It would've become a cage soon enough," I reply. "Yeah, I get it. For what it's worth, I hated having to keep you here like that. Frankly, I'm glad that your father offered Ciara's hand to Sergei, and he decided to make his move on her. At least it gives him less of a reason to keep coming after you in order to hurt me. Now you can have some peace and the ability to move around more. With bodyguards, of course."

Eileen shifts to look up at me. "Of course. I guess it's the best out of the worst possible outcomes, right?"

"It does put a pin in the internal war prospects, if only for a while," I respond. "Your father's condition makes things worse, unfortunately, but I'll take a breather wherever I can get it."

"I know what you mean," she sighs deeply. "I just wish Ciara had more sense."

"She's hurt and she's spoiled. She's also entitled and stubborn. All you can do is mend whatever you can mend and let her come to you should she ever need your support."

"I'm scared for her. I wasn't even that close to Sergei, yet I could tell precisely how duplicitous and dangerous that man was. Ciara isn't an idiot. She's not blind either."

"Her ego is the size of Wrigley Field, Eileen. She's absolutely blind at this point. But there are some hard lessons that she's going to have to learn on her own, whether you like it or not."

Eileen sits up, her beautiful breasts capturing my attention. Her skin glows in the morning sunlight that pours through the windows. I lick my lips, suddenly craving more of her. As much as I'd love to make the most of what's left of our time together, she needs to get ready to go.

"Your father is back at home, right?" I ask her.

"Against the doctor's advice, yes."

"At least you can go see him now without worrying about the family drama."

Eileen gives me a sad look. "It's a shame it took Dad's health to bring Ciara back into the fold. And even that's not a certainty, not while she's engaged to that monster."

"She knows what she's doing, babe. Marrying into the Bratva isn't the worst idea, but there aren't any eligible Karpovs left. Ciara is making a play for the rising power within the organization. Unfortunately, she's betting on the wrong horse, because soon enough, I plan to knock Sergei down a few pegs. I just need to make sure he doesn't have the other families' support when that happens."

"It's all so complicated."

I shrug. "It wouldn't be if you changed your mind about taking over the Donovan business. Ciara wouldn't be able to challenge you, not while Ronan's will still has you at the top."

"We talked about this, Anton. It's not what I want. It never has been."

"It's like being a monarch. It's mostly in the title. You could appoint someone you trust to do the actual management and handle the leadership."

Eileen shakes her head slowly. "I was never made for this. It's why I'm so eager to plunge into my café business instead. Ciara is perfectly capable of handling the Donovan business. It's her future husband who worries me."

"At the end of the day, you'll always be safe, my love." I reach out and pull her back into my arms. "Whatever happens to the Donovans from now on is on them."

"It sounds logical enough."

"But it doesn't feel that way, does it?"

"No."

As I plant a kiss on her lips, I can feel her temperature rising. She moans against my mouth, and for a moment I think we are about to slip into a hot and steamy quickie. A knock on the door, however, has us both scrambling out of bed.

"Mr. and Mrs. Karpov." Ian's voice comes from the hall. "Pardon the intrusion, but there's a guest downstairs for Mrs. Karpova."

"Who is it?"

"Your stepsister."

I've got an unpleasant feeling about this. As soon as we reach the living room, I realize that my feeling was right on point. The look on Ciara's face is a dark omen. Her smile gives me the fucking creeps.

Instinctively, I take Eileen's hand in mine.

"How's Dad?" Eileen immediately asks.

"He hasn't come out of his room yet, but Dr. Rattner just left. There are no visible changes, but it will take a while for the treatment to have an effect."

"What brings you here then?" I inquire.

"I'm making the rounds all over Chicago to officially announce my engagement to Sergei Kuznetsov," Ciara says. "It feels like the right thing to do."

"With your father still gravely ill?" I ask, raising an eyebrow.

She gives me a wry smile. "Anton, darling. It is my father's desire to see me married and well settled before he passes."

"My God, Ciara. He's not dead yet!" Eileen snaps.

"No, he isn't, but it's not looking great either," she says, her voice trembling with emotion. "He wanted to see both of us married, and I'm doing this for him. Sergei and I set a wedding date for next month. We were going to wait a bit, but Dad wanted it sooner rather than later, just in case. His words, not mine."

Eileen sighs heavily, tears brimming in her eyes.

I reach for her hand, giving it a soft squeeze. "Congratulations then, Ciara," I say.

"You will be receiving an invitation soon. I approved the design earlier this morning. They should be ready to send out by tomorrow afternoon."

"Thank you. Eileen and I will be honored to attend."

"Eileen is going to be a guest, not part of the wedding party. I've already selected my maid of honor and my bridesmaids. I wanted women I could trust."

Eileen nods. "That's fine, Ciara. Whatever makes you happy. And congratulations on the engagement. We'll be happy to be there on your most special day."

"One more thing," Ciara says, her tone lower, colder. "I had an interesting conversation with Sergei and Dad last night over dinner, and I thought you and Anton should know. He plans to challenge the Karpov leadership soon."

My blood runs cold.

I thought I'd put a lid on that. I still have the support of the bigger and more powerful families, but whatever this stunt is, it leaves a sour taste in my mouth.

"Sergei told you that?" I ask.

"Yes."

"And what did your father have to say about it?"

"Dad would never support—" Eileen starts to speak, but Ciara cuts her off.

"Dad said it's the Bratva's issue to deal with, not ours. We'll support whoever sits at the head of your table, no questions asked."

"Why are you telling us this, Ciara?" I ask, carefully analyzing her expression. There's a hint of fear in her eyes and a nervous twitch at the corner of her mouth. It's subtle, but I still notice it. "Sergei is your future husband. He might consider this a betrayal."

Ciara gives me a hard look. "*Future* husband. He's not my legal husband yet. And Eileen is still my family, despite our animosities. You're now my brother-in-law. I thought you might find the information useful, whether you can do anything about it or not."

"What about you?" Eileen replies, visibly worried.

"Sergei's intentions aren't exactly a secret. He never asked me to keep my mouth shut about it." Ciara tries to shrug it off. "I trust that he'll get what he wants, one way or another. I just didn't want you to be blindsided, that's all."

"I appreciate that," I say. "Thank you, Ciara."

"For the record, you don't deserve this olive branch," she replies.

I nod slowly. "I do not, yet you give it, nonetheless. Someday, I will repay the favor," I tell her. "In the meantime, please reach out for whatever you might need, be it for the wedding or anything else. I want you to know that this," I add, gesturing around me, "will always be a safe space for you, no matter what."

"I'll remember that." She takes a deep breath and puts on a pleasant smile. "Now, if you'll excuse me, I need to visit the Fedorovs next."

"Will you be telling them about Sergei's intentions as well?" I ask.

"No. That was for your ears only."

I give her another nod as Ian politely escorts her out of the mansion.

Once I hear the front door close and Ian's footsteps echoing throughout the hallway, I allow myself a deep sigh. "Well, shit."

"Anton, did she seem scared to you?" Eileen asks me. "I didn't want to ask her outright. She's as stubborn as Dad in that sense; she'd never admit it."

"If she's not scared, she's definitely worried," I reply. "I think there's a part of her that is finally beginning to see the kind of man she's about to marry."

"Then why is she still willing to go ahead with it?"

"After the embarrassment we caused her? She's probably trying to save face, grateful that she's still able to marry someone within the Bratva," I reply. "Your stepsister is a highly desirable woman and could marry whomever she chooses, but Sergei does have power and influence within the organization. He also has several key businesses behind him. Otherwise, I would've taken him out of the picture a long time ago."

"Do you think this is a power play on her part?"

That's a good question, but Eileen might not like my answer. I promised her complete honesty and full transparency, though, so I'm telling her exactly what I think.

"I think she's riding the fence, waiting to see if the Karpovs stay at the helm or if Sergei has an actual shot at taking over. If he gets his way, and she turns out to be a Karpov supporter, it could cost her and the Donovan businesses in the long run. If I maintain leadership, then at least she's at peace, because she warned us, and so cannot be deemed a traitor or a liability."

"Dad was right. For all her flaws, Ciara is a good strategist."

I can't do much other than speak to the Bratva families again, if only to reassure their loyalty.

Hopefully, I still hold the majority.

CHAPTER 24

EILEEN

That was quite the news that Ciara delivered. I'm just not sure where it will land her in the long run.

In the meantime, I can only focus on the things I can control. My stepsister isn't one of them.

"My God, this place oozes potential!" Laura exclaims as she walks into the café.

For now, it's still an empty space, rife with possibilities. Laura shines like a diamond in the middle of it, with her peach pantsuit and cream-colored heels.

"I didn't expect you," I say, giving her a warm smile. "What are you doing here?"

"You don't sound happy to see me," she replies, pasting on a fake pout.

"On the contrary, I'm very happy to see you! I could use the extra pair of eyes!"

"I figured as much when Andrei told me he had to swallow his gargantuan ego to help Alex close this deal," she laughs. "So, first and foremost, congratulations! This is long overdue. Second, what are we thinking?"

I look around once again, wishing she could see the image I have in my head. "Ian is helping me out with the measurements. The interior decorator has already been here, and we agreed on a preliminary game plan."

"Okay. Talk to me. What's the game plan?"

Ian gives Laura a warm smile before he goes back to his notes, carefully measuring every wall and angle until the page looks like something out of a mathematician's wet dream. The man is definitely detail-oriented and multifaceted, I'll give him that.

"Well, I'm thinking cozy, but not *too* cozy. Warm and welcoming, but not a replica of the coffee shop down the street."

"Obviously not, this is Gold Coast," Laura replies. "You need warm but snazzy as hell. People in this area are as uppity as they come."

"I'm close to finalizing a deal with several countries for their single-origin beans, courtesy of the Fairtrade Foundation."

"Yeah, that's great and all, but I'm interested in the café itself and the décor. Are we doing café tables and chairs, or cozy booths and sofas with mellow jazz music?"

"It would be somewhere in between," I reply. "I'm thinking of a lounge section over there," I point to the eastern quarter of the room. "Tables and chairs over by the western windows, close to the kitchen and easier for the waitstaff.

The coffee bar is going to be right here, smack in the middle, a big, circular centerpiece," I finish, twirling around in the center of the room.

Laura's eyes widen with excitement. "Oh, that sounds marvelous."

"I think so, too. It will have coffee beans from around the world, a nice selection of fine teas, and artisanal hot chocolate."

She nods excitedly. "Excellent. What about food?"

"The bar will have a pastry section filled with a variety of pastries baked fresh every morning. Italian cakes, French croissants, Danishes, etc. I was thinking about offering some breakfast sandwich options, too, for people on the go. Everything else will be on the bistro menu. I'm also looking into getting an in-house master chocolatier—there's room next to the roastery for a confectionery space. Something unique to our café. It could be the start of a gourmet brand."

"What's your color scheme?"

I laugh lightly. "Oh, wow, I feel like I'm at a job interview."

"More like *Shark Tank*. Talk to me," Laura replies, an excited expression on her face. It warms my heart to have her support and enthusiasm.

I give her a curious look. "*Shark Tank*? Are you interested in making an investment?"

"Maybe. You've got spunk and a fabulous entrepreneurial spirit. Anton wouldn't have bought this place if he didn't have faith in you. We never got around to looking at that vision board of yours, though, and I don't remember all the details. So, walk me through it. I just may have a chocolatier for you."

"Oh?"

"An ex-colleague of mine from Paris. He just wrapped up a ten-year contract at Hotel Costes, and he's looking to put his roots down back here in his hometown."

"And the good news just keeps on coming." I smile broadly. "It was salmon and gold, for the most part."

"What was?" Laura asks.

"The color scheme," Ian and I reply at the same time.

I give him a warm smile. "You remembered."

"With plush cream-colored seating, I believe?" he adds.

"Ditch the yellow gold, go for white gold," Laura suggests. "Do off-white or ivory and emerald-green seating. Play with the bold contrast across the entire lounge area. The dining space should follow along the same lines, with cream, powder pink, and lime-green chairs. White marble tables with white gold for the metallic details. Oh, I can already see it coming together," she gasps with delight.

I join in on the fun as we casually stroll around the room, our gazes lost in the future. I point to the ceiling. "Tom Dixon lighting. You know, those minimalistic orbs?"

"The white-gold ones and throw in a black smoked-glass version here and there."

"For contrast, yeah, I see where you're going with this."

Laura pauses to affectionately look at me. "Anton is the luckiest son of a gun, I'll tell you that much."

"What makes you say that?" I laugh, feeling my cheeks blush.

"Because we're going to be on the same page when it comes to renovating the Karpov mansion. I've got that on my project sheet, and I'm going to need your stylish brain to back me for what I'm about to do with that place."

"In that case, it sounds like you're the lucky one, not Anton."

Laura thinks about it for a second. "No, he's the lucky one. You are literally the first woman he's ever brought home that I actually adore."

"You're too kind."

"I'm honest. I don't care much for your stepsister."

"I don't think Ciara cares much for herself either, sometimes." I sigh deeply.

"How is she doing?" Laura asks. "We're all pretty jittery about that engagement of hers, to be honest. Even some of the families in the Bratva have expressed concerns on the matter, but Anton and Andrei are doing their best, trying to calm them regarding the possibilities to come."

Just then, I hear the doors open. I turn to see who it is.

"Paddy!" I exclaim as I recognize my father's most trusted security enforcer. "What are you doing here?" I rush over to hug him.

"Eileen," he exhales sharply as we pull away from embracing.

My heart thunders as I see the tears pooling in his eyes. "Paddy, what's wrong?"

"It's your father. Ciara wanted to call you, she wanted to tell you herself, but she's already overwhelmed by all the preparations that need to be handled."

"What about my father?"

I already know. I can hear it in the tremor of his voice. I can see it in his eyes. The grief. The heartbreak. Instinctively, I reach out to Laura, needing someone to hold on to for the awful words that I know I'm about to hear.

"He passed away this morning, Eileen. I'm so sorry," Paddy says.

Standing still, I take a deep breath as the news hits me. I would've been shocked had I not seen Dad's health declining over the past few months. The grief is still unbearable, though.

"My condolences, Eileen," Ian says, coming closer and placing his hand on my shoulder. His voice is soft and gentle, his gaze oddly comforting as I look at him. "Truly a terrible loss. How can I help?"

"I... I don't know."

It's the truth. My mind is drawing a complete blank. I want to cry. I want to scream, shout, and curse at the universe. But my babies are counting on me to take care of both my mental and physical health. They cannot be collateral victims of the burning grief that is itching to consume me.

"We should let Anton know," Laura suggests. "And we should take you to see Ciara." She looks at Paddy. "I assume she's at home?"

Paddy nods. "Aye. Ciara wants to hold the wake tomorrow and the funeral on Saturday."

"Yes, I need to see Ciara," I manage to say.

It's all I can manage.

CHAPTER 25

EILEEN

I'm numb.

I've been numb since my father's wake.

I sit quiet and still while the chaplain talks about my father, sprinkling a few bible quotes in here and there before the family tosses their final roses and handfuls of dirt on top of his casket.

I shudder when it's finally over and my father is laid to rest. I stare at the fresh flowers left on his grave—an abundance of white lilies—his and my mother's favorites. My eyes are puffy from crying, and I have a headache, but Anton has been my rock, my comfort, my everything, through it all. He stands beside me, his hand resting on the small of my back.

"They had lilies at their wedding," I tell him in a low voice.

"Your parents?"

I nod slowly. "I saw the photos in the family album when I was a kid. A sea of white lilies. My mother seemed lost among them in her white bridal dress."

"Maria was a beautiful woman. I doubt the lilies outshone her that day."

"You remember her?" I ask, looking up at him.

"Bits and pieces, really. But yeah, I remember her. Maria's passing sent a shockwave through the Bratva families. I know Ivan loved her deeply. How's your stepsister doing?" he asks after planting a kiss on my temple.

I look around and spot Ciara bidding a few people goodbye —members of the Fedorov family who came to pay their respects. My stomach churns as our gazes lock, and I can see the fear and anger in her eyes. "I'm not sure. Ever since Dad died, it's like Sergei took over the Donovan family. We barely said two words to each other at the wake. Every call I've made to the house has been rejected. I was told to leave a message."

"He's hovering, even now," Anton mutters.

We watch as he shakes hands and smiles at the dwindling guests. The leaders of the Russian dynasties, to be specific. He looks confident and downright perky, but whenever Ciara looks up at him, he puts on his grieving face. I can see right through the curtain, and it sickens me.

"I'm worried about her, Anton."

"You have every right to be, but I'm not sure there's much you can do at this point. The cards were dealt, and she made the engagement official. They're keeping the wedding date for next month, despite having just buried your father," he says.

Andrei and Laura join us.

"How are you holding up?" Laura asks me, gently giving my arm a squeeze.

"I'm doing okay. Better than I thought I'd be, but then again, I've got you all keeping me sane," I reply with a timid smile.

"And your stepsister?" Andrei asks, his gaze set on Ciara and Sergei.

"I was just talking about her with Anton. You know what?" I pause, noticing how tight Sergei's grip is on my sister's upper arm. She winces from the pain as he pulls her away from an Irish couple, the McDowells, who stopped by to offer their condolences. "I don't like this. I can't just stand by."

"Eileen, wait," Anton tries to stop me, but it's too late.

I dash across the clearing, cautiously stepping between the headstones as I make my way over to the area where they're standing, near the section where the chaplain held our father's service. Ronan's portrait still sits there, surrounded by flowers with white ribbons.

"I need to talk to my sister," I tell Sergei.

He gives me a cold smirk. "Whatever you have to say to her, you can say in front of me."

"It doesn't concern you," I hiss.

"Eileen, there are still people here," Ciara whispers. "Now isn't the time for a scene."

"I'm not trying to make a scene, I'm just trying to talk to you," I shoot back.

Sergei steps between us, but all that does is piss me off. "You're out of line, Eileen. Ronan is gone, and you're not the head of the Donovan family. Ciara is."

"Good. In that case, I want Ciara to tell me whether we can talk or not."

"Clearly, she doesn't wish to be bothered right now."

My blood boils and I look at my stepsister again. My heart breaks as I catch a flicker of fear in her eyes, but she shakes her head, trying to play it cool.

"It's not a good time, Eileen. I'd like to be left alone so I can thank the remaining guests and then go home to grieve."

"We need to talk about what's going on here, Ciara."

Sergei scoffs, firm and defiant in his position, determined to bring out the worst in me. "And what is going on here, Mrs. Karpova?"

"You are not yet married, therefore, you have zero say in my family's affairs. I suggest you back the fuck off and let me talk to Ciara."

"Eileen, shut up!" Ciara bursts into tears. "Just leave it alone!"

"No."

"I'll have you escorted off the grounds," Sergei hisses.

"I would love to see you try," Anton interjects.

I glance over my shoulder to see him approaching, Andrei and several of our bodyguards with him. As if summoned, other members of the Bratva begin to approach as well, along with plenty of the Donovan and related Irish families. They're all curious, concerned, and ready to take this to the next level if needed.

"Anton, I don't know what sort of agreement you thought you had with Mr. Donovan, but it is no longer in effect. The Donovans have pledged their full support for the Kuznetsov family, for me, specifically," Sergei declares, loud enough for everyone to hear. "And your wife is being a nuisance to mine."

"It's my father's funeral, you utterly disgusting prick, and Ciara isn't your wife yet. So, take it down a notch. You don't own the Donovans!" I hiss.

"Oh, but I do. And Ciara can confirm," he says, widening his eyes, his inner psychopath shining through.

"What do you mean?" Andrei asks.

Ciara averts her gaze, her cheeks blushing red with shame.

My stomach drops and I'm damn near breathless. "Ciara, what did you do?"

Sergei's smug smile speaks volumes. Paul Mattis, his business partner, snakes his way into the conversation, pulling out a document from his inner suit jacket pocket. I immediately notice what appears to be Ciara and Dad's signatures on it. I can feel my knees caving in as I read the top line.

"Fiduciary powers," I mutter.

"That's right. Ronan decided to hand the reins over to me with his dying breath, and Ciara agreed," Sergei replies.

Paul nods, a disgusting grin on his face. "I bore witness, and it was notarized accordingly."

"Dad would never do that. Ciara, what the hell did you do?"

My knees give out, but Anton holds me close and snatches the paper from Paul's hand. "This doesn't look like Ronan's signature," he says.

"Challenge it in court, if you have the balls," Paul sneers.

"Until then, I'm in charge of the Donovan businesses as a trusted fiduciary. And I'm also Ciara's fiancé, which fully legitimizes me to tell you all to fuck off, so she can grieve in peace. These past few days have been hard on her," Sergei says.

Andrei shakes his head. "Seriously, Sergei? This is what you've resorted to? Fraud? Manipulation? What do you have on the poor girl to have subdued her like this?"

"She loves me."

"Bullshit," I reply and look at Ciara. "Tell me you didn't agree to this."

"I did," she hesitantly replies. "And you need to accept it. Dad's gone. Somebody needed to take over."

"Yeah, you! That was the plan! That's always been the plan. It's the only reason I backed away, because I trusted you to take over!"

"I'm going to be a Kuznetsov wife. My children will lead the Donovan family when they come of age. Until then, Sergei is in charge."

"Spoken like a true puppet," Andrei says.

Sergei takes a step forward. "Mind your tongue, Andrei. Soon enough, you'll be answering to me."

"Eileen can still contest this garbage," Anton cuts in. "Technically speaking, she's very much at the top of Ronan's last will and testament."

"Not anymore. I had the old man add an addendum there, as well," Sergei says. "Again, good luck fighting us in court."

"We'll see you in the streets," Andrei growls.

Anton firmly pushes him back. "Don't. Not here, not now."

"What is the meaning of this?" the chaplain intervenes, red-faced and furious. "A man was just laid to rest less than twenty feet away! Show some respect!"

I know Chaplain Carter. He's buried his share of Donovans, Fedorovs, and Kuznetsovs, as well as others from Chicago's most dangerous and powerful families. He knows where this discussion will lead if he doesn't put a lid on it. He's got his sacred collar to shield him, though. Nobody's going to touch him.

"He's right," I say, my voice barely above a whisper. I can't take my eyes off Ciara, though. That's not my sister anymore. Something happened between the day we reconnected and the morning I got the news about Dad's passing from Paddy. I know Sergei is at the center of all of it. "We can't do this here."

"We'll do it another time, don't worry," Sasha Popov cuts in. He's Oleg's son, and he's a fierce supporter of the Karpovs. "Sergei just declared war."

"I didn't declare anything; I merely stated my intentions," Kuznetsov bluntly replies. "And you'd do well to think twice before you pick the losing side. There is more support behind me than there is behind your precious Karpovs."

"You're not going to get away with this," I warn him.

He gives me a hard look. "A woman in your condition should be careful of her words."

"Keep threatening my wife, Sergei, and I might have to apologize to the good chaplain here for what's going to happen next," Anton growls.

"Gentlemen, please," Chaplain Carter insists. "This is holy ground."

Sergei nods curtly, motioning for Paul and Ciara to follow him. "Come on, we've got a funeral dinner to attend." He pauses to point at me. "You're uninvited. All of the Karpovs, too."

Ciara tries to change his mind. "Sergei, darling, she's still his daughter."

"Did I stutter?"

She stills, her face pale, then nods once and follows him down the stone path leading back to the eastern gate. I watch as my stepsister walks away, helpless and quiet. The life I knew was falling apart, crumbling around me in the clutches of Sergei's evil hand.

Murmurs erupt behind us. Concerns about Kuznetsov and the threats that were made. I can't really focus on any of it, though. I just buried my father and lost my stepsister in the span of an hour, and I don't know how to deal with any of it.

"Ciara fucked up," Anton tells me, keeping his voice low while Andrei speaks to the others. They're understandably startled and worried. I am, too. "But I don't think your father signed that document. Or at least, he wasn't of sound mind when he signed it. He may have been ill, but he wasn't stupid."

"I know."

"He never would've handed the Donovan businesses over to Sergei."

"He still wanted me to be involved. That was part of the reason why he insisted that we get married, aside from the obvious," I rub at my baby bump. "He trusted you to help steer the businesses in a better direction. Dad didn't trust Sergei. Not very much, anyway. Then again, that could've changed in the months that we didn't see each other. I'm just not sure anymore, Anton. I can't believe any of this is happening."

He takes me in his arms. I find comfort in his embrace, as always, but this time, I don't think it's enough to keep my head above water.

"We'll figure it out, Eileen. Whatever Ciara did, we can fight it in court."

"Paul Mattis all but begged you to do exactly that. They must have some ace up their sleeve. I'm guessing it's that addendum to my father's will."

He thinks about it for a moment. "Let's go home, baby. Whatever it is, we'll handle it, but you need to get some rest first."

It sounds encouraging enough, but judging by the look of concern on Andrei's face, I worry that trouble is just getting started. My dad always used to say that it gets worse before it gets better.

Oh, Ciara, you proud and foolish girl, how could you do this?

CHAPTER 26

ANTON

Eileen's father was right about one thing—it does get worse before it gets better, and we can't afford any more losses.

In the week since Ronan's funeral, three different Karpov businesses were targeted—two cyberattacks and a small factory fire—the source of which we've yet to uncover.

"You can't sit there and tell me you haven't made any headway," I tell Jonas Aslanov, Ilinka's eldest son and second in command. "Is she really siding with the Kuznetsovs, now?"

"She said it felt like the safer bet once the Sokolovs and the Aronovs switched their support to Sergei and Paul." Jonas offers a tense shrug. "I tried to talk her out of it, Anton, I swear."

"Does she understand the repercussions?" Andrei asks, seated in the chair next to Jonas, on the other side of my desk. "If we withdraw our funding, all of her charity galas will fall. Nobody's going to touch her."

"Sergei has a few senators in his pocket. He promised her uninterrupted charity events for the next four years, at least," Jonas says. "His Senate buddies need juice for their reelection campaigns, and their districts fall under the Kuznetsov turf. He can put his money where his mouth is."

"And if Ilinka decided to stick with us, he would've made it harder for her to go ahead with those events, because of the same senators, who have ties in the local council and connections to the federal government. Which would've led to funding cuts. He would cripple her," I conclude, shaking my head in dismay.

Jonas gives me a wondering look. "Would you be able to prevent that?"

"Not right now."

"We should've twisted a few more arms for D'Arcy and Bennet," Andrei mutters. "Had they won those Senate seats, we wouldn't even be worrying about who can do what to Ilinka Aslanov's charity funding."

"My mother lives for those functions and for the billions she raises to help so many good causes," Jonas says. "She would rather sleep with the devil than lose any of it. She always says that it's all worth it."

"In this world? I can't really blame her." I sigh deeply.

"It doesn't help us. Who do we have left, now?" Andrei asks me.

"The Fedorovs, but even they're shaky at this point. The other families are too small to count once Sergei pulls his numbers together for the next council meeting."

The odds are not in our favor, and Jonas knows it.

"Either way, you have my sympathy," he says.

"Your support would've been more welcome," I reply. "I have no use for your sympathy."

"We go where the power is, Anton."

"I'll remember that when the tables turn."

I can see the flicker of fear in his eyes. Deep down, Jonas is aware that they're betting on the wrong horse, spurred by fear and nothing else. Sergei Kuznetsov has proven that he's unable to lead the Bratva—having to resort to cyberattacks and acts of sabotage to weaken us is all the evidence I need that he isn't mature or intelligent enough to hold the grand seat.

"Though other fools and madmen have held my chair before me, before my father, those were not better days," I tell Jonas. "Every time Sergei promises that he'll help restore the Aslanov's former glory, he neglects to tell you how bad it really was in that era. There's a reason why you have little family left on your father's side."

"It's my mother's decision, Anton. I can't overturn it."

He stands, giving Andrei and me one last nod before he heads out.

The heaviness of what we just learned settles in as my brother and I exchange glances.

"Do you have a contingency in place for Laura if the shit hits the fan?" I ask.

"Yeah. There's a security detail prepped and ready as well. What about Ian?"

"He knows the drill. He hasn't left Eileen's side since we got back from the funeral. If I'm not with her, he is, and he's got a dozen former FSB gentlemen at his beck and call, if needed."

"I hate that it's come to this." Andrei sighs deeply. "Ciara made a fatal mistake."

"We can't help her, not right now."

"He will kill her, you know. I'm pretty sure he had a hand in Ronan's health declining the way it did, and dare I say, his sudden death."

I give him a hard look. It's something my brother and I have discussed before, suspected. "I've yet to share that suspicion with Eileen, so I hope you've kept it to yourself."

"Laura is aware, but Eileen won't hear a thing from us."

"Good. She doesn't need the aggravation. Not without evidence, anyway."

Andrei sits straighter in his chair, suddenly more energized. "You know, we could investigate that whole thread. Discreetly, of course. What was the physician's name again?"

"Rattner."

He pulls out his phone. "Let me handle this. If Kuznetsov is going to play dirty, we might as well do the same. I don't think we can afford to be cautious at this point," he says while texting someone.

"You're right, we can't."

A rapid knock on my office door brings our conversation to a halt.

"Come in," I respond.

Kacey, one of our assistants, enters slowly. I don't like the look on her face. "Sir, we just got a call from the brewery."

"Which one?" I ask. "We own five."

"The South Side one. Fire and police services were called."

Shit.

~

My brother and I stand on the other side of the street watching the terrifying blaze. Our entire building is engulfed in roaring flames, black smoke billows from the shattered roof to the sky. Dozens of firefighters struggle to stop the inferno from spreading as explosions boom throughout the brewery, orange tongues lashing out as rescuers guide the last of our employees to safety.

A triage point has been set up at a safe distance. Three more ambulances arrive, while multiple police officers do everything they can to keep the bystanders safe. Paramedics treat those suffering from smoke inhalation, providing oxygen masks and checking vitals. In the meantime, I'm trying to process how the fire could have started as I watch the horrifying aftermath.

"Two people are dead," Andrei mumbles. "According to Officer Friendly over there, six people are still missing. I haven't seen anyone else come out."

"The arson investigation unit will come in once they have it under control and the fire is completely out," I reply.

"Sergei is going to pay for this."

"He's getting more brazen."

"It's fucking war, Anton. We need to start responding accordingly. Insurance will cover the loss, but it still puts this location out of business for at least six months. This was our top producer, too, dammit."

I give him a long, tired look. "He knows where to apply pressure, but he's not invincible, Andrei." I take a deep breath. "We'll double security at all other business points. And you'll have all the support you need to follow that line on Rattner. Let's uncover some useful dirt on this fucker before he burns something else down."

"Or worse, before Ciara gets served a steaming mug of polonium tea. I wouldn't put anything past Sergei right now."

I thought we had it in the bag. Perhaps I was naive, or perhaps I had too much faith in the other families. They weren't raised like we were. They bought Sergei's act, right down to the last number. But it's still just an act.

I need to find big enough cracks in his mask so I can drive a mallet through them. You don't threaten the woman I love and expect to live a long, fruitful life.

"Rally the other families," I tell Andrei. "We need a sit-down with them immediately, before the next council meeting. I'll reach out to the Benedettos and every other ally we can muster. The Bratva's turmoil will reverberate across the board. The Camorras should know."

My brother gives me a cold grin. "Oh, that's dirty. I like it."

"The Italians don't like Sergei. Might as well take advantage of that."

"The others won't take kindly to outside support, though."

"Then they shouldn't have allowed Sergei to drag the Donovans into this, fiduciary powers or not," I reply.

If there's one thing I learned and will forever uphold from all the teachings from our father, it's that if the enemy goes low, we meet them there and destroy them with everything in the Karpov arsenal. Going high when someone goes low only leads to humiliation and early death.

We're Russians. Slavic fucking warriors.

We might as well act like it.

CHAPTER 27

EILEEN

"How is everything coming along?" Anton asks as we sit in the backseat of his town car on our way to my café, Ian behind the wheel. It's touching to see him trying to be upbeat and focused on me when I know he's got so much on his mind. The recent string of fires and sabotage attempts against his businesses have left a deep furrow between his brows.

"We're almost done, actually," I reply with a warm smile. "The furniture arrived earlier this week. I've got the interior decorator popping by in a couple of hours to help me with the layout before I order the appliances and have the rest of the kitchen equipment delivered."

"And it only took you, what, two weeks?"

I nod excitedly. "Yeah. Granted, Laura and Ian have been incredibly helpful every step of the way. I thought we'd have to wait another week for the light fixtures to be delivered, but Laura managed to pull some strings, and in less than forty-eight hours, we'll have light. A godsend, that woman. But most importantly, I have you to thank. You provided all the funding we needed, allowing us to make sure we could accomplish everything in the shortest timeframe possible."

Anton gently squeezes my knee. "Anything for my bride, you know that."

"I'm so grateful. Had I not had your support, Anton, I would've had to scrounge for pennies and think twice about the smallest details. I would've prioritized the coffee stock before anything else, but the place probably would've looked like a semi-posh café wannabe spot for Gold Coast commuters."

"I'm so proud of you, Eileen. I know this is a dream come true for you, and, given the double buns you're carrying and the toll it's taking on you, both physically and emotionally, I am genuinely impressed that you were able to pull this whole thing off in such a short period of time."

"It was a team effort."

"No, no, don't be modest," Ian politely interjects. "You put in most of the hard work. Own it and be proud of it. You deserve the accolades."

Glancing out the window, I watch the shopfronts whizz past as we make our way through River North. I love this city, warts and all. It's my home, and I know it's underbelly better than most. Ciara and I were lucky to be raised as Donovans. Many of my father's underlings struggled harshly to reach the top of the food chain. We were born up there.

"I don't know about that. Technically speaking, it kind of got handed to me," I mutter.

"You were given a barren space, and you turned it into what is likely going to be a very successful business and a wonderful customer experience," Ian insists. "Do not sell yourself short."

Anton agrees. "You had the resources and the capabilities. Ian's right. Be proud of yourself, especially under these circumstances." He pauses and looks out the window. "Have you heard from Ciara?"

"No," I shake my head slowly. "She hasn't returned any of my calls or messages. It's been two weeks, Anton. I'm frightened for her."

"My intel confirms she's still alive," he says. "She hasn't left the Donovan property; she was seen earlier this morning in the back garden."

"How do you know?"

Ian scoffs. "We had to send a drone over in order to avoid detection. The entire mansion has been taken over by Kuznetsov's men."

"What about Paddy and the rest of our security detail?" I ask.

"We don't know," Anton replies. "Andrei is making inquiries across the city. Morgues, hospitals, anything."

"God, this is awful."

"It could be worse."

"Really?" I give him a confused look. "How? How could any of this be worse?"

Anton looks at me, and I see the dark shadows settling in his deep, hazel eyes. A grim reminder of what he has seen and lived through, long before our paths ever crossed. "It could be an all-out war in the streets of Chicago, like back in the '30s or even the '70s."

"Or the '80s, when crack entered the scene," Ian reminds us.

"You're right; that was a particularly gruesome decade," Anton sighs. "Point is, it could always be worse. We're gathering evidence against Kuznetsov as we speak. One way or another, I am taking that bastard down, and I will do everything in my power to get Ciara out of it before she gets hurt or worse."

"In the meantime, we move on," Ian says. "You've got the café's grand opening party to organize. A soft launch next week, and an official opening in about a month. That's what Laura suggested, anyway."

I was on board with that timing until the brewery fire. Now, I'm not so sure. "It might be dangerous to hold a public event in this current climate," I respond. "Kuznetsov's goons might target us."

"I doubt that, knowing we'd all be there, the Karpovs and other high-ranking members of the Bratva," Anton says. "He's a monster, but he's not a fool."

"He's not the brightest pea in the pod, either," Ian mutters. "I heard from my buddies in the CPD's Arson Unit that they're hot on a trail that involves Paul Mattis. Paul to Sergei is just a stone's throw, isn't it?"

"Well that's a positive lead," Anton says.

"We're on to something. And we're fortunate to have some support within the CPD. They're not fans of a potential Kuznetsov administration either. They know how Sergei's people operate."

"The fact that the Karpovs have been running the Bratva for the past few decades is why the morgues weren't overflowing."

"You'll get him, I know you will," I tell Anton.

He gives me a soft smile, his happy expression fading as he looks somewhere over my shoulder. A cold shiver travels down my spine as I follow his gaze.

"Oh, shit," Ian mumbles.

"What is it? Oh." I lose my breath altogether once I realize we're parked outside my café.

"Eileen, stay in the car," Anton says and jumps out. Ian is quick to join him.

I step out despite his command. My heart breaks into a million pieces as I slowly try to take it all in.

My café has been horrifically vandalized. Some of the windows smashed, others with paint thrown all over them, a milky white that spreads like disease.

From my vantage point, I can see the interior damage. Every damn couch and chair was torn wide open, the fluff from the stuffing all over the place. More broken glass and spray paint. Ugly slurs painted across the walls in bright pink, neon green and yellow, and toxic orange. The decorative mirrors have all been broken, their frames in pieces.

The bar, my beloved coffee bar, is a dreadful mess.

"Oh, I think I'm going to be sick," I whisper, leaning back against the car. My legs feel as if they're about to give out.

Anton and Ian take out their guns and agree to split up. Ian goes around the back to check the service entrance on the other side of the building, while my husband steps through the smashed double doors and checks the interior.

I can hear the broken glass crunching under his shoes. It's a sickening sound.

"Clear!" Ian's voice echoes from inside.

I meet them by the bar. My beautiful coffee bar. Even the pastry displays were obliterated. There's paint in the sink and all over the marble worktops. My salmon pink and white gold finishes scream at me, vandalized beyond recognition. A lot of hate went into this. So much hate, in fact, that I can almost feel it in the pit of my stomach.

"I'm so sorry, baby," Anton whispers as I burst into tears.

He holds me close as I let it out, wailing and sobbing, while Ian calls the police to report the horrendous crime that happened here. We all know who did it, and we know why. We have the motive and the suspect, but without tangible evidence, the cops won't be able to do much.

"He did this," I say.

"I know."

"He has to pay, Anton."

"Oh, trust me, my love. He will. A million times over."

Ian gives us both a troubled look as he touches a spray-painted corner of the bar. "This is fresh, sir. We missed them by minutes, at most."

"What?" Ice thickens in my veins. "You mean they were just here?"

"Your CCTV system isn't installed yet," Anton looks around with a frown.

"We had the technician scheduled to come in today, along with the guys from the internet company," I say, shuddering in my husband's arms.

Ian takes a deep, heavy breath. "Had we arrived just a few minutes sooner—"

"This was timed close to perfection," Anton says. "You and Ian were due to get here half an hour earlier, but you got here later, waiting for me, because I wanted to see the place."

"What are you saying?" I ask him, though deep down I think I know precisely what he is getting at.

"Had I not made you late, chances are you would've been here when Kuznetsov's goons came in. I think they tossed the place, because they couldn't be seen waiting around. It's close to opening for a lot of the businesses up and down this busy street. They missed their window, so they did a number on the café, instead."

The look on his face is lethal.

"Kuznetsov has just declared an all-out war. Either he thinks he's got something to bury us with, or he's attempting a dangerous gambit. But I can assure you, Andrei and I have done a damn good job of covering our trail over the years."

He's either insane or desperate for absolute power. Maybe a little of both. Either way, I was the intended victim. If his men really were here waiting for me to arrive at my usual hour, there's no telling what would've happened to me or my babies. Instinctively, I cradle my bump.

I am in clear and present danger.

"Anton, do you trust me?" I ask.

He gives me a curious look. "Of course."

"Then I need your support. There's something I have to do. And only I can do it."

He doesn't seem confident anymore after hearing that.

It's going to be a struggle to get him on board, but I need to give Ciara one last chance to do the right thing before Anton meets Sergei in this soon-to-be bloody war.

CHAPTER 28

EILEEN

"I really don't like this," Ian whispers.

We're surveilling the Donovan mansion from across the street, discreetly parked between two neighbors' cars. The lights are off, and we sit in complete darkness, monitoring Kuznetsov's security movements.

"I know Mr. Karpov reluctantly agreed to this, but I still don't like it," Ian insists.

"And you have every reason not to. Nevertheless, I have to do this, Ian. Before all hell breaks loose, before Anton and Andrei bring out the big guns, I have to at least try to talk to Ciara, to see if there's a way we can stop Sergei from the inside."

"We haven't exhausted our other options yet."

"Come on, Ian. We both know that every day that goes by that Ciara is out of my reach translates into one day closer to doomsday," I reply. "If something happens to her, the Donovan boys won't give a shit about the Kuznetsov's firepower. I know those men better than Sergei. This could escalate within hours into something unstoppable. Any other options won't be on the table anymore, and Anton knows it. That's why he agreed to this. Reluctantly, but he still agreed."

He sighs deeply. "Alright. Fair enough. She's still your family, and I know Mr. Karpov would do the same to reach his brother if they were in your situation. I can get you through the service door, but you will have no protection in there."

"Do we know if there are any Donovan men left in there?"

"Only Kuznetsov soldiers for the time being. I photographed and documented each of them. We've yet to find Paddy, by the way. Still in the wind."

"What about his family?"

"They claim they don't know anything. They're either lying to protect him, or they honestly don't know where he is."

I look toward the house, noticing two guards stationed outside the gates. "Do we have a location for Ciara within the mansion?"

"Yes," Ian replies as he hands me a pair of military-grade binoculars. "First floor, west corner."

"Ah. That's Dad's study," I mutter as I look through the binoculars and spot movement in that window. Judging by the size of the shadow, it's definitely Ciara. "I wonder if she's alone."

"Here's the panic button," Ian says, slipping the small device into my jacket pocket. "All you need to do is press it, and in less than ninety seconds, police will be knocking down the front door. We're prepared to make quite a scene in order to get you out."

I give him a warm smile. "I know that house inside out. Every nook, every cranny, every secret passage."

"Secret passage?" he sounds surprised. "There was nothing noteworthy on the blueprints when I checked them. It took some arm-twisting even to get my hands on those."

"That's why they're secret." I wink at him. "Dad, bless his soul, was just as paranoid as Grandpa and all the other Donovan men before him. Paddy is the only person outside the Donovan family who knows about the passages and the tunnels. Get me through the side door, and I'll be able to access those from the inside."

"You can't do it in reverse?"

I shake my head. "They're meant for escaping, not for infiltrating the mansion. There are key code panels only accessible from the inside."

"And you know the codes."

"Of course."

"That means so does Ciara."

I give Ian a sad look. "Yeah, but she hasn't used them so far."

"Perhaps she told Sergei about them, too."

"She wouldn't. She'd want to keep at least one means of escape to herself if she needed to."

"God, I hope you're right." He exhales sharply. "Come on, let's go. They're changing shifts now. This is our window of opportunity."

Sure enough, we see two other men in black suits approaching from the other end of the street.

Quietly, Ian and I get out of the car and bolt across the road, sneaking past the parked SUVs and through one of the neighbor's poorly secured front yards to make it to the service alley. About thirty yards ahead, I see the secondary gate, a Kuznetsov guard casually strolls away from it.

"He's on his phone," Ian whispers. "Go now. I'll wait here."

"Okay." I give Ian a wink and run up the alley, light on my feet.

Carefully, I lift the metallic latch and slip through the gate. I hear footsteps approaching. The guard must be coming back. Dad gave me a skeleton key that opens every door when I turned eighteen, and judging by the worn look on the lock in front of me, Sergei hasn't gotten around to changing any of them.

Good.

I turn the key and breathe a quick sigh of relief before disappearing inside.

I look around. I hear more footsteps, but they're distant, guards likely patrolling the hallways and the living room at the front of the house. The windows on that side are huge, making that part of the perimeter more exposed.

It gives me the opportunity to sneak into one of the staff's quarters at the back of the mansion. Paddy's room, to be specific. A chest of drawers and an armchair sit against the western wall. I carefully pull the furniture aside by a few feet, mindful of my condition. Once I'm done, I find myself smiling as I stare at the small wooden door I just uncovered.

"Come to Mama," I whisper as I press my code into the tiny keypad mounted where the lock and the doorknob should be. There's a click, followed by the door opening.

I go in.

It's damp and dark, but I use the flashlight on my phone to move around after I close the door behind me. I hope and pray that none of the guards will go into Paddy's room anytime soon.

I pause in the narrow corridor. Ahead, two sets of staircases give me two different options. One leads to the east wing of the mansion, the other to the west. Ciara was last seen in Dad's study.

West it is.

Quiet as a mouse in the walls, I follow the secret path until I reach the door I'm looking for. I stand outside of it and listen for a while. I can hear Ciara's voice. It sounds like she's on the phone with someone. My heart feels like it's damn near about to leap out of my chest.

"How much longer do I have to stay here, Sergei? People are getting suspicious," she says, then pauses. "That's not going to work. The only reason why you have any of my family's support is, because they don't know what a two-faced bastard you really are. If they don't see me at all, they're going to worry. You don't want the MacDonalds to worry, Sergei, trust me."

She pauses again, then begins sobbing. I can only imagine what horrible things he must've responded with.

"Okay, okay. Just... please, let me out, even if it's just for something simple. I'll be good, I promise. You saw me at the funeral. I didn't say a word. I played my part."

After a few seconds, Ciara hangs up, slamming the phone against the desk. I recognize that sound. Dad used to pound that desk, too, whenever he was angry. It breaks me to hear Ciara like this, but hopefully, it means she'll listen to me, if only for a hot second.

I gently knock on the secret door. Silence

I knock again and I can hear her gasp.

I knock a third time. Rushed footsteps coming toward the door.

"Eileen?" she calls out.

"Keep your voice down," I hiss.

"Shit, sorry. Hold on."

I patiently wait as she punches her code into a similar security pad on the other side of the door. When it opens, tendrils of dust flutter between us for a brief moment. My eyes squint against the warm light in Dad's study.

Ciara looks at me with wide eyes, her skin pale. "What in God's green earth are you doing here?"

"Obviously trying to save your ass," I reply. "Come on, let's go."

"I can't."

I give her a confused look. "Why not?"

"He's got access to everything, Eileen. I won't last a day outside these walls."

"We can protect you."

She shakes her head. "No, you can't. And I think you already know that. If I leave now, the whole thing's going to blow up, and none of us will be safe again. Eileen, he's amassing power within the Bratva. Anton won't be able to protect me. Right now, he can still protect you, because you're his wife. But I willingly, consciously, and stupidly signed all of my financial and legal power over to him."

"Oh, Ciara..." I exhale sharply, squatting down in the doorway. I remain in the passageway, just in case I have to disappear quickly. Ciara kneels in front of me, and I take a good look at her. Puffy eyes. Slightly cracked lips. Her hair hasn't been washed in days. "What the hell happened? How did we get to this point?"

"He... I don't know, Eileen. I thought he was decent enough. I have no idea how he coerced Dad to sign those fiduciary papers."

"Dad didn't sign those. It's not his signature."

She scoffs and stares at her hands. "I suspected that much. I guess I wasn't ready to admit it."

"It will take some time to prove it, time we don't have right now. What is going on in the house? Where is Paddy?"

"Paddy is most likely on the run. Sergei was going to terminate him and put one of his men in charge of Donovan security," she replies. "But he's not going to be able to do that now that Paddy is in the wind. There are still loyalists among the Donovan boys, and Sergei knows he can't get them to submit without Paddy's body."

"Jesus Christ."

"He held a gun to my head." She begins to cry. "To sign the fiduciary papers. I didn't want to. Even when I saw what I thought was Dad's signature, I still didn't believe it was real. Dad didn't trust him."

I nod slowly. "What can I do to help you, Ciara?"

"I'm so sorry," she says. "You warned me, but I was too busy being angry with you. I was so hell-bent on making you miserable. I've always been a terrible sister, haven't I?"

"Captivity seems to be a good time for introspection," I mumble.

"And then some. I've had plenty of solitude. Hours and hours to sit on everything and retrace my steps, figure out where I fucked up. And I fucked up so many times, Eileen. Will you ever forgive me?"

"Stop talking like you're dying, and tell me how I can help."

She gasps and looks at me as if she's seeing me for the first time. "Are you insane? You shouldn't be here. Where's Anton?"

"On the edge of his seat, waiting for a positive conclusion to this stunt that I convinced him to let me pull. I need you to focus. Tell me how to take Sergei down."

Ciara takes a moment to think about it, her gaze darting all over the room. "Okay. I don't have access to his quarters. He's taken over Dad's bedroom."

"I'm guessing it's where he keeps sensitive information?"

"Yes. He made me give him the security code for Dad's vault," she says. "I can try to get in there, but I don't know when or how. Or if I can still use the same code. He could've changed it."

I shake my head. "I doubt it. He didn't change the locks on the access doors. He's clearly cocky as hell. It might work to our advantage."

"I promise I'll try. If I can get into the vault, I'll use the tunnels myself. I'll escape. But I can't walk out of here empty-handed."

"Okay. Tell me whom he's been meeting with lately."

"All the big families in the Bratva. He keeps trying to bend the Fedorovs in his favor, but I hear Ivan rejected three of his offers. Sergei seems desperate to get Fedorov support," she says, then gives me a wry smile. "I guess it was a good thing to marry a Karpov, after all. That Fedorov blood of yours seems to be working in your favor."

"And yours, too. Every second that Sergei doesn't spend at the head of the Bratva is a second I can use to destroy that cocksucker."

"Oh, shit," she gasps, eyes widening as she suddenly seems to remember something. "Paul Mattis came in really late last night. I was in my room. I wasn't allowed to come out, but I could hear them arguing. Paul said something about Homeland Security having eyes on the Kuznetsovs. I heard them say the words 'national security.' That could be something, right?"

"I'll definitely pass that on to Anton."

We both hear footsteps approaching.

"Shit," she whispers. "Go, now."

"What about you?"

"I'll be okay; I promise."

"Ciara..."

"No, Eileen. I love you, but I can't go with you yet. I owe it to you and Dad to at least try to fix this, ideally without getting myself killed in the process. I'll be in touch, one way or another. Just go before that goon sees you. He checks up on me every ten minutes or so."

I give her a nod as I squeeze her hand, then let her close and lock the door as I carefully make my way back to Paddy's room. She was genuine. I felt it. I felt her fear; I felt her regrets. For a moment, it was like I had my sister back.

We still have a long way back to a proper reconciliation, but first, I need to remove that wretched stain that is Sergei Kuznetsov from our family.

I find Ian waiting for me, hiding in the shadows. We hurry back to the car and quietly leave the area as I tell him everything I learned. Ian listens intently, one eye on the rearview mirror at all times, making sure we aren't being followed by anyone.

Sadly, the farther we get from the Donovan mansion, the safer I feel.

"I've got a few contacts within the NSA," he says as we leave my old neighborhood altogether. "I can reach out and see if they have any information where Sergei is concerned."

"You think maybe we can get some dirt on him?"

"At least something to present at the next Bratva council, for sure. Or, even better, perhaps we can supplement whatever the NSA is cooking up against him with information and leads of our own. If Ciara can get into his vault, we could lock it in completely."

Hopefully, before the bloodshed begins. I think we are all aware that the doomsday clock is ticking now that Kuznetsov has control over my family. The Irish will probably try to fight back, but Sergei is quite notorious for his way of handling rebellions of any kind. I've heard stories from Ian and Anton—stories that make the hair on the back of my neck stand up.

***

"Tommy Benedetto!" I exclaim as I walk into my husband's home office to find Tommy by the window, nursing a double scotch. "What brings you here?"

"A buddy of mine from the NSA texted me," he says.

I'm momentarily speechless as Anton gets up and takes me in his arms, planting a firm kiss on my lips. "I'm glad you made it out of there in one piece."

"I asked you to trust me, and I'm glad you did," I reply, then look at Tommy. "What's your deal with the NSA?"

"Ian doesn't know that my contacts in the NSA rank higher than his," Tommy chuckles. "I'm here to help."

"How so?"

Anton motions for me to take a seat on the sofa. He joins me, his knee glued to mine. I welcome the comfort of his presence and his touch. After the day I've had, being close to my husband is pretty much like hugging the sun.

"Well, my buddy confirmed that they're looking into the entire Kuznetsov family. The circumstances of their deaths—"

"Whoa, whose deaths?" I interrupt.

"Two of Sergei's siblings. Possibly three. They're trying to open a line of comms with the Russian Secret Service, but it's murky waters. It's been hard to get reliable intel across these days," he says.

Anton frowns. "I thought Sergei's older brother passed away and that the others went back to Russia."

"Who'd wanna leave the cornucopia that is the Chicago Bratva to go back to Moscow where the market isn't as profitable?"

"I figured they were oligarchs. That social class does well over there."

"Sergei isn't as good at managing his family's finances as most are led to believe, and his daddy wasn't any better," Tommy replies. "There's a reason why they were never able to dethrone the Karpovs. Come on, man, how come I know more about the Kuznetsovs than you?"

Anton chuckles. "You'll have to forgive me. Your NSA friend is clearly better informed. So tell me, what are we dealing with, exactly?"

"Sergei's brother, Anatoly, was fished out of the river about four months ago. Another sibling, Jakub, is off the radar completely. The NSA is currently trying to track him down. They're close to establishing a partnership with the Russians on this, provided they extradite Sergei."

"As long as he's out of the Bratva here, I'm good with that," Anton decrees, and I nod in agreement. Anything is better than nothing at this point.

"Therefore, whatever you have on Sergei and his family, anything at all, any kind of dirt, send it my way and I'll pass it on. There won't be miracles overnight, but if they can share information with the Russians, they might be able to pick up a paper trail, something to help them nail the bastard down."

"What about you and your family?" I ask. "Rumor has it that Sergei is planning to make his takeover of the Bratva official. He'll want your support."

Tommy shakes his head slowly, a shit-eating grin on his face. "Let me tell you something, Eileen. What Sergei is doing now is pretty old-school—resorting to physical aggression, vandalism, destroying your buildings—it's all just enough to get a reaction out of you. If you give him that reaction, the Benedettos will have no choice but to support whoever leads the Bratva, whether it's Anton today or Sergei tomorrow.

"But if you play it cool, if you keep yourselves away from him and figure out a *legal* way to burn his ass, you do it. Because then, the other families will have no choice except to support you," he adds.

"How so?"

"Do you remember the Trattoria Rosa dinner from 1985?" Anton asks me.

I nod once. "Some kind of edict was signed then, right?"

"A peace treaty, to be specific, between the great families of Chicago," he says. "The three big ones of the Bratva—us, the Fedorovs, and the Abramovics, along with the three big ones of the Camorra—Benedetto, Mancini, and Angeli."

"It included the three heads of the Irish, as well, which means your father," Tommy tells me. "Three from the Colombians, three from the Mexicans, three from the Japanese Yakuza, and three from the Triads. A total of twenty-one signatures from the twenty-one most powerful men in Chicago's mob world."

"A peace treaty. Okay, yeah, I remember Dad mentioning something about that."

"A peace treaty that became law. Written, and, funnily enough, notarized, solely for the families' peace of mind," Anton adds. "It means nothing to actual law enforcement, but it means everything to us. And according to that peace treaty, if all attempts at peace have failed, and if a member of the aforementioned families has died as a direct result of violence perpetrated by a member of another family, then all the families—"

"Are obligated to stand with the aggrieved," I finish the statement for him. "Which means that unless Sergei makes a direct attempt at my life, or at the life of any other Karpov, then the other families cannot support our claim against him."

"Furthermore, the treaty extends to the leadership of each of the organizations," Tommy adds. "If the Karpovs are chosen to lead the Bratva, we support them against any other family within the Bratva. If the Kuznetsovs take over and are recognized as the new leaders, we'll have no choice but to support them."

"Oh, that is so twisted."

Anton offers me a bitter smile. "It's the way of our world. And it's not about what's wrong or right either, it's about who holds the power. If Sergei gets a violent reaction out of me now, it will lead to war within the Bratva. I cannot win that war without the other families' support, and that will give Sergei the power he needs to take over my seat. If that happens, we're fucked in every possible way except the good way. I cannot allow that to happen, not to me, not to my brother, and certainly not to you."

"He's got a hold on one of the three big Irish families, too, but he doesn't have the full support of the others," Tommy reminds me. "That's why he's flinging turds at Anton, trying to get a reaction out of him."

I take a deep breath, my mind wandering through every possible scenario. "The Donovans, the O'Reilly's, and the MacDonalds are still one unit over the Irish organization. You're right about one thing. Sergei hasn't swayed any of them yet, not fully, anyway. My voice may not count in a vote since I'm married to a Karpov now, but I could make a few phone calls, nonetheless. Ask Sean O'Reilly to come by the house for a cup of tea or Edwin MacDonald for a slice of steak and kidney pie."

"As long as you stay here," Anton says. "It has become imperative."

"Ah, back in my cage, then," I chuckle softly.

"I'm sorry."

"No, it's okay, I get it," I tell him. "Given the circumstances, I honestly get it. I will limit my outings as much as possible, and I will always have Ian, at least, accompanying me if I have to go out."

Tommy nods in agreement. "I'll liaise with the NSA in the meantime. I'm telling you, if we can gather enough evidence against Sergei and slap the other families over the face with it, you'll keep your seat at the head of the table. Kuznetsov may be a ruthless fucker, but he's not suicidal. He'll have no choice but to flee before the Feds get him."

"Or before some envoy straight out of Moscow gets him." Anton's eyes twinkle with newfound enthusiasm.

I've got a feeling he just stumbled into a new and exciting idea. Whatever it is, I fully support him. My moral code will have to take a nap for a while, I suppose.

This has become a game of survival, and I'll be damned if I'll let Sergei destroy our lives.

CHAPTER 29

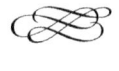

EILEEN

The days that follow are eerily quiet.

Kuznetsov is nowhere to be found, though the Donovan mansion is still very much under his control. Ciara hasn't reached out, but I know she needs time and a safe way to get into his sensitive documents. She'll call or text me when she has what we need to bury that bastard—unless Tommy's people from the NSA call first.

Either way, it has become a matter of when, not if, we take him down.

Until then, I keep my word to Anton and limit my outings. It's beautiful outside, so I at least allow myself to enjoy afternoons in the garden. Sitting on the edge of the pool, I dip my bare feet in the water while the early summer breeze blows through my hair. I allow my body to soak in as much sun as possible.

"Your lemonade," Ian says as he brings an ice-cold pitcher and a chilled glass out to me.

The minty top note hits my nose first. I look up at him through my shades and smile. "Thank you ever so much. Any news from Anton?"

"He and Andrei are meeting with the Popovs as we speak. The initial support for Kuznetsov seems to be waning, but I wouldn't place any bets yet."

He fills my glass and adjusts the sunshade.

"Do you think you might be able to set up lunch on the terrace for Laura and me today?"

"I think I can make that happen," Ian replies with a smile.

"Thanks, Ian. You're the best."

My phone pings.

"Oh," I mumble, checking the screen.

It's a text from Ciara.

I'm in trouble. Help me.

Shit.

I immediately call her, but I'm sent straight to voicemail.

What's going on?

Sergei suspects something.

Did you get into his vault?

It's quiet for a while, and I'm getting nervous, my heart beating faster with each minute of silence. Finally, three dots appear again.

I did. But he's got eyes on me all the time. I can't get out of here.

What can I do?

I need a diversion.

Okay, leave this to me. Hang in there, sis. I got you.

Anton isn't reachable by phone or email. I've left him messages, so he's been informed, at least, and he'll learn what I'm about to do when he reads through everything. In the meantime, Ian and I prepare to head out.

"I just need to get close enough to the mansion so we can create a diversion."

"I know, but it still doesn't feel right."

"All we have to do is be there when Ciara comes out of the tunnels. I told her to take the route that leads into Mr. Kristofferson's yard, which is right next door. We'll be in the car, waiting, right outside his gate."

"It sounds simple enough."

"Then what is it?"

He checks the magazine and slips it into the gun, then makes sure the safety is off before holstering it under his jacket.

"I don't know, Eileen. Call it a gut instinct, if you will. I specifically don't like the fact that Mr. Karpov didn't green-light this move."

"Have you been successful in reaching him?"

"No."

"Time is of the essence here, Ian."

Just then my phone rings. "It's Ciara," I tell him.

Quickly, I answer. "Hey, what's up? Where are you?"

"I ran..." Her voice is fractured. She's breaking up.

"Ciara, where are you?" I repeat while Ian gives me a worried look. "I can barely hear you."

"I... got... out... on my way... your coffee... place..."

The line goes dead. I stare at the screen for a few seconds.

"Where is she?" Ian asks.

"I think she's on the way to my café," I tell him.

He gives me a puzzled look and then drives us across the city to Gold Coast, to the pitiful remnants of my café.

"She must've gone inside," I tell Ian. "I texted her the passkey for the back door."

My heart hurts whenever I come here. The façade was repainted, and the windows were replaced, but we still have a lot of work to do inside. Nevertheless, Ciara needs me, so I gather the strength I need to get out of the car and follow Ian through the service alley that leads us to the back door.

He inputs the code into the electronic lock. After a click, the access light turns from red to blinking green. We go in, and I am immediately struck by the smell of spray paint again.

"That smell. I should leave the air conditioning system on for a day or so," I say as we make our way through the dark corridor and head for the main hall.

"Call out to her," Ian says, walking in front of me, one hand on his holstered weapon.

"What's wrong?" I ask.

"Just call out and stay back."

I do as he asks. "Ciara?"

A rustling sound causes both of us to pause in the main hall's double doorway. Ian places his arm in front of me then looks around. He draws his weapon and my skin crawls all over, the hairs on the back of my neck rise as I listen carefully.

"Ciara?" I call out again.

FLIT. FLIT.

Ian twitches and falls to the side.

I scream, watching the blood bloom on his shirt. "Oh, my God!"

"Fuck," he hisses as he fires back.

I hear footsteps pounding, but I don't see the man until it's too late. He's big and dressed all in black. He charges at us, then kicks Ian so hard he passes out.

"No!" I cry out and try to run away, but not before I feel the muzzle pressing at the back of my neck. I freeze on the spot. "No, please."

"Relax; he wants you alive," his thick Russian accent fills me with dread as I realize this was a setup.

"Where's my stepsister?" I ask as he binds my hands behind my back with a zip tie.

"You'll be reunited soon enough."

I don't like the sound of that. I don't like the sound of him. And I don't like the look of Ian, passed out and pale, bleeding from what appears to be two gunshot wounds—one to the left shoulder and one to his side.

"Oh, Ian..." I whisper.

"Worry about yourself, Mrs. Karpova."

I'm taken to a structure somewhere on the other side of town, far outside the suburbs, by the looks of it. It's quiet and dark at this hour. I'm gagged and bound as I am unceremoniously dragged out from the back of a black van and up the front steps of the house.

It's a two-level building with white marble flooring and huge, French-style windows. Based on the state-of-the-art security system and over a dozen Kuznetsov goons present, I'm guessing I'm in a Kuznetsov safe house.

"You'd better not scream or do anything stupid," my giant kidnapper says as he removes my gag. "Or I will put this back and add a black eye."

"You're too kind," I mutter, my mouth dry and my blood boiling as I look up at him. "You're a real gem, threatening to hit a pregnant woman."

He shrugs and gives me a sneer. I notice a long scar on one side of his face. "I don't care that you're pregnant, and I don't think the boss cares either."

"Sergei? He should care. He just declared open war against the Karpovs," I reply.

"It's a new age, Mrs. Karpova. We will rule soon enough," he says, pushing open a door behind me.

He gives me a shove, and I stumble into the room where he locks me in. Immediately, I turn around and start banging on the door, determined not to go down quietly. "You son of a bitch! Let me out! Now!"

"Quiet!" he shouts, pounding a fist against the door, causing it to shudder.

It startles me, and I take a couple of steps back. This is not where I'm going to die. No way in hell I'm letting Kuznetsov win. There has to be a way out of this mess. There's always a way out.

"Eileen?" A weak, familiar voice causes me to spin around.

Ciara sits in a chair by the window.

"Oh, my God," I whisper, stunned by the sight of her.

Her face is bruised. There's not enough concealer in the world to hide the vibrant red and blue splotches around her eye, stretching down her cheek, all the way to her chin. There are bloodstains on her white blouse. Her lip is split and cracked, and clearly tender whenever she tries to speak. She looks so weak, so pale.

"Ciara," I breathe as I rush over and kneel in front of her. "What happened?"

She gives me a pained look. "He caught me snooping. He beat it out of me... the plans we made... I'm so sorry."

"It wasn't you texting me, was it?"

"No."

"You called me, though."

Ciara shakes her head slowly. "No, he forced me to say those things, to ask you to meet me at the café."

"That son of a bitch."

She nods, wincing in pain. "I'm so sorry."

"It's okay. It's not your fault."

"It *is* my fault."

"No, Ciara, it isn't." I gently tuck a lock of hair behind her ear. It pains me deeply to see her like this. She may not be the world's greatest stepsister, and her mouth and ego might often get the better of her, but she didn't deserve any of this. We each did the best we could with what we were given.

She sobs quietly, barely able to look me in the eyes. "I should've been more careful. I should've rejected Sergei's offer, Eileen. Dad said I could say no, that he'd find me another match."

"But you said yes. I know why and I understand. I don't like it, but, hey, we've all made mistakes, right? I mean, look at me," I laugh nervously, and she glances down at my bump. "Don't get me wrong, I love these babies with everything I've got, and I can't wait to bring them into the world, but this wasn't exactly planned. We make mistakes, Ciara. The trick is we need to learn from them."

"I'm going to get you and the twins killed."

"No, honey. This is on Sergei. Besides, I'm not dying here, you hear me? Neither are you."

"Eileen, we're trapped. Sergei is on his way over and he's going to kill us both once the marriage certificate is signed. I'm to blame. I can admit it. It's my fault. I'm a terrible human being; that's why Anton didn't think twice to toss me aside for you. Deep down, I knew—"

"Had he not learned about my pregnancy, he would've married you."

She gives me a long look, her tired eyes filled with shame and grief. "I wanted to rush the wedding the first time, because I saw how you two looked at each other. I was afraid he'd change his mind. And when you fainted, I was so scared he'd pull away that I was in an even bigger hurry afterward. Then he made the new deal with Dad and… God, Eileen, will you ever forgive me?"

"For being insecure? For not being true to yourself? Because that's where all of this stemmed from. It's not my job to forgive you. It's yours to forgive yourself. In order to do that, however, we need to survive."

"I'm sorry."

"Stop apologizing. Right now we have to put our effort and energy into getting out of here alive, so we can take that monster down once and for all."

"You don't even know the half of it, Eileen. Of what Sergei really is."

"What do you mean?"

"He said something earlier. God, how could I be so blind?"

"What did he say?"

The door swings open. "Ah, my favorite ladies!"

The devil himself stands before us, hands casually resting on his hips. He looks annoyingly pleased.

"The Donovan sisters reunited," he adds, taking a step forward. "Has Ciara told you yet? She's got that sick look on her face. The same look she had when I told her. It's priceless."

"Told her what?" I ask.

"Your father didn't go out on his own," he says.

It's a good thing I'm kneeling, because I think my legs would've given out upon hearing what he said. The smug look on his face causes my blood to boil, but I need to focus, I need to get Ciara and myself out of here before it's too late. Therefore, whatever Sergei says to rile me up or to hurt me, I cannot allow it to get to me.

"What did you just say?" I ask, my voice slightly trembling.

Ciara is a mess, holding onto my hands for dear life. She's terrified of him.

"There's this thing called thallium sulfate. Incredibly useful and easy to procure when you're a man of my means," Sergei says. "Ronan was sick, but it was nothing that a dietary change and a healthier lifestyle couldn't improve. Hell, he probably could've overcome it altogether if he picked up a dumbbell and threw an exercise routine into the mix."

"You poisoned our father," I say, the words coming out through gritted teeth. "I know what thallium sulfate is. It's undetectable."

"His doctors were stumped. All those tests. But that's the thing, Eileen. When you don't know what you're looking for, you're not going to find it."

"You piece of shit."

"Watch your mouth!" he snaps, then smiles again. "Besides, he had it coming. You and I were going to be the greatest couple in all of Chicago. You would've been by my side while I went about my mission to destroy the Karpovs. Look at you now, on the wrong side of the fence. But don't worry, you and Ciara will be joining your father soon enough."

"So, what exactly are you going to do?" I ask Sergei, trying to buy some time to come up with a plan.

"You should've stayed with me," he says, each word dripping with fury and contempt. "I didn't want to settle for your sister."

I give Ciara an apologetic glance. "He's off his rocker. You know that, right?"

"Ronan was still rooting for you to take over the Donovan business. It's why I made the marriage proposal in the first place," Sergei continues. "I never bought the Ciara angle. She doesn't have your resilience, your clear head. More than once, she proved herself to be a spoiled brat. It's a pity, too, the girl is smart, just not smart enough."

"I'm going to make you eat those words," Ciara hisses, fury finally pushing her fear aside. Good. I need her angry.

I squeeze her knee. "Don't engage him."

"See? This is what I mean. So easy to rile up. I was devastated when Karpov swooped in and won you, Eileen. The only reason I proposed to Ciara instead was because I needed another way into the family. If you weren't going to come to me willingly so that I could finally grab the Donovan estate, I had to try a different approach."

"Why are you so desperate to get my father's fortune? You're a powerful and influential man, Sergei. You don't need us," I say.

"He does need us," Ciara groans.

"I'm going to kill *you* first," Sergei replies, pointing a finger at her. "It'll be ruled a suicide. Plenty of witnesses to confirm that you were unstable. You have been unstable ever since Karpov left you for your stepsister. Then your father died. It'll be a tragedy."

"You make it very hard not to promise you a world of pain, Sergei," I shoot back. "Enough with the gloating."

"That's all he's got. Gloating. He is out of money, Eileen. He's been broke for a while now. Getting rid of his siblings seemed like a good idea until he realized that they were the ones keeping the Kuznetsov businesses running. Once he was left on his own, Sergei proved exactly how incompetent he truly is. One by one, his companies started going under. Throw in a gambling debt, and here he is. The mighty Sergei Kuznetsov is nothing more than a loser and a flop."

He is about to lunge at her, but I get up, stopping him in his tracks. Hesitating, he scowls at Ciara.

"Is that true?" I ask him.

"It doesn't matter."

"What are you going to do, Sergei? Kill us both and expect to get away with it? Have you forgotten about the treaty?"

For a moment, Sergei appears uncertain. Ciara is right. These are the actions of a desperate man who lied and who has to keep lying in order to save his own ass. It puts me at a slight advantage, provided I can buy us some time.

"Ciara's death will be ruled a suicide. You'll be diagnosed with a heart condition because of the pregnancy. There wasn't anything anyone could do," he mutters, completely dodging my question.

"Do you really plan to kill me and my unborn children? Sergei, I'm trying to reason with you here. My stepsister and I are still alive right now, and it's in your best interest to keep it that way, because nobody's going to buy your story. Anton already knows the truth. Your men left Ian back at the café."

"Shut up!" he snaps. "Shut the hell up!"

He's losing it. Good. It means he's getting closer to the edge and he's not thinking straight anymore.

I lower my gaze, the blood rushing through my veins as I struggle to keep myself calm and composed. I cannot allow him to see fear or despair on my face. Finally, after a lengthy, heavy silence where all I can hear is his ragged breathing, Sergei inhales sharply and walks back to the door.

"I'll let you know when the marriage certificate gets here," he says. "Paul will bring it over as soon as the judge signs it."

He gives me one last glance over his shoulder. He's screwed, and he knows it. He was playing fast and loose this whole time. This puts him in a whole new light. I thought he was calculated and five steps ahead of us. I was wrong.

Go figure.

It's time for Sergei to meet his fate.

CHAPTER 30

ANTON

Every atom in my body is about to explode.

It's taking a tremendous amount of energy and self-control not to let that happen. Every deep breath, every movement I make contains all the rage that I must keep from blowing outward, from obliterating everything and everyone in my path.

"He has her," I say, my voice angry and cold as I make my way up the stairs to the second floor of the private hospital. Andrei is with me.

"He has both girls. That's what our intel is saying so far."

"Any traceable phone numbers?"

"Our people are combing through everything we've gathered so far."

"Time isn't on our side," I grimly remind him.

He nods once as we reach the second floor and follow the nurse's instructions to Room 201. We find Ian resting, his eyes closed. He looks rough but turns his head and opens his eyes when we enter.

"You look like hell," Ian remarks upon seeing me.

He's right. I'm not at my best. I haven't slept or shaved in almost two days, and my clothes are wrinkled. I'm in a constant fight mode with one objective on my mind, and that's to get my wife back, alive and unharmed.

"Pot, meet kettle," Andrei chuckles dryly, then moves around Ian's bed and cordially shakes his hand.

He's pale, dark circles under his eyes. The loss of blood did more damage to his body than the actual bullets, from what his doctor told us. But he will pull through, and for that, I'm grateful. Ian has been a pillar of our family for so long, I could never replace him.

"It's a good thing you came to when the paramedics showed up," I tell him. "A passerby saw you on the floor, maybe a few minutes after you went down. They heard tires screeching in the back alley, but they didn't see the car or the driver."

"I told the paramedic to bring me to this location. I figured you'd want me here. Hell, I'd want me here," Ian says, still groggy from the anesthesia. "Nothing beats a private hospital, especially in my condition. I told myself that if I'm to die, I might as well do it on your dime, in pristine luxury."

I can't help but smile. "I'm glad you're okay, Ian. Really."

"I'm sorry, Anton," he says, pain darkening his gaze. "I tried to keep her safe, I tried to—"

"Let's face it, there is only so much we can do to keep Eileen from doing something once she has her mind set on doing it, especially when it comes to her family." I sigh deeply. "It's not your fault, and it's not hers either. Sergei just knew what buttons to push and how to push them. I'm still not sure what role Ciara played in all of this."

Andrei shakes his head slowly. "I don't know. Honestly, I'm inclined to believe Eileen when she said Ciara really did have a change of heart."

"If that's true, then Sergei is holding them until he finalizes the legal proceedings," I say. "He won't need either of them after that's done."

And that spells death.

Ian grunts softly as he pulls himself up, Andrei helping him get comfortable with the pillows. "They were very discreet about the whole thing," he says. "They knew they couldn't lure Eileen to the café without good reason, and it had to be convenient for them."

"Location-wise, you mean," I reply.

"Yes. It must mean they have a place somewhere outside of the Gold Coast area," he concludes. "Something quiet, perhaps. Inconspicuous."

"Somewhere to keep Eileen and Ciara until he gets the marriage license signed and legalized by the judge," Andrei says, then takes out his phone. "We need to put a wire out on all the judges in Chicago."

"That's too many," I reply. "Besides, anyone with a license to officiate can handle this for Sergei. People can get these off the internet nowadays."

Ian disagrees. "Considering the legal ramifications and the sheer size of this theft that Sergei is hell-bent on, I think he'll want to go through a judge. Likely, someone who's pliable toward the Russian or the Irish organizations. He would need familiarity with the officiant to power through with the certificate and notarization."

"Andrei, do it. Put a wire out," I tell my brother.

"They're alive," Ian tries to comfort me. "You'd have found them by now if they weren't."

"That could change from one hour to the next," I mumble.

"In the meantime, you need to gamble and go all-in," he replies.

I give him a startled look. "What do you mean?"

"Summon all the families. Emergency council meeting. Bring all the evidence that you've gathered. Let Andrei speak on your behalf while you're out there looking for Eileen. Make sure it's a big enough circus to draw attention to Kuznetsov's and Mattis' movements."

"He's got most of the Bratva families on his side," I remind him. "It would be moot."

"Not if he's looking to kill the Donovan sisters, especially a pregnant one," Andrei says once he's off the phone. "No, I'm with Ian on this. I will bet you a million bucks or more that most of the families siding with Kuznetsov at this point have no idea how many laws he's breaking under our treaty. Let me do this. I'll go in, do a whole number, slam my fist into the table, do a fucking slideshow of everything we've uncovered up until now. It'll be enough to cast doubt, at the very least."

"It might even get some of his sympathizers to change their mind and give us important information," Ian adds.

A knock on the door causes the three of us to go quiet.

Tommy Benedetto walks in.

"What are you doing here?"

"I've had eyes on Ian since he was brought here," Tommy replies with a wry smile, then gives Ian a friendly nod. "Glad to see you're not dead yet."

"I'm a persistent SOB, what can I say?"

"This isn't a courtesy visit," I mumble. "What is it, Tommy?"

He takes a deep breath and lets it out slowly. Slow enough to get my anxiety crackling again. "I've got some information from my NSA contacts," he says. "You're not gonna like it, though."

"About his activities?"

"And his whereabouts. I've got a line on him, Anton. But we need to be really careful about how we proceed here."

"Why?"

"He moved the Donovan sisters deep into Triad territory last night. I don't know all the details, but I do know you can't just go in there, gung-ho, and shoot your way through," Tommy replies.

Andrei frowns. "Can't you find out? You Camorra boys have some favors to curry with the Lee clan, from what I recall."

"That's why I'm here. I'm meeting one of the Lee boys for coffee in about an hour," Tommy says, then narrows his eyes at me. "Think you can come with me but refrain from causing a scene? We need him to tell us what he knows. I can't get in hot water with the Triads, Anton. Regardless of our treaties and agreements, we have to be careful and play nice."

Sergei is hiding in Triad territory precisely because he knows how hard it is for us to penetrate the Chinese web. The Russians and the Chinese are great at doing business together above the line, but when it comes to shit off the grid, we've had some bloody skirmishes over the years.

"Our history with the Lees doesn't exactly work in our favor," Andrei reminds me.

"I'll do it," I say. "I'll go with Tommy. You gather the Bratva council. See who shows up. Whoever is unable to meet you at the Upton Conference Center will probably be too busy supplying Sergei with tactical and financial support."

"That will give us a good idea if there's anything left to salvage," Andrei mutters.

"And, most importantly, we'll be able to see how much damage Sergei has already done to the organization. At least I'll know what I'll be coming back to once I save my wife and put a bullet in that fucker's head," I reply.

Something will shake loose from somewhere. And when it does, it will reveal a trail for me to follow. That's all I need. A trail, a scent. And then he's all mine. I would've forgiven any attempt on my life or my businesses; competition among the families is often fierce. I understand a man's rabid desire to succeed more than most.

Sergei isn't playing with my life. He's playing with my wife's and our unborn children's lives.

I cannot forgive that, nor can I respond with anything less than every ounce of lethal force I have at my disposal.

∼

Howard Lee doesn't look happy that I'm joining his coffee date with Tommy. As soon as he sees me and Tommy walk through the café door, he gets up from the table, ready to bolt.

"Tommy," I warn my friend.

"I got this," he replies and goes ahead of me.

I can't hear what they're saying to each other, but I wait with whatever shred of patience I have left. Tommy was right about one thing—I cannot burn every bridge to get to Sergei. Some of them must be crossed, and that requires paying a toll.

Looking around, I notice the place is quite busy. These people don't have a clue about what's going on here. Howard Lee came in with a neutral position in mind; it's not a trap. He really is here to talk.

Finally, Tommy gets him to sit back down. I join them, but I can tell that Lee is still extremely nervous about my presence.

"Hey, Howie," I say with a casual smile.

"Just listen to what he has to say," Tommy tells him.

Lee nods once, then shifts his focus to me. "Mr. Karpov."

"Anton, please," I reply. "We're friends here, I promise."

"Surely, you understand the delicate situation I'm in," he says.

Tommy and I exchange glances. Lee managed to say a lot with a few words but it's a good thing. It gives me a clear direction forward, while worst-case scenarios of what Eileen is enduring constantly replay in the back of my mind.

"Here's the thing, Howie. I understand Sergei's got you doing business with him. Big business with a lot of money involved. I'm guessing he promised you'd make way more than you ever made with the Karpovs."

"And the Fedorovs put together," Lee mutters.

"Wow, that's mighty ambitious coming from a man who is virtually broke." Tommy chuckles dryly and takes out his phone, showing Lee several key screenshots. "He's been lying to you, Howard."

"That can't be," Lee says, an expression of disbelief on his face.

"Sergei Kuznetsov has been running quite the con. Promising money he doesn't have in order to gain access to favors and market segments that he wouldn't be able to touch otherwise. He's been working the Donovans for a while now, and he's *this* close to getting his grubby hands on their estate," I say, squeezing my forefinger and thumb close together for emphasis. "That's what Sergei is using to do business with you. Money that isn't his."

Lee gives me a hard look. "It's still money."

"It comes at the cost of my wife's life. She's pregnant with my children, twins."

"Not to mention her stepsister," Tommy adds. "That's four innocent lives, Howard. If you allow that to happen, you'll give us no choice but to reconsider our business arrangements with the Triads going forward."

"You wouldn't."

The Camorras' and the Triads' history is about as long and fruitful as ours, minus the bloodshed. The Italians and the Chinese seem to get along okay, probably because they learned from my forefathers' mistakes. You can catch more flies with honey than you can with vinegar. Threatening to pull your whole business out of the Triads' reach is quite the grievous threat.

Tommy probably doesn't have that kind of authority, but Lee doesn't know that.

"I would. You see, there are lines we do not cross, Howard," Tommy says. "Hurting women and children is one of them."

"The treaty our organizations signed years ago still stands," I add. "If Sergei hurts my wife, he's directly attacking a Karpov, in which case, you would all be required to support us. If you don't, every other member and co-signatory of that treaty would be entitled to cease doing any business with you. The Chinese are mighty in Chicago, I'll give you that, but you don't have the juice to take on the Russians and the Italians together. I know you are well aware of that."

"I thought we were sitting down for coffee, not issuing threats."

"Howie, it is what it is. I just need your help," I say, sitting back in the booth and slightly raising my hands in mock defense before turning serious again. "He's got my wife. I need to know where he is." My raised hands turn to fists that I slowly lower onto the table, my expression one of angry determination. I can almost feel my eyes turning cold and black.

"How would I know?" he asks innocently.

I've been around liars my whole life. I can spot deception from a mile away.

I give him a small smile, though my eyes remain cold and unyielding. "He asked for your help. He knows I'd find him anywhere in Bratva territory. Sergei needs a safe place to hide while he obtains the legal paperwork he needs to conclude this giant con that he's been playing. He came to you, didn't he?"

"What if he did?"

I lean forward. "Do you have children, Howie?"

"Are you threatening my children now, Mr. Karpov?" He meets my gaze, stern and unafraid.

"No, I'm merely trying to explain that I'd very much like to have children of my own. I just told you that my wife is pregnant with twins. If anything happens to them, it will be on your head. And I will make sure that your children, that your entire family, knows it. I will also make sure your children know what their legacy is. From what I hear, patricide is quite common among the Triads."

Tommy releases a heavy sigh. The waitress approaches our table to take our order, but he waves her away. We won't be staying here much longer.

"I cannot betray a business associate," Lee insists, albeit weakly. His walls are almost down. He just needs one last bit of encouragement.

"Have you received any funds from him yet?" I ask.

He shakes his head slowly. "No. They're in escrow."

"He's not your business associate until money passes through your hands. If there's been no transfer yet, then there's no partnership. It's the 'yet' that I'm banking on. Howie, I'm only asking for some information here. I need to know where to find him."

"I need an incentive," is his reply.

In the old days, I would've just pistol-whipped the shit out of him until he sang like a fucking soprano, but these aren't the old days anymore, and there's too much at stake.

"Whatever business deal you had with him, I'll take over," I tell him.

"We're talking two hundred million dollars' worth of merchandise that you'll be buying from me," he says.

"Make it three hundred." I shrug. "Unlike Sergei, I literally have money to burn."

"Are you serious?" Tommy gives me a troubled look.

I shrug again. "If that's what it takes for me to get my family back in one piece." I glance again at Lee. "So, there you go, you now have an incentive. I should add, however, that if this incentive doesn't satisfy you, I will have no choice but to resort to less pleasant methods. I'm losing my patience here, Howie. Help me, and you will help yourself."

He thinks about it for what feels like forever.

"Time is running out," I add. "My wife and unborn children need me."

"Fine," Lee finally relents. "Sergei called me late last night. Said he needed a place to stay. A safe place that's off the radar. He sent a courier to my door with a bunch of diamonds, payment for doing him this favor, he called it."

"He's selling off the Donovan family jewels," Tommy says.

"Where did you tell him to go?" I ask Lee.

"I have a few locations throughout the city and on the outskirts. I figured he'd want easy access into the city, though."

"Where is he?"

"East Side."

CHAPTER 31

ANTON

From the moment I get the location from Howard Lee, everything starts moving—and fast.

It only takes us a few hours to put a good team together.

"Andrei has about sixty percent of the organization inside Upton Conference Center as we speak," Tommy tells me.

We're half a block down from our target in a gritty and dangerous part of the city. There are very few lights along this stretch of road. Hookers and dealers work every corner, while the occasional John drives by looking for a good time. Junkies constantly wander about looking for their next fix.

I've got my earpiece in, listening to Ian's men confirm their positions while I give Tommy a long look. "Why are you here, really?" I ask him.

"Let's get one thing clear—I'm not a participant. My dad would kill me himself. But you saved my life once, Anton. You gave me a fresh start, and I was able to patch things up with your brother. The least I can do is keep an eye on this thing and call for backup if you need me."

"Backup?"

"Yeah, backup. Worst case? The cops. You've got good lawyers on your payroll, don't you?"

"And what's the worst case beyond that, because we both know it could go bad in a hurry," I ask, ignoring his question.

Tommy nods. "The Mancini's have expressed interest in lancing a boil like Sergei Kuznetsov, provided they can rely on your discretion. Turns out that the deal he made with Lee is causing a bit of a dent in my uncle Leo's business. I guess we're all connected to this fucker, one way or another."

"Sergei is so desperate to come across as the smartest man in the room that he can't see past his own ego. He never was able to see the greater picture. It will be his downfall; I will make sure of it."

"Either way, I've got you," Tommy says. "And I made sure to get the word out through my NSA buddies to pass it along to a couple of eager beavers in the FSB that Sergei might be getting sent back soon. They've offered to assist with a pickup and transport to the airport."

"That's so nice of them," I mutter.

Things aren't going to end well for Sergei. Andrei has sent multiple messages stating that, so far, the evidence he has provided the families regarding Sergei's operations seem to have pulled more than half of them back to our side.

Circumstantial at best, yet it did the job. Good. I want that fucker to burn.

"Robin to Eagle." A voice comes through my earpiece. It's Declan, Ian's best friend and former MI6 and SSA operative.

"Go ahead, Robin," I reply.

"Target confirmed," he says. "Kuznetsov is inside. Heat scans show us two dozen live bodies in there."

"Any sign of my wife and her stepsister?"

"Top floor, back office. Judging by the heat signatures, it's them. Eileen and Ciara are both alive, sir."

"Good. We proceed as planned. I'll be out in one minute."

"Roger that, Eagle. I'll be waiting."

I check my weapons and the rest of my equipment one last time, then shake Tommy's hand. "If something happens, I want you to know it was a pleasure," I tell him.

"Just go get your wife and let me be the godfather to your twins," he replies. "Take that psychopath down once and for all."

Here's to wishful thinking, because I'm preparing for the worst.

Kuznetsov isn't the deadly one, though. It's his team I'm worried about. They're ruthless assassins, most of them born and bred in the former Soviet Union, several in the military and the FSB before they came to America.

My wife is in there and I'm getting her out alive.

No matter what.

Tommy stays behind, comfortable in the passenger seat while I make my way up the road. I stick to the shadows cast by the derelict buildings and once-booming factories and manufacturing plants. This part of town used to keep the whole city pumping tons of money into the state's coffers. But the market crash eventually found its way here and nobody was spared.

Declan meets me across the street from the address of the warehouse that Lee gave us. Clad in black and joined by eight of his most capable mercenaries, he gives me a reassuring nod. "We're ready, sir," he says.

"There's more of them than there are of us," I remind him.

"Quality trumps quantity, sir."

I appreciate the confidence with a slight nod. "Points of ingress?"

We go over the building blueprints together, agreeing on the steps we'll take in order to get inside. We will neutralize every hostile in sight.

The more I look at these lines of white on dark blue paper, the tighter the knot in my stomach becomes. Eileen is up there. Scared and vulnerable. At least she's got Ciara with her.

"I'm first through the door," I instruct. "Declan, you're with me. The rest of you know what to do. Keep your eyes sharp and your earpieces in, no matter what. We need to be as quiet as possible."

Declan shows me the silencers mounted on each of their semi- and fully automatic weapons. "Discretion is part of the package, sir. But do we have a contingency plan in place?"

"Cops are the best choice should the worst happen."

"And the absolute worst?" he asks.

I give him a wry smile. "You have a bad history with them."

"Mancini."

Declan's younger sister was killed in a turf war between the Mancinis and the Lopez gang about eight years ago, somewhere on the South Side. I know from Ian that he doesn't play well with the Italians, in general, but that he has a particularly sharp bone to pick with the Mancinis. Hopefully, it won't get that far.

"Alright, let's roll." I give the order.

A minute ticks by in tomb-like silence as Declan and I make our way across the warehouse yard, careful to stay in the shadows. Ian's voice comes through my earpiece.

"Nest to Eagle."

"Ian, what the fuck are you doing?" I hiss, my gaze darting all over the place.

We spot movement about fifty yards ahead, two guards lingering outside the front entrance—a massive set of double doors made of corrugated metal. The lights are on inside.

"I'm still in bed recovering, sir, but I figured I'd be of help," he says.

Declan can hear him, too. "You're off your rocker, Nest."

"Right back at you, Robin. But at least I'm being useful. The warehouse was fitted with a CCTV system a few months back."

"How do you know?" I ask.

"I hacked into Lee's phone and email when you and Mr. Benedetto sat him down for coffee."

I give Declan a startled look while we remain still in a dark corner. "How the hell did you do that?" I reply in a low voice, but I'm sure Ian can sense my outrage.

"Don't be mad, Sir, but I planted several apps on your phone that allow me to access other devices by proxy. I didn't think I'd ever have to use them, but I was comforted to have a contingency in place, should anything happen to you."

"Nothing happened to me."

"No, but I can still use your phone to help Eileen."

"Fair enough. Tell us about the security system," I concede.

"I just disabled it. They won't see you coming. I left some standard empty segments looping on their screens. I doubt they'll notice the time stamps."

Declan exhales sharply. "He got himself hooked up with a laptop at the hospital not two days after getting shot. The man is unbelievable."

"And you're welcome," Ian replies. "Best of luck, gentlemen."

"Yeah, we'll talk about those apps you installed without my consent when I get back, but thanks, Ian."

Declan and I approach the front entrance from two different angles.

The guards fail to spot us until it's too late. Declan shoots one in the head, and I get the other one in the neck. They both drop dead. I briefly stare at their bodies and the pools of crimson blood spreading on the ground, wishing there had been an easier and better way to do this.

But there wasn't.

Slowly, we go inside.

"Looks quiet," Declan whispers.

Indeed, the ground floor is a vast space of nothing. But I don't like it.

"It's *too* quiet," I whisper.

POP. POP.

Bullets whizz past us.

They either heard us come in or their outside boys didn't check in when they were supposed to. It's on, whether we like it or not.

Declan is quick to spot one of the shooters at the top. He fires back. The assailant drops from a considerable height with a sickening crunch of his bones. More of Sergei's people come at us from various locations within the dark warehouse.

I shoot at everything that moves without discrimination.

"Ground floor, birdies!" I call out through my earpiece.

Immediately, four of our men join the gunfight.

I hear the bullets as they ping across the room from multiple directions. Sparks fly. Wood gets blown to splinters while Declan and I split up and take cover.

"More incoming!" one of our own says into my earpiece. "Six, maybe more. They're packing heavy, sir."

"Keep them down here!" I order as I catch a glimpse of a familiar figure.

Sergei Kuznetsov slowly approaches, though he doesn't look so brave and defiant anymore. A stoic expression shadows his face while his men keep firing and taking bullets. He seems to be looking for a way out.

I move away from the fireworks, trusting Declan and his men to handle the situation while I inch closer to Sergei.

"Hey, asshole!" I shout after him.

He sees me and turns white. "No!"

"What did you expect?" I reply and start firing.

He ducks out of the way, then trips and stumbles up a narrow stairway leading to the upper floor.

"Son of a..." I mutter and start running after him.

Something slams into me from the side with the full force of a linebacker. I'm thrown against the wall, the wind knocked out of my lungs. For a hot second, everything turns white as I hear the rushed sound of Sergei's footsteps as he climbs the metallic ladder.

The guard I'm wrestling with is big and packed with hard-as-rock muscles. His left hook catches me in the side of my head, making my ears ring.

My instincts kick in. My main weapon is on the floor out of reach, knocked out of my hand when he rushed me. I have another one I can reach, if only—

I grunt as he kicks me in the gut.

It feels as though I was hit with a battering ram.

My vision turns red as I catch my breath. I'm furious as I start hitting back. Unlike my aggressor, however, I'm not banking on force. I'm banking on quick and deadly. I need to catch up to Sergei before it's too late.

I know where he's going.

CHAPTER 32

EILEEN

"Something is happening downstairs," I tell Ciara.

We both hear the noise. The shouting. The incessant popping of automatic weapons. Footsteps thud past our door. My heart races as I look around the cramped office that we've been stuck in for who knows how long. Everything happened so fast from the moment they moved us out of that house.

"What do we do?" Ciara asks me. The bruises on her face break my very soul whenever I look at her. "We are not safe in this matchbox."

"No, we're not," I agree.

I try the windows first, but they're bolted. I grab the fire extinguisher and try to break the glass with it, but it doesn't budge.

"This glass is most likely bulletproof, dammit," I curse as I set the fire extinguisher down. My arms feel heavy. My legs are shaking. The adrenaline and fear are doing quite the number on me.

"We could bust open the door," Ciara suggests with a trembling voice.

"Yeah, but Sergei's goons—" I pause mid-sentence as the door opens.

A guard comes in with a grim look on his face. His gun is cocked and ready in his hand as he looks at Ciara, then at me. "Boss says we're leaving," he tells us.

"Hold on, what's happening downstairs?" I ask.

He points the gun at me. "Not your business. He doesn't need you anymore. Just Ciara."

"Wait, no!" Ciara cries out and lunges at him.

My mind moves fast while Ciara struggles with a man three times her size. I don't know where her courage or recklessness comes from, but I have to think quickly and act accordingly in order to help her.

He manages to peel her off him and throws her against the wall. Ciara falls on her side with a painful thud while I grab the fire extinguisher again. I roar as anger and fear collide within me, and I hurl the damned thing at his head.

CONK.

To my astonishment, I hit my target.

Hard.

His skull cracks open, blood trickling down his face as he gives me a stunned glare. I approach and kick him in the balls for good measure. He passes out on the floor while I rush over to Ciara and help her get up.

"Are you okay?" I ask her.

"I think so. You?"

"Yeah. I'm high on adrenaline. Come on, let's go."

We head out the door, but we don't get far.

POP.

SMASH!

A bullet whizzes past us, shattering the glass of a fire emergency panel next to my head.

"Oh, shit," I gasp and freeze, one hand tightly gripping Ciara's wrist.

"Don't even think about it." Sergei's voice echoes behind us.

I can see the ground floor from here. So many fallen bodies. So much blood.

Gunshots still ringing out.

Slowly, shaking like two leaves in the wind, Ciara and I turn around to face him. He looks terrible. Pale-faced and scared out of his mind. He can barely even hold his gun.

"Eileen!" Anton's voice has my heart jumping.

I look down and see him fighting his way past a mountain of a man. He's come to rescue me. To rescue us. All we have to do is stay alive for a little while longer. There are more of Sergei's men dying down there than ours.

Our men are like stealth hunters, killers in black with precise targets and cat-like movements. Sergei's goons don't stand much of a chance. Their only advantage was in their numbers, but those seem to be quickly dwindling.

"What's the deal, Sergei?" I ask with a calm voice. "You're not getting out of here alive. Surely you know that by now."

"There's another exit right at the end there." He grins an evil grin, pointing toward the open corridor behind me. "All I need to do is take you out."

Ciara gets in front of me. "Did you get the marriage license signed then?"

"Not yet."

"Then you can't kill her, not without killing me first," she says, raising her chin in defiance.

"Oh, my God, Ciara, what are you doing?" I blurt out.

She gives me a hard look. "What I should've done a long time ago. I'm protecting my sister."

"You think I'm not going to kill you anyway?" Sergei laughs hysterically.

"Not while you still need me to sign the marriage certificate. You've come this far, right?" she replies, fully aware that he absolutely does still need her.

Time is the one thing that Sergei doesn't have anymore. There's something off about him; he doesn't look right to me.

"True, but I don't need to kill you to get to your bitch of a sister," he hisses then shoots Ciara in the leg.

I scream as she cries out in pain and drops to the ground.

Instinctively, I cradle my belly, lower my head, and brace for the worst. For a second, I can't even breathe.

A gunshot rings out.

I'm still breathing. Nothing hurts; I'm not bleeding anywhere.

Slowly, I raise my head and look around. Ciara is at my feet, panting and moaning from the pain while blood seeps through the torn fabric of her jeans.

Sergei falls to his knees, his eyes wide and glassy with shock. His lips part as his last breath leaves him. Crimson spreads across his chest.

"Oh, God," Ciara manages as she watches him collapse in a puddle of his own blood. "Oh, my God, Eileen, are you okay?"

"Yeah, yeah..." I manage and kneel beside her. "I don't know where the shot came from, though."

"Fuck, this hurts. That mother—"

"I know. I am so sorry."

"Not your fault," she groans and tears my sleeve off. "I need this."

I tie it just above the gunshot wound in her thigh. Judging by the blood flow alone, it doesn't look like Sergei hit an artery, but we still need to slow the bleeding down. I listen to her throng of curses as I tie my sleeve tightly around her leg, then pull it even tighter.

Footsteps approach.

I look up.

"Anton" I whisper.

"Well, at least we know where the shot came from," Ciara mumbles.

"Eileen, are you okay?" Anton asks me as he rushes over to us, concern etching his features.

"I think so. I'm not hurt anywhere."

"I am," Ciara chimes nervously with a pained chuckle.

Anton checks Ciara's leg, then puts his gun away before wrapping me in his arms.

I cry like a little girl as I lose myself in his embrace, finding the safety I'd missed over the past few days. "I thought I'd never see you again."

"It's over, Eileen. It's finally over," he says.

I have longed to hear those words for what feels like forever. I hold Anton tight and thank the heavens that we made it back to each other in one piece. My stepsister will live, and we will rebuild our relationship and our lives... We will all heal from the damage that Sergei has done.

"I love you so much, it hurts," Anton whispers in my ear. "I would rather burn the whole fucking world down than to ever lose you, you hear me?"

I have no choice but to look him in the eye. "I believe you. I love you so much, Anton."

"Good, because we've got quite the shitstorm coming at us," he bluntly replies.

I feed on the warmth in his gaze. The beating of his heart, his sighs of relief, his loving smile. I feed on his mere presence to stop myself from passing out, from collapsing after the ordeal that Ciara and I just endured.

Red and blue lights flash throughout the building.

"Cops?" Ciara asks, sounding somewhat alarmed. "You called the cops?"

CHAPTER 33

EILEEN

I barely register everything that unfolds once the adrenaline wears off.

I find myself sitting in the back of an ambulance next to Ciara. The paramedics take good care of her, while I give a rather standard statement to one of the police detectives. Anton asked me to tell the truth, or as much of the truth as I could without implicating the Karpovs.

He's doing the same about twenty feet away from me.

Declan, Ian's friend, is in the back of another ambulance. His injuries are much worse than Ciara's. They're getting ready to rush him to the emergency room of the nearest hospital. My heart breaks over and over as I replay everything in my mind, every moment.

"So, you're telling me that Sergei Kuznetsov played a con on everybody," Detective Contreras says, sounding rather skeptical.

"Yeah, pretty straightforward, now that we have the bigger picture," Ciara says. "Ow..."

"Hold still, I need to get this IV line in," one of the paramedics gently cajoles her.

She sits up. "You have to let them go. They did nothing wrong! They saved our lives."

"Who, Anton Karpov? I'm sorry, that's not my call," the detective replies.

"Who called you, then?" I ask him.

He narrows his eyes at me. "A gentleman by the name of Paul Mattis alerted us to the situation. He stated that Mr. Kuznetsov was in fear for his life. He sought refuge here."

"That son of a bitch," I scoff and shake my head. "He had a backup plan in place the entire time to screw us over. Listen Detective, Sergei Kuznetsov poisoned our father. He conned his way into our family. He conned his way into several other businesses, as well. He was going to kill us."

"Do you have any evidence to back up your claims?"

"The bullet in my sister's leg and the bruises on her face don't count?" I blurt out. "The fact that we were rescued from an old, abandoned warehouse doesn't raise any red flags? My friend Ian was shot, and I was abducted. I mean, come on..." I can't believe this is happening.

I stand up, my legs still shaking, but at least my vitals are good. I'll need to see a doctor soon to make sure the babies are okay, but I've got enough spunk and anger left in me to do everything I can to protect my family. What's left of it, anyway.

"You can't arrest him," I say to the other detective, just as he's about to slap the cuffs on Anton.

"I'm sorry, who are you again?" He gives me a tired scowl.

Anton laughs lightly. "That's my wife, Detective Johnson. And she's got a point. You can't arrest me."

"We found you lighting this place up and dropping bodies like it was some kind of video game. Ten people are dead and another eight are in critical condition," Johnson replies. "Not to mention the head of a powerful Russian family is in a body bag. Of course, I'm going to arrest you."

"They fired the first rounds. We were defending ourselves. I was trying to get my wife and sister-in-law out of there in one piece," Anton replies.

CSI technicians buzz around like busy bees—taking photos, bagging evidence, and placing numbered squares wherever they find something, while detectives and beat cops take testimonials from Declan's and Sergei's crews, trying to capture statements from everybody there.

More vehicles arrive, cop cars and medical examiner vans. The echoes of the violence that occurred here linger in the cool night air, sending shivers down my spine.

"This is wrong on so many levels," I declare. "We were the victims here."

"Until we figure out who did what, we're going to have to do this by the book," Detective Contreras insists. "We'll take you and your stepsister to the hospital. Then, once you're both cleared by the doctors, we'll finish taking your statements. In the meantime, Mr. Karpov will ride with my colleague down to the station."

"No, you can't do this!" I snap and try to put myself between Anton and Detective Johnson. I don't stand a chance.

"Baby, don't worry," my husband tells me. "It's going to be okay. Just call Andrei. He'll know what to do. Please let the doctors check you out first, though. I want to make sure that you and our babies are okay."

"Anton..."

"Trust me," he replies with a reassuring smile.

I have no choice but to settle into the back of the ambulance, clutching Ciara's hand for a modicum of comfort, while Anton is roughly shoved into the backseat of Johnson's squad car.

"This is beyond sickening," I mutter.

"Hey, we survived," Ciara whispers. "Everything else we can handle, okay? The truth is still on our side. As for Paul Mattis, I'm going to make sure he..." she pauses as soon as she realizes that Detective Contreras is still within earshot. She gives him a nervous look, then smiles at me. "Stay here, I need you."

"I'm here, Ciara. I'm not leaving you again."

"I'm the one who left, Eileen, and I'm going to make it up to you."

I could tell her that that's not the case, but I would be lying. It was Ciara's pride and stubbornness that got in the way of common sense and reason. Had she not been so blind, she probably would've spotted at least some of the red flags.

But there's no point in going down that road now.

CHAPTER 34

ANTON

The days that follow seem like a dream.

The cops aren't listening. My lawyers are intent on building a plea deal for the charges that the DA is already rushing to throw at me. It's not until I see Andrei—three days after the shootout—that the world starts making sense again.

"Where the hell have you been?" I hiss.

We're in my jail cell, guarded by a uniformed police officer who makes it a point to stare at me and eavesdrop on every conversation. Except for meetings with my lawyer, those are still protected. I know that I am quite vulnerable in this place, and it causes me to be on edge all the time.

"Orange is not a good color for you, brother," Andrei sighs as he takes a seat in front of me.

"Yeah, well, ending up in here in an orange jumpsuit wasn't exactly part of the plan," I mutter. "What's going on? Talk to me."

"It's a bit messy, but I think I have a solution," he says. "First, I need to fully explain the problem we're dealing with."

"Okay, Andrei, explain the problem. Fully."

"The council meeting went about as well as you could expect. We were able to get some of the families back on board, but we still have some major holdouts. Paul has been lobbying against us, pulling the rest of the Kuznetsovs under his umbrella. The Abramovic, the Sokolov, and the Popov crews are still siding with the Kuznetsovs. And they're still asking for you to step down. This time, however, with Sergei obviously rotting, they want Paul at the head of the table."

"You've got to be fucking kidding me."

"I wish. Tommy Benedetto slipped out when he saw the cops coming that night, and I've yet to reach him. Declan is recovering, but he's under arrest, too. Legally, it's not looking good for us, brother. For you, in particular. Paul covered many of Sergei's tracks, so it's hard for our side to prove that you weren't going in there to assassinate him. They're trying to make it look like a failed mob war, and they want to take the Karpovs down," Andrei says.

"What about Eileen and Ciara's testimonies?"

"Considered and recorded, but they won't do much against that mountain of bodies that you fellas dropped."

"It's not like we had a choice."

"I know that. Had we been the ones to call the cops first, we would've had better control over the narrative. It still would've sucked, and it would've been a pain to clean up, but—"

"I'm still looking at a trial and prison time."

"Yeah, afraid so."

"You said you had a possible solution."

Andrei gives me a strained smile. "You're not going to like it."

"Try me, because all I want is to get out of here so I can be with my wife and my family."

"As I said, Tommy has been impossible to reach, but I did get a call from one of his NSA buddies. He was right—his contacts are ranked higher than Ian's," he chuckles. "They put me in touch with someone from the FBI's Chicago Field Office. An offer was made."

"An offer was made," I repeat after him.

My stomach drops. I know what that means. I also know that I cannot compete with an ambitious DA who was just handed a nice case against us. There's too much evidence. And the fact that Paul Mattis called the cops does reset the narrative in his favor, no matter how much proof we come up with against Sergei.

And even that doesn't guarantee that I'll avoid prison time.

I will do whatever it takes to be a free man.

I've got too much to lose now.

A week later, still unable to contact Eileen under my newly revised agreement with the FBI, I take my brother and organize another council meeting at the Upton Conference Center. This time, I made sure to let it slip through the Bratva grapevine that I was about to renounce my seat.

"Would you look at that?" Andrei mutters as we watch Paul Mattis and the other treacherous pieces of shit walk into the meeting room. "You were right."

"I said I'd quit. Of course, they showed up," I reply, comfortable and calm in my seat.

I'm still at the head of the table, though. Negotiations with the Feds took forever. For a moment, I wasn't sure we'd get anywhere. Fortunately, Andrei came through for me, as always. He may not be the wisest nor the most clearheaded, but when the shit hits the fan, my brother always shows up.

"Looks like we're all here, right?" I ask as my gaze slides across the massive conference table, setting the tone for what is likely to be a very uncomfortable conversation. "We're not expecting anyone else, correct?"

"You killed Sergei, so no," Paul bluntly replies.

I give the weaselly bastard a wry grin. "Right. Welcome, ladies and gentlemen. Let's get started."

"Why are you out?" Ilinka Aslanov asks me before I can say another word. "I was told you were denied bail, that you'd be stuck in jail until your trial."

"Yet here I am." I grin, confidently dressed in one of my favorite suits.

"Get on with it," Paul says. "Resign, so we can move on."

"Why would I resign?" I innocently ask. "I have done nothing but good and right by our organization. Our finance department can easily confirm that. You each have a copy of our turnover reports in front of you," I add, nodding at the folders that Andrei has left at every seat at the table.

It took us a while to plan precisely how this meeting would unfold, and I have to admit, it's already going better than I had expected. With one eye on my watch, I wait for their reactions.

Peter Popov is already drunk and easily riled up. "What are you talking about? You don't have the majority support. Not anymore. We don't want you in that seat, Anton."

"You've caused a lot of trouble with the police," Max Abramovic adds with a sharp, overly confident grin. He'd be quite the heartthrob if he weren't such a psychopath. I guess it's why he and Sergei got along so well. "We can't have that kind of stain on our face, not after the treaty we all worked so hard to enforce."

"We're expecting a resignation today," Dmitri Sokolov replies. "Nothing else."

I look around the table again. "Ivan and Petra, thank you both for being here today," I address the Fedorovs first. "Ivanka, you, too. I have always had faith in your judgment. Oleg Sokolov, you've got quite the mouth on you, but your honesty is brutal and sorely needed in these trying times. And Andrei, my beloved brother, I'm forever grateful for your support. It's true, Peter," I add, giving the Popovs a cool grin. "I don't have a majority anymore, but that's about to change."

Dmitri chuckles. "Really? How so?"

"I'm going to change your minds. By the time we're done, there's going to be a shift in the votes submitted at this table," I declare. The city of Chicago smiles at me from beyond the glass windows. "So, let me start at the beginning. Let me, in fact, start with the treaty."

"The Trattoria Rosa dinner of 1985," Andrei chimes in.

"Precisely. The treaty was drawn up and signed that night. I've taken the liberty of enclosing a copy in each of your folders. Do me a favor and go through it, paying special attention to what the fourth edict says."

Ilinka frowns as she takes out her copy. "Any attempt on the life of a family member, by blood or by marriage, is considered a declaration of war."

"Correct," I say.

"Nobody tried to kill Eileen," Paul is quick to interject.

"I'm afraid I have a witness who can contradict that claim," I reply.

"Ciara Donovan? She's a crazy, scheming bitch," he scoffs. "Easily disputed."

"Well, not really. She's got a gunshot wound that confirms Kuznetsov's intentions," I rebuff. "And I believe that by the time the CPD concludes their investigation, there will also be CCTV footage to back that up."

Peter Popov scoffs lightly. "Even so, Sergei Kuznetsov is dead. A life for a life. The price has been paid."

"Not really. You see, I am offended by your accusations that my activities brought the police to our doorstep," I say, nodding at my brother to play a recording on his phone.

Suddenly, the room goes quiet as we all hear Paul's voice on the recording.

"9-1-1, what is your emergency?" the dispatcher asks.

"Yes, hi, my brother is in fear for his life. He's at 233 Sutherland Avenue, on the East Side. Multiple assailants with weapons have charged into the building. They're gunning for him. You need to send someone there fast. He's alone and scared!"

Ilinka gasps, eyes wide with horror.

Andrei stops the recording.

Tension fills the air as all eyes turn to Paul.

"That's supposed to be confidential," Paul mutters as his face drains of blood, beads of sweat blooming across his forehead and temples. He knows he's in deep shit now.

"How did you—"

"It doesn't matter." I cut him off. "What matters is that I'm not resigning today. In fact, I'm reaffirming my leadership over the Bratva by exposing the charlatans and the traitors in our midst, starting with Sergei Kuznetsov and Paul Mattis. My brother has already served you all with compelling evidence regarding his treachery and his machinations, not to mention the financial damage that he has caused to his own businesses."

"Resign," Max Abramovic insists.

I cock my head to the side, visibly amused. "Did you know that there's a RICO investigation actively looking into your activities in Lincoln Park, Maximilian buddy?"

"They have nothing on me."

"They do now," I reply.

As if on cue, the door opens. In walk a dozen FBI agents, waving their warrants around.

I nod to Peter next.

"You've been running some shady dealings down in Bronzeville that I chose to close my eyes and ears to for far too long, Peter. That also ends now."

"Dmitri Sokolov," one of the agents declares, cuffs already out. "Get up. You're under arrest."

"Under what charge?" Dmitri gasps, downright enraged, while the other agents promptly arrest Max and Peter.

"Little Village," I remind the Sokolovs. "That dirty family secret you thought nobody knew about? I knew about it."

"Anton, what are you doing?" Ilinka asks me, genuinely alarmed. "Turning on your own like this? Handing us over to the Feds? Are you serious?"

"I'm not handing *you* over to the Feds," I tell her.

With their rights read and their wrists cuffed, Max Abramovic, Peter Popov, and Dmitri Sokolov are escorted out of the room by the FBI agents. Their supervisor gives me a curt nod. "You're good, Mr. Karpov. Thank you for holding up your end of the bargain," he says.

"To my surprise, it was a pleasure doing business with you," I reply with a cool grin.

Once they're gone, there's a lightness to the room that wasn't there before.

Max's second-in-command, Sasha, looks rather confused and scared. Peter's son, Perry, is just as distraught, already on the phone texting their lawyers. Dmitri's twin sister, Iulia, gives me a slight nod, though she's working really hard to keep her fury in check. She understands what just happened.

And so does Ivan Fedorov, who starts laughing wholeheartedly. "So, is that it then?" he asks me. "Those of us who betray you go to federal prison? You've clearly got the FBI in your pocket now. Is this a show of force?"

"Not at all. Max, Peter, and Dmitri were the least useful members of the organization, and our greatest liabilities, whether any of you are willing to admit it or not," I say. "All I did was clean house. It was sorely needed. Hey, Paul?"

"What?" He's wide-eyed and pale, sitting in his chair in disbelief.

"There's another team of agents waiting for you downstairs. Don't think for a second that you're off the hook. You're going to be dealing with the NSA, though. You, and the entire Kuznetsov organization, to be specific. You're out of the Bratva altogether, and the Kuznetsovs are no longer welcome at this table. Any attempt at creating a competing force will be met with the full weight of the Bratva."

"You're screwed six ways from Sunday." Andrei laughs.

"Let's not make fun of their troubles," I joke. "But yeah, you're fucked, because you're the one who brought the police and turned this whole thing into a federal case. This is on you, Paul, and you will pay the appropriate penalty. To everyone else left at this table, is there still a request for me to resign? Or are we moving on?"

Quietly, Paul removes himself from the meeting, rushing out the door like the terrified little mouse that he is. He won't get far, though. I estimate he'll be getting his own set of bracelets in less than a minute.

Ivan Fedorov gives me a hard look. "You consorted with the Feds."

"I had no other choice. It was either that or jail time for something that is fully acceptable under our treaty. Fuck their laws. It's *our* laws that I'm focused on defending. And what Sergei and his followers did... well, I couldn't let that stand. Not when he tried to kill my wife!" I begin shouting. "So, yes! I will bury each and every single member of the fucking Bratva if any of you even think about gunning for anyone in my family ever again! Is that clear?"

My voice booms across the room and a heavy silence follows.

Ilinka breaks it. "Understandable and acceptable. You have our support."

"You saved my niece," Ivan says to me. "You have our support."

"And ours," Oleg Aronov adds. "I may not be your biggest fan, but you are fair."

Sasha Abramovic raises a trembling hand. "You have our support as well," he says.

"The Popovs stand with you," Perry chimes in.

Iulia Sokolov takes a deep breath. "It's better than the federal galleys, I suppose."

"Ah. There we go. Minds changed. Votes changed. And we're all better for it, right?" I quip with a bright smile as I reclaim my seat at the head of the table. "Now, let's move forward with the issues at hand and how we're going to deal with each of them. I need to get home to my wife."

CHAPTER 35

EILEEN

"I don't get it. Why won't anyone tell me anything?" I lament as I walk into the living room with an iced tea in one hand and a dainty lace fan in the other. The summer heat waves are starting to do a number on my already swinging moods. "I hate being kept in the dark like this!"

Ciara watches me as I settle into the armchair. With her leg still tightly bandaged, she gets to claim the sofa wherever we lounge in the Karpov mansion.

"Remember about six months ago when you hooked up with this devastatingly hot guy after he practically kidnapped you?" she casually asks, nursing a lemonade of her own. She takes a sip and crinkles her nose. "This would taste so much better with a splash of rum in it."

"You're on painkillers." I roll my eyes, trying not to laugh. "And yes, I remember. Said a devastatingly hot guy actually saved my life that night."

"And do you remember how he also got you pregnant?"

I'm laughing now. "Okay, where are you going with this?"

"Well, you're still pregnant and stressing yourself the hell out. Calm your tits. Andrei said he was okay, and that he was going to be home soon. In the meantime, we get to hang out and recover from the Kuznetsov trauma together. By the way, this is turning out to be the longest we've been around each other without bickering. Tell me you've noticed."

"Oh, I've noticed, and I'm glad." I soften as I gulp down half of my iced tea.

"Me, too. It's been a rough ride."

"Dad didn't help us much either."

"He did the best he could. We certainly gave him hell for it."

"I guess we weren't too easy to handle."

Ciara takes a deep breath, and we both sit in silence for a while. "Thank you for letting me stay here," she says. "I just... I can't go back home. Not yet."

"I completely understand. You can stay here for as long as you need, Ci. Nobody is rushing you anywhere."

"Well, I am rushing. Just not back home," she says. "Listen, I want to call a meeting early next week. Paddy's out of hiding."

"A meeting?"

"The Donovans, the MacDonalds, the O'Reillys. The whole organization is in disarray after Sergei's slimy takeover attempt. And our family doesn't currently have a leader to take the main seat," she says. "With your approval, of course. Just wanted to run it by you first."

I give Ciara a long, warm smile. "Ciara, you're the leader that this family needs."

"We both know that's not true. I failed on so many levels. Come on."

"Sergei had everyone fooled, our father included," I insist. "Ci, I have your back. If you ever need my vote or my support, I'll be there. But I'm building my dream here with Anton. I never wanted to lead the Donovan organization, you know that. That was always you."

"But Anton was convinced he could get you to—"

"They were all convinced they could sway me back into the fold. Maybe someday I will. I don't know. But only if you decide to step down willingly. Otherwise, this is your turf, Ciara. Your future. Your organization. If you want me by your side, I'm there. But I have faith in you. I know you can lead them. So, yeah, call the meeting. I'll sit in and support whatever you decide to do. And tell Paddy he needs to get his ass down here and have lunch with us. He is sorely missed."

Ciara giggles. "Paddy said he'll support me, too."

"You'll do well with him having your back. He was right to leave when he did, though. You have to know when to pick your battles. Sergei would've killed him."

"Indeed. Then we'd be crying over him as well."

We both sit up upon hearing the front door open.

I bolt from my chair just as Anton comes into the living room. I'm starstruck by how good he looks in that suit. I'm even more enticed by the satisfied smirk stretching across his face and the fire burning in his hazel eyes. His gaze softens as it meets mine.

"Hello, Mrs. Karpova," he says.

"Mr. Karpov, so glad to see you again."

"Ciara. I see you're still alive and kicking," he gives her a playful wink.

"Alive, yeah. Kicking, not so much, but with a little bit of physical therapy, I will be soon enough," Ciara replies. My heart grows with each step that Anton takes toward me.

"I'd love to sit around and chat some more," he says, never taking his eyes off me. "But my wife and I have some catching up to do."

"Knock yourselves out, I get the TV all to myself for once," Ciara quips.

I can't help but laugh. Anton closes the distance between us and sweeps me off my feet, causing me to squeal and say, "Oh, God, Anton, I'm heavy!"

"Good thing I'm strong," he replies as he scoops me up in his arms and carries me out of the room. A minute later, we're on the upper floor, hungrily kissing each other as we stumble into our bedroom. "I've missed you so much, baby."

"I love you," I tell him. "I was so scared that I wouldn't be able to see you again."

"No way. Have you met me?" he replies, mercilessly tugging at the straps of my dress.

It falls to the floor, and I'm left standing naked in front of my husband. I help him out of his suit, our mouths fused as we whisper sweet things to each other. The fire that burns between us reaches a whole new level, passionate lust gathering in my core as he lays me on the bed and spreads my legs.

"I have been thinking about this for a while now," he growls, letting his tongue slide between my wet folds.

I whimper and grab the satin sheets as Anton ravenously eats my pussy.

He brings a hand up to fondle my tender, full breasts, while the other focuses on my wet, hot opening. Suckling my clit hard, he penetrates me first with two, then three fingers. I cry out in ecstasy, my orgasm unraveling with lightning speed as days' worth of longing are finally sated and released.

"Oh, God, Anton, yes!" I manage as he comes up, his lips wet with my juices.

I sit up as he lies on his back on the bed. I straddle his hips and lower myself onto his thick shaft, both of us groaning as I slide down his length. He grabs me by the hips, thrusting upward as I rock rhythmically on his cock.

It doesn't take long before another climax rockets through me.

We're both so hungry, so desperate, so eager for that ultimate release.

He comes hard soon after, and I welcome every drop of him inside, my core tightening and pulsating as another orgasm explodes through me, the sound of his climactic grunts and the hazy look in his eyes too much to bear.

I collapse on him. "We're just getting started. You know that, right?" he mutters and nuzzles my ear as I drape myself over him.

"You're damn right. I've got quite the appetite these days," I reply.

∽

"Close your eyes," Anton says.

We're in the backseat of his town car, Ian behind the wheel.

"Okay, I'm getting a bit of a déjà vu feeling here," I giggle as I close my eyes. "What is going on?"

"You'll see when we get there."

Ian chuckles. "You're going to love it, I promise."

"Ah, well, if Ian says I'll love it, then okay."

"Wow, thank you for the confidence," Anton quips.

We reach our destination, and Anton helps me out of the car. The smell of roasted coffee beans immediately smacks my nose. I gasp and breathe it all in, my eyes still closed as I try not to laugh. Anton holds me close and gently guides me up the steps.

"I think I know where we are. The surprise isn't really—"

"SURPRISE!" Too many voices explode at once.

I freeze on the spot, leaning into Anton as I open my eyes. I knew he was working on the café to get it up and running for me—Ian gave him away a week ago. But I had no idea how far he'd come with it, and I certainly wasn't expecting a surprise party.

"Oh my gosh!" I exclaim upon seeing Laura and Andrei, Ciara, Paddy, and many members of the Russian and Irish mob present. "Oh, wow."

"I know you were aware I was working on this, but I think I still managed to knock the wind out of you with this one," Anton says, his eyes sparkling with excitement as he walks me into the newly refurbished café.

"I don't know what to say."

I really don't. Not only was my café renovated and refurbished, but it's even gotten a few gorgeous upgrades. Different light fixtures and a whole new design on the central bar—both of which I know I talked to Ciara about. They've been working together on this, clearly, and it came out like a dream.

"Are those servers?" I gasp, watching several uniforms glide by with drinks on their trays and smiles on their faces.

"From a catering company, just for today. I wanted you to see what it's going to look like when it's fully operational," Anton replies, his hand resting on the small of my back. "After the nightmare you went through, you deserve a beautiful dream. And it's been a pleasure and an honor to have a hand in this."

"He didn't do it alone, though," Laura says as she comes in for a hug.

"He had plenty of help," Ciara adds with a wink.

Andrei pats him on the back. "He would've been helpless without us."

"Helpless," Anton agrees.

"*Almost* helpless," Paddy chimes in, gently squeezing my shoulder. "Congratulations, kiddo. Your da would be so proud, I'm sure of it."

"So, is this like a grand-opening party?" I ask, shyly looking around. "I mean, I know most of the people here."

Ciara laughs. "Of course. Every high-ranking member of Chicago's underworld is here to celebrate with you. Look at that, the Italians made it, too."

I follow her gaze to find Tommy Benedetto walking in, a bottle of French champagne in each hand, grinning like the devil.

"Hey! We're gonna drink these after the mini-Karpovs pop out!" he says.

"Tommy!" I giggle and rush over to hug him.

To say that I'm happy would be an understatement. After the storm, it's nice to feel the sun on my face again. Anton did say that the troubles wouldn't last forever, but when you're deep in the muck, it's kind of hard to see much of what's ahead.

Today, however, I see it all.

"It's the least I could do for everything you've given me," Anton tells me as I admire the coffee bar, the party joyously unfolding around us. "I want you to be happy, Eileen."

"I am happy."

"Happier."

"I am the happiest I could possibly be," I insist.

He plants a kiss on my lips, and I welcome his taste, his love, his protection.

This has been a long time coming.

EPILOGUE I

EILEEN

Two months later...

I'm still in shock.

"Do you, Ciara Donovan, take Ian Masters to be your husband, before God..." The pastor continues with the vows while I try to wrap my head around the whole thing. Only half an hour ago, Ciara was dragging Anton and me into this tiny chapel, begging us to do a favor for her. Little did I know.

"...until death do you part?"

"I do," Ciara declares, tears of joy streaming down her cheeks.

Ian lovingly looks down at her, wearing the kind of smile that assures me it's the real deal with these two.

It really is.

It's been two months since the Sergei incident, and here we are, witnesses at Ciara and Ian's impromptu wedding.

"Did you see this coming?" Anton whispers in my ear.

I shake my head. "Nope. You?"

"I knew Ian was smitten, but I had no idea it was this serious."

Out of such tragedy, good things came. We survived. I'm close to being ready to deliver my twins—Lord knows, my ankles and my back won't last much longer. The C-section is scheduled for tomorrow, which is why Ciara was in such a rush to get us here today.

Talk about timing.

The café is doing great. The official opening party was even better than the soft launch that Anton put together.

My husband has consolidated his rule over the Bratva. And Ciara... well, she's definitely going places.

"Do you, Ian Masters, take Ciara Donovan..."

I can see Ian shaking with genuine emotion.

I'm so happy for them.

Shocked aplenty, but happy. He may not be mafia royalty, but I've seen how far Ian will go to protect the people he cares about. I know he'll do even more for Ciara. My stepsister needs loyal, strong men around her. With Paddy and Ian flanking her, she'll do just fine as the Donovan in charge. I've no doubt the others will fall in line effortlessly.

"I do," Ian says.

"By the power invested in me, by the state of Illinois, you may kiss the bride," the pastor says with a bright smile.

And kiss the bride, he does.

"Congratulations!" I tell the bride and groom as they turn to face us. "Wish you'd given us a heads up, though. I would've loved to organize an actual wedding, an actual wedding party—"

"Oh, no, we didn't want any of that," Ciara says, shining like the sun in a simple but beautiful white gown, pearls resting at the base of her slender neck. "This right here... this is perfect."

"Seriously? I'm basically in the only dress left that still fits me," I nervously laugh.

Ciara hugs me and plants a kiss on my cheek. "Okay, first of all, you look gorgeous. You've always been gorgeous. You could wear a potato sack, and you would still be gorgeous, and I'm sorry I never told you that."

"Thank you."

"Second, after our wedding debacles, do you really think another attempt at a fancy wedding would've been a good idea?" She raises an eyebrow. "No, I insisted on something small and private. We've got enough going on as it is. Ian agreed."

"I wish you both a wonderful life together," Anton tells them and cordially shakes Ian's hand. "I swear to God I didn't see this coming, but I am glad you're both part of this family now."

"And you're a part of ours," Ciara says. "The Karpovs and the Donovans, tighter than ever."

"Technically, I'm not a Karpov," Ian chuckles.

"Not by name, but you've been one of us for a long time," Anton replies.

I point a finger at the happy couple. "I'm still reeling from the shock. How were you so good at keeping it a secret?"

"Former British intelligence, remember?" Ian says with a cool smile and a wink.

Ciara gasps, remembering something. "Oh, shit, Laura's gonna kill me."

"For not inviting them?" I ask.

She nods. "Oh, yeah. She's going to throw a hissy fit and then some. We need to make it up to her, baby," she tells Ian.

I gasp too, albeit for a different reason.

"Oh, I think I've got something to keep Laura distracted with," I manage, grabbing Anton's arm. "Baby..."

"Your water broke," he says matter-of-factly.

"Holy crap!" Ciara exclaims. "We need to get you to the hospital, like now!"

Ian is already in action mode, snatching the car keys from Anton's pocket. "I'll drive. Anton, help Eileen to the car. Ciara, call the doctor and let them know we're coming."

The contractions start.

"Fuck!" I cry out.

"I've got you, baby," Anton says as he holds me up.

EPILOGUE II

EILEEN

"How the heck do they grow up so fast?" Ciara asks.

"I'd like to say that three years go by in a flash, but it doesn't really feel that way to me," I reply. "Then again, I'll enjoy every second of every day that I get to spend raising them."

We're lounging in the afternoon sun on a late summer Sunday. The back garden of the Karpov mansion unravels at our feet with its lavender and hydrangea bushes, the sycamore trees casting their long shadows across the deep green. Anton and Ian keep the twins busy—Anton's got Lachlan on his shoulders, while Ian has Ronan. They're in the pool, splashing and laughing and having heaps of fun.

"They look so cute with their bright orange swimming vests." Ciara can't stop laughing.

"Our husbands are so cautious when it comes to my boys; it's so endearing."

"We got lucky, didn't we? You with Anton, me with Ian."

"Or maybe they're the ones who got lucky." I raise an eyebrow at her.

Ciara nods in agreement, then checks her phone. "Ah, good. Andrei and Laura are headed back from the conference center. So, it'll be the six of us for dinner tonight."

"I'm going to leave you and Anton to discuss business after dessert," I tell her. "He's got a proposal he wants to run by you."

"A proposal?" She gives me a curious look.

"Yes. He asked Tommy Benedetto to come over, too."

"Care to share some details?"

"I don't have any." I shrug. "But I trust you three will handle it. You've been rocking this whole mob boss thing, anyway, Ci. I knew you would."

"Honestly, I wasn't sure I'd be able to hack it. Not after what Sergei did."

"I knew you'd bounce back. A little insecurity never hurt anyone. Today, the Donovans are stronger than ever, thanks to you and Paddy. Anton's got his ducks in a row with the Bratva, and there are rumors that Tommy Benedetto is being groomed for a top leadership position, as well. It's looking more and more interesting, I'll be honest."

"Have you told him yet?" she asks me.

I shake my head slowly. "Not yet."

"You should."

"Give me a minute." I laugh and get up.

Ciara gasps. "Wait, like, a literal minute?"

I don't answer. Instead, I slip out of my cover-up and join my boys in the pool, the cool water quick to seep through my one-piece bathing suit, sending a slight shiver down my spine. Anton and Lachlan are the first to turn around and eagerly greet me.

"Momma!" Lachlan exclaims, reaching out.

The twins are like two peas in a pod, ridiculously identical. It took me a while to securely tell them apart when they were babies, and somehow, it's getting even harder now. They're both curly-haired little monsters, the spitting image of their father, but I see the red highlights whenever they're out in the sun, their green eyes allowing their Donovan side to shine through.

Dimples deepen on their cheeks whenever they smile, and I melt every time I hear them laugh.

"How are my guys doing?" I ask, shuddering while I adjust to the water temperature. Anton comes closer, with Lachlan safely on his broad shoulders.

"Causing mischief, as usual," my husband replies.

"Momma, look!" Ronan cheers and slaps the water with his feet, splashing it all over Ian's face.

"You'll make a fine boat engine someday," Ian quips.

I laugh lightly. "You got yourself into this the minute you caved into Ronan's demands," I tell him. "Your only option now is to let him wear himself out."

"Oh, his batteries are dwindling, worry not."

"How's my favorite wife?" Anton asks me, then plants a kiss on my lips.

"Your favorite wife?" I give him a confused look. "Is there a less favorite wife I should worry about?"

Anton thinks about it for a moment. "Well, there's Andrei, my work wife. He's the nagging type. You made these two little rascals, and you make me happy on a daily basis. So, yeah, you're my favorite."

"As if I couldn't love you more," I say, practically swooning.

"Mommy loves Daddy!" Lachlan declares.

"She most certainly does, baby," I say, keeping one eye on Anton. "So, my darling husband, I'm your favorite because I made two boys, huh?"

Anton gives me a wry smile. "I didn't call you a baby factory."

"What if I am, though?"

"What?"

I shrug lightly. "What if I am?"

"What if you're what?"

"You seem confused," I sigh deeply.

Ian's jaw drops. "Holy moly..."

"Mmm-hmm."

"Wait, what?"

I laugh. "Well, if I'm your favorite because I made two babies, what do you say if I make us a third?"

There it is. The spark of realization. Then the ensuing joy. The purest kind of joy.

Ciara laughs wholeheartedly from the comfort of her chaise lounge. "I get to be the godmother this time."

"Are you for real?" Anton asks me, his voice barely a whisper.

Lachlan and Ronan are too young to keep up with the conversation. Besides, they're also too busy giggling and splashing in the water. But Anton is catching up, and he is damn near jumping out of his skin.

"Eileen."

"Yeah, we've got a third one on the way," I tell him, holding my breath for a moment.

"As if *I* couldn't love *you* more." He looks over to Ciara. "Hey Aunty Ci. Give us a hand here for a hot second?"

"Yep, yep!"

Gently, he carries Lachlan over to the edge of the pool, where Ciara is quick to take him. Ian brings Ronan closer to them, as well, while Anton comes back and swoops me in his arms, the water splashing everywhere around us.

"Are you for real, Mrs. Karpova?"

"I am, Mr. Karpov."

"Then, yeah, you're absolutely, totally my favorite wife," he says and kisses me deeply.

I feel his love blooming in my heart, every atom in his body resonating with mine as the sun's golden light glazes us both in shimmering happiness. It's been such a crazy, wonderful ride so far. Despite the bumps, the ups and the downs, I wouldn't have it any other way. Bringing a third child into the world we're building together feels like the natural course of things.

It makes sense.

Our love makes all the sense in the world, and each of our children is living proof of it.

The End

Printed in Dunstable, United Kingdom